A Bitter Root

A Bitter Root

Kelsey Greye

*Aunt Violet,
With love,
Kelsey Greye*

Wesbrook Bay Books
Vancouver, B.C.

Published by Wesbrook Bay Books, Vancouver, part of The Wesbrook Bay Group.

www.wesbrookbay.com

wesbrookbay@gmail.com

Edited by Beverley Boissery

Cover Design by Graeme J. Friesen

Interior Design by BDG Atwood

First edition.

ISBN: 978-1-928112-39-6

Dedication

To my God and Father in heaven, who steadfastly roots bitterness out of my heart as I grow to know and love Him better. And to Jorin and Dorothy Green, who have been instrumental in the process by gently speaking words of truth and grace into my life while loving me as I am. Thank you.

1

Pale threads of sunlight filtered through the early morning mist, striking surprising sparks of gold in the shallow pools of water scattered across the cobblestone streets outside the boarding house. It was quiet, too early for the voices of flower sellers and sandwich hawkers to fill the air with the din of commerce and too late for the raucous laughter of inebriated men making their way back to respectable homes after late night visits to areas of London that fed desires best left unmentioned. The door to the house opened and a man, tall, lean, and wearing an expression of mingled annoyance and amusement, emerged. Ignoring the faint, pleading call issuing from within, he shut the door behind him and hurried down the steps toward the street, assiduously avoiding the small puddles that would have soiled his shining black boots and impeccably creased trousers.

Reaching up to smooth his dark hair, Inspector Jack Ramsey allowed himself a momentary flare of frustration at his ill luck. He frowned as he strode down the street. *Couldn't I find a room that would suit for more than six months? At least my notice has been given and I am finished with it.* A noise from behind caught his attention and he glanced back.

"Oh, for heaven's sake," he muttered, stopping and turning to face his former landlady. "Mrs. Edison. Pray tell, why are you following me?"

The middle-aged woman marched up to him and jabbed his chest with her finger. "Why am I following you?" Her voice, already high-pitched, reached a range Ramsey had not thought possible. "First, you insult my darling niece, freshly come from the country to help me with my work. Next, you turn up your nose at the breakfast she and I slaved in a hot kitchen to have ready for you at the ungodly hour you insist on rising, and then," she stopped momentarily to punch his chest once more, "you announce that you're giving up your rooms without even the courtesy of giving me enough notice to find someone to take your place. How am I supposed to pay my expenses when my tenants up and go without so much as a second thought, you selfish prig of a man!"

Ramsey winced, his hand automatically straightening his already perfectly aligned collar. The insult, while crudely phrased, wasn't entirely untrue.

"I hardly think that attacking my character is the appropriate response to a slight, real or imagined, Mrs. Edison," he told her in a tone guaranteed to quell the most fiery temper. "Perhaps my announcement this morning was somewhat abrupt, but I'm certain the fact that I shall pay the remainder of the month's rent will soften the blow to your pride."

"*My* pride?" Mrs. Edison's already red face flushed such a shade of scarlet Ramsey glanced around, wondering if he would need to call for a physician before their conversation was over. "It's *your* pride at the root of all of this!" She waved her arms wildly as spittle flew from her lips to land perilously close to Ramsey's boots. He edged backward, trying to stay out of range. "Treating my dear Edith as though she's not good enough to wipe your boots when she's a fine girl who will make some lucky man the best of wives! And to think, I encouraged her mother to send her to me in the hopes that the two of you would make a match of it. Not now, sir, not if you paid me a thousand pounds!"

Ramsey shuddered involuntarily. The thought of arriving home to a wife bearing such an uncanny resemblance to his former landlady in face, form and disposition was frightening. "I don't see how you can hold me responsible for your assumptions, Mrs. Edison. I'm not in the market for a wife and have always made it perfectly clear that I desire peace and privacy wherever I choose to room. As that is not something you desire to provide, I shall depart so that you can find a tenant who will appreciate your matrimonial efforts."

He turned on his heel, carefully avoiding the curious and amused gazes of passersby, and left the woman sputtering in the street. He felt his cheeks redden in response to the jeers of a group of barefoot little boys dressed in what amounted to rags and a fresh wave of irritation filled him. *If this was all intended to humble my pride, Lord, it's unfortunate that it couldn't be done without the added pain of public humiliation.* Receiving no answer from Providence other than an unsettling sense of cosmic amusement, Ramsey quickened his pace.

He wondered what he would find waiting when he arrived at 4 Whitehall Place, better known as Scotland Yard and home to the London Metropolitan Police Force. In his youth, he'd never imagined that he would one day be proud to be part of Sir Robert Peel's innovative attempt to bring peace and security to the people of London. The "Peelers," as they were commonly known, were a group of men from a variety of backgrounds with a variety of skills. Ramsey's own strict, middle class upbringing, meticulous nature, and thorough education at the hands of the same schoolmaster uncle who raised him gave him the ability to question the upper classes regarding crimes affecting them without causing nearly the outrage that some of his more humble colleagues garnered. As grateful as he was for the benefits of his upbringing, he suspected the lack of affection between his uncle and himself was at least part of the reason he'd formed no lasting attachments as an adult other than a couple of friendships with men in professions connected to his.

Ramsey crossed Trafalgar Square to the accompaniment of panicked pigeons fleeing a small band of well-dressed boys, who were in turn fleeing a small army of plainly attired governesses.

"Master Harry," one of the women shouted, attempting to match pace with her charge despite the length and weight of her skirts. "You naughty boy. Leave those poor birds alone. If you throw one more stone, there will be no bread and cheese for you when we return home, I promise you that."

"Mama will not let you starve me," retorted a little boy so stout and round-cheeked it could not be doubted that he spoke the truth. "I will tell her that you were too busy talking to the other governesses to mind me properly and you'll lose your post unless you give me all the bread and cheese I want. And cakes too!"

Ramsey was tempted to stop and arrest the greedy little pig for attempted extortion just to see what Mama had to say about that, but it would hardly have helped the beleaguered nanny. He passed the pair, the boy's disdainful expression causing a distant memory to flash through his mind. Ramsey's cousin Paul had often stared at him with the very same mingling of haughtiness and scorn, as though wondering what a creature like Ramsey was doing inhabiting the same world, let alone the same home, that he did. His aunt and uncle's grudging tolerance of the illegitimate child of a loose woman had caused their own son to treat Ramsey as an unwanted, though necessary, burden.

The shame of possessing a ruined sister would have driven his uncle to drink had he not possessed a rigid code of morality and a terror of the consequences of such licentious behavior. Ramsey rubbed his wrist as he turned onto Whitehall, the faint ridges circling his wrist a physical reminder of Uncle Morris' cruel attempts to eradicate the strain of wickedness he feared his young nephew had inherited from depraved parents. Ramsey pushed aside the unwanted images from his past: shadows creeping across the nursery wall while he watched, wrists bound to the bed post with thin strips of leather lest he rise in the night and commit some obscene act of violence against the family. It had been of no consequence that he'd never exhibited behavior of that sort. His blood was tainted and thus, child or not, he could not be trusted.

It's a wonder I became a law enforcer rather than a lawbreaker, he thought, not for the first time, smiling when he remembered the look on his uncle's face when he'd announced that he was joining the London Metropolitan Police Force. Ramsey slowed as he approached the building that housed the force, unconsciously smoothing his hair and straightening his coat. A cacophony of sound greeted him as he passed the duty desk. He nodded at the man behind it, and entered the main reception area where sergeants and constables were busily compiling notes, comparing cases and directing inquiries to the appropriate superior.

"Inspector Ramsey, sir," called one sergeant upon seeing him, "I've got that information you requested on the Rivers couple." He lowered his voice as Ramsey came close to his desk. "Nothing definite, but your suspicions that they're heavily involved in organized crime seem to have a solid foundation. Do you want to assign someone to keep an eye on them for a few more days?"

"Good work. Let me think on it, Jenkins," Ramsey told him. "I've no doubt whoever we sent would see evidence of criminal behavior but I suspect that the Rivers wouldn't take kindly to any threat to their freedom. Confirming my suspicions isn't worth the life of a good man, not if we can find out what we need to another way."

Understanding dawned in the sergeant's gaze and he nodded. "Whatever you say, sir. I'll await your instructions."

"Thank you, Jenkins. For now, you'd best turn your attention to other matters. I assume that you have enough work to busy your hands?"

"I do, indeed. More than enough, what with poor beggars stealing just to eat and factory workers so tired out that they come home and raise a fist to anyone that asks them for something, usually the missus or their little ones, as luck would have it."

"I know it." Ramsey's frown deepened at the sad truth. "Do your best to make a dent in it, then. That's all we can do."

He moved across the room and down the hall to his private office. He'd just unlocked the door when he heard his name.

"Inspector Ramsey." He turned to see a constable rushing toward him, face flushed with what could have been either exertion or excitement. "You've a visitor." He reached the office and lowered his voice, glancing furtively over his shoulder toward the large open area. "She's a real lady, she is, sir. I asked her if I could help her but she said no, it was a matter of life or death and she needed to see someone with more authority than me." His face flushed more deeply with what Ramsey assumed to be embarrassment. "Of course she didn't mean it to be cruel. She's quite upset, sir, that's all."

Ramsey privately thought that emotions were hardly justifiable cause for anything, cruelty or otherwise, but saying so would hardly be beneficial to the young constable.

"Wait five minutes and then bring her in, Constable," he said, ignoring the other man's obvious sense of urgency. "I need to prepare myself to hear whatever it is she wishes to say."

Not waiting for confirmation, he walked through the doorway

into his office and shut the door behind him. As always, the sight of neat stacks of paper, perfectly aligned pencils and tidy baskets for filing settled him. Enough light filtered the window to illuminate the room, so he left the gas lamps in wall sconces unlit and sat down at his desk. A serious crime was like a drug to him, and he was an unapologetic addict. Nothing stirred his blood more than a complex mystery and the ensuing hunt for the culprit.

He looked up as a knock sounded and the door opened. The constable was preceded by a heavyset woman of between thirty and forty wearing a dark, severely cut green gown of fine wool.

"Lady Arabella Rosings, sir." The young man's voice shook nearly imperceptibly with excitement. "This is Detective Inspector Ramsey, Lady Rosings. He's the best there is at solving crimes and making certain whoever's done wrong pays for it."

Lady Rosings raised a brow, barely lowering her chin in a nod clearly intended to dismiss the constable without exerting the unnecessary effort of speaking to someone so beneath her level. His cheeks reddened and he bowed clumsily, with a nod to Ramsey before exiting and closing the door behind him. Ramsey studied the woman coolly, amused to see her own cheeks redden in either embarrassment or outrage at his candid assessment.

"Please sit down, Lady Rosings," he said after a moment. "And when you're ready, you may tell me why it is you require my assistance."

Her lips thinned in disapproval, exaggerating the lines of discontent etched into her broad, stern face. She gathered her skirts and sat, carefully arranging the layers of silk and satin around her. The movement was likely automatic but Ramsey appreciated the attempt to keep her gown from the unseemliness of creases. Silence stretched between them as Lady Rosings scrutinized him in return with surprisingly shrewd hazel eyes. Apparently coming to some internal conclusion, she folded her hands in her lap and began to speak.

"I'm here on behalf of my sister, Lady Georgiana Kingsley, Inspector," her voice was formal but Ramsey thought he detected an underlying thread of emotion. "She was lately removed from London and hidden away at an asylum for the mentally deranged in the nearby countryside. I want you to investigate the matter for me."

"I'm afraid I can do nothing, Lady Rosings, without asking questions I believe you will find rather intrusive."

The older woman stiffened her already ramrod straight spine. "Ask what you must. I will answer your questions as honestly as I can, but I was not present during the situation that prompted Georgiana's husband to send her away."

"I see. Suppose you tell me what you know and why you feel so strongly that your sister does not belong in an asylum?"

"Of course." She took a deep breath, the briefest flash of vulnerability and fear covering her features before she composed herself. "Just over a month ago, my sister was hosting tea in her home following an afternoon of Whist. From what I can gather from those who were present, she was in the middle of a conversation with her good friend, Lady Hollister, when she suddenly leapt up from her chair and began shrieking. She began to flail her arms wildly, crying that ghosts and specters were attacking her, and then fell to the ground, convulsing. They were so violent that her gown was ripped and her hair came completely undone. And this in mixed company!" Mingled horror and shame covered Lady Rosings' face and she paused to regain her composure. "It took both the maid and one of the gentlemen present to restrain her until the convulsions ceased and they were able to coax her upstairs to her bedchamber. Her husband, Lord Francis Kingsley, sent for the doctor, who sedated my sister as soon as he arrived. News of the spectacle quickly spread through our social circles and the following day, Francis packed Georgiana off to the countryside."

"Were you surprised by Lord Kingsley's actions?" Ramsey would hardly have expected anything different from a man of title and fortune.

"Certainly not," responded Lady Rosings with an indignant sniff. "I was shocked, however, to hear the news of my sister's death shortly after the emergence of her apparent insanity."

"Her death?" Ramsey's clear grey eyes narrowed. "When, and in what manner, did that occur?"

"Only three weeks after she was removed from London, her body washed up on the shores of the Thames. She was," Lady Rosings' cheeks paled and her lips tightened again, "in a state of undress and marked all over her body with burns and bruises."

"Where precisely did the body wash up?" Ramsey felt a wave of pity for the woman, along with a burgeoning curiosity, as he recalled the postmortem of a victim. A young man in that case, but the injuries were the same as Lady Rosings described and the body had also been pulled from the Thames.

"She was found on the shore near Vauxhall Gardens," said Lady Rosings. "An elderly couple walking by the water found her and called for assistance."

Ramsey sat back, rubbing his chin. *Not only was it the same river and manner of death but the same location.* The only difference was that the young man's body was pulled from the river by a young courting couple enjoying a trip down river in a punt. Well, enjoying, that is, right up until they found a dead body.

"If I understand what you've said, your sister was found dead at least a week ago. Is that correct?"

She nodded.

"And yet you're only now coming to Scotland Yard for assistance?

Do you not believe that the local police are investigating the matter fully? I can assure you that we take murder very seriously."

"I believe that they are investigating the matter, yes," Lady Rosings paused, "yet I also believe that my brother-in-law has convinced them that my sister's character was such that this end was to be expected. From what I inferred from a certain Inspector Hamilton's heavy handed questioning, they conclude that my sister somehow escaped the place she'd been taken for her own safety and made her way back to London to meet with some unknown man who then killed her. They seemed to believe that her mental breakdown was prompted by the immense guilt of becoming romantically involved with a man other than her husband."

"I see." Ramsey knew Inspector Hamilton well and, while the man was competent, he was too easily swayed by the opinions of the wealthy and titled for Ramsey's liking. He would have to tread very carefully but the potential connection with the case involving the young man pulled from the river might be enough to gain some footing. "I cannot promise, Lady Rosings, that you will like what I uncover but I am willing to look into the matter further. You may leave it with me. If and when I discover anything of import, I will come and inform you. Until then, I'm afraid you will have to wait and pray that the truth is found."

"I suppose I can't ask for anything more than that," Lady Rosings gathered her skirts and stood. "I will await word from you and will pray daily that you both find my sister's killer and bring down all the judgment of God and man upon his head." She began to move toward the door but stopped, turning back. "If I wasn't clear enough, Inspector Ramsey, let me be perfectly frank. I am so certain that my sister's husband did this horrid thing to my dear Georgiana that if you find irrevocable proof he did not, I will confess to the deed myself."

"I understand, but may I ask why you're so very certain?"

A deep sadness covered Lady Rosings features. "When Georgiana married Francis, she had all the same hopes most girls of seventeen do when they dream of their future husband. During their courtship, he showered her with gifts and she was blinded by the romance of it all, unaware that he was only concerned with her sizeable dowry. Once they married, Georgiana received nothing but criticism, not even a trinket when she bore Francis an heir. That is," her eyes were hard as they met Ramsey's, "until the day before the Whist party."

Ramsey made a notation on the paper he'd been using to jot information down during the interview. "What is it that Lord Kingsley gave your sister that day?"

"I'm not exactly certain, but Georgiana mentioned in a letter she wrote me the evening before her episode occurred that Francis had shocked her by coming home with some sort of fragrant lotion that he insisted she apply before retiring. She was quite sarcastic," Lady Rosings' chin lifted, "as was unsurprising, given their relationship. As distasteful as I find it to speak ill of the dead, my sister's murder is more important than my sensibilities. She wrote that she suspected it was the same scent his mistress wore and he wished to imagine himself with her in the dark of the night rather than his wife."

She turned and left the room in silence. Ramsey studied the notes he'd taken during the interview, feeling the familiar stirring of excitement in anticipation of the hunt for answers. The day was going to be far more interesting than he'd anticipated.

2

The small bell above the doorway chimed as a short, stocky man with a full head of bright red hair walked into the shop. A myriad of scents assailed him: sweet, savory and sharp. They should have been at odds with each other but somehow everything combined to give a pleasing sensation of vitality. Flynn's Healthful Herbs was situated on a narrow street just off the busy market thoroughfare. It was small, but large windows, high rafters and spotless wooden plank flooring gave it a welcoming, airy feel. He moved toward the counter just as a very pretty girl of about twenty bustled through the curtain that closed the preparation room off from the main part of the store. At the sight of him, her wide smile grew even larger.

"Papa!" she hurried around the counter and threw her arms around him, hugging him tightly. "What are you doing in London? We weren't expecting you."

He held her tightly and then stepped back to study her. Her green eyes twinkled on a mobile face crowned with hair the exact shade of his own.

"I had some business to take care of for Mr. Douglas and the estate so he told me to be sure and come see you. Tell me, Annie, how are you and your sister getting along? Your mother will expect a full report and woe to me if I fail to bring her one."

"Very well, Papa. I love working with the customers, even though there aren't nearly enough handsome young men who come in and Gracie, well, you know what she's like." Her lips formed a pout that melted away as he patted her hand consolingly. She lowered her voice, "You know she's at her happiest mixing up her potions and lotions. As long as I keep anyone from trying to venture through the curtain to interrupt her, business runs smoothly for us both."

"Suppose you go and tell her that an old man is here and wishes to consult her about a tincture to heal a heart lonely for his two thankless daughters who have gone off and left him. You know what a soft spot our Gracie has for those who are alone in the world."

"Alone in the world, are you – with Mama and five children still at home. You are absolutely incorrigible."

"You'll do it, then?" He smiled as Annie rolled her eyes.

"Of course I will, Papa. How could I say no to such a pathetic-looking old man?"

Ignoring his indignant huff, she whisked the curtain aside and stepped through into the back room, automatically breathing deeply at the scent of fresh peppermint. Standing with her back to the entrance was a tall woman with hair a few shades darker and less vivid than Annie's. Her supple hands measured, crushed and mixed with an almost artistic grace.

Annie watched as her older sister worked steadily away, grinding mortar and pestle, adding boiling liquid from a nearby flask bubbling over a small flame and then stirring the mixture to a thick paste. Setting the bowl aside, she carefully covered it with a thin piece of muslin and turned around. Warm brown eyes looked inquisitively out of a face that was both sensitive and intelligent, and her wide, pleasant mouth moved easily into a self-deprecating smile at the sight of her younger sister.

"I'm sorry, Annie, I didn't even hear you come in. You know how involved I get when I'm working." She shrugged, her shoulders moving smoothly under the blue and cream plaid of her simple day gown. The apron that protected it was liberally spattered with a variety of colored stains and streaked with green dust. Annie made a mental note to take it to the laundress before it was beyond repair.

"There is an old man out in the shop who wishes to see you, Gracie. He was quite insistent that he needs something for a broken heart."

"Annie. You know as well as I that there is no herb or concoction that can heal what only God is able to. I'm surprised at you for even suggesting such a thing."

"Oh Gracie, he looked so despondent. Please, won't you come and at least talk to him?" She gave her sister a pleading look, biting her lip to keep from laughing.

"I suppose; but if he leaves insulted and angry, the fault is yours. You know that I haven't the patience to deal with gentlemen, be they old or young. Or customers in general, for that matter."

Grace didn't bother to remove her apron, giving her hands a swift brush over the fabric to wipe any remaining dust and paste from her fingers before swishing through the curtain to the front of the shop. She stopped short at the sight of her father standing at the far side of the counter, his grin widening as his eldest child's affronted look melted into warm affection.

"Papa!" she exclaimed, moving quickly to greet him with a kiss on his weathered cheek. He held her close and breathed in the scent of herbs lingering on her hair and clothing, the same scents that had clung to her since she was a child, the result of her never-ending experiments with remedies. It had been fortunate for Grace's long-suffering family that her uncle had been in need of an assistant in his fledgling apothecary. Their country village of Thatcham in the Berkshires west of London was certainly no liberal oasis but people were surprisingly charitable toward Grace's involvement in preparing their tonics and lotions, despite her sex. She'd spent many happy hours in that apothecary learning the properties of different plants and herbs and hounding her mother, the village midwife, with all manner of questions.

Eventually, her Uncle Connal had lent her enough money to set up her small London shop specializing in natural remedies and practical advice. Flynn's Healthful Herbs did such good business that she'd not only paid him back but had been able to use some of the profit to help her brother James with expenses while he studied medicine. James had come to London with her to lend his name and authority to her endeavor, since a woman owning a business, especially one so like an apothecary, was inconceivable in their modern times of 1847.

Stepping back, Seamus Flynn studied his eldest child. *She looks happy*, he thought with a small pang because it meant that she would not be returning to her family. He was proud of her success and knew that London had been her dream since she was a child. She had passed that dream along to James and Annie, much to their parents' consternation. Knowing the three of them were together made it easier but he still missed having all his children underfoot.

"Where is young Jamie? I was hoping that the four of us could sup together before I leave this evening."

"That sounds lovely, Papa," said Annie, giving his arm a squeeze. "Jamie should be done with his rounds at the hospital by half past six and we close the shop at six precisely. What time must you leave?"

"I will simply have Mr. Douglas' driver, Billings, bring the carriage to whichever dining establishment you suggest and I can leave straight from there. He told me not to worry about him. Apparently he has brought along a copy of Mrs. Radcliffe's *Udolpho* which will keep him occupied as long as necessary. My only fear is that he will drive us off the road trying to avoid imaginary specters after putting such foolishness in his head. I will be too busy sleeping in the carriage to notice erratic driving and won't be the wiser unless I wake up in heaven instead of in Thatcham."

Both daughters laughed, picturing the burly, bearded coachman held captive by the gothic horror novel.

"Annie, do you remember when James tried to read it as a break from his medical texts?" Grace's laughter made it hard for her speak. "He woke us up in the wee hours of the morning for four days straight by frantically knocking at our door. He could not even bear to snuff out his candle to sleep. He ended up curled up on our floor for two weeks until the frightening dreams abated and now swears he will never read such a novel again."

Annie's eyes danced at the memory. "Well, Papa, at least we know that Billings will be wide awake on the journey home, even if you are not."

"Come now, my girl, enough poking fun at the poor man. Where shall we have our supper? I'm afraid I need to get on with Mr. Douglas' business if I'm to meet you at seven."

"How about The White Stag? The food is good and plentiful and the place is respectable. Sometimes James takes us there rather than bother Mrs. Lydiate for our dinner."

"That sounds perfect. Annie," Seamus gestured his daughter toward the door. "Come, give directions to Billings, will you? You know my sense of direction leaves something to be desired. The last time I tried to lead us, we ended up six miles beyond our destination without ever passing through it."

Giggling, Annie preceded her father out the door and into the street leaving Grace shaking her head. She had just turned to go back to her work when the bell tinkled, and heavy, shuffling footsteps announced a customer rather than Annie's return. Pasting what she hoped would pass as a welcoming smile on her face, she turned around and fought to suppress a groan at the sight of the man standing just inside the shop. Hiram Wiggins' lips pulled back from his teeth in what only the most generous soul would term an affable expression. He was a large, muscular man with cruel eyes and heavily pomaded, slicked-back dark hair. His failing attempt to appear congenial only emphasized his intimidating features.

"Mr. Wiggins," she said, trying to inject a smidgen of politeness into her voice. "What can I do for you today?"

He moved closer and she caught a whiff of the cheap, sour-smelling cologne he doused himself with, overlaying a permeating air of sweat and body odor. She took a step back, trying not to gag.

"Have you given my proposition any more thought, Miss Flynn? I will not wait forever for you to change your mind."

"Mr. Wiggins, you have come in every day for two weeks asking me the same question and I have given you the same answer." Grace's eyes flashed as her temper rose, frustration from repeated encounters with the man pushing it nearer the surface than usual. "While I understand you desire large quantities of bleeding heart plants and belladonna, unless you tell me whom you wish to treat with such things and why, I will not sell them to you. Both can be fatal if the dose is too large. Besides, I don't stock the amounts you require and have no plans to do so anytime in the future. Please take yourself and your business elsewhere."

The man's eyes narrowed and he stepped closer, using his size to try to cow her.

"I think, Miss Flynn," he hissed through yellowed teeth, "that you had better reconsider. You wouldn't want anything to happen to that pretty sister of yours, would you?"

A chill raced down Grace's spine at the threat and her face flushed.

"Do I understand," she said slowly, teeth clenching as she fought for control, "that you plan to harm my family if I choose not to supply you with lethal herbs?"

He took out a large knife from a sheath at his waist and began to clean his fingernails. The sunlight streaming through the windows caught the metal, the sharpness of its reflection mirroring the keen edge he toyed with idly.

"These are dangerous times we live in, Miss Flynn. One can never be too careful or have too many friends."

Grace's stomach roiled at the intimate lowering of his voice. She slid a hand into a small pocket in the side of her full skirt.

"Let me be perfectly clear, Mr. Wiggins," she said, her heated tone matching her temper-reddened cheeks. "I will never allow you to purchase anything in this shop, not even the sprig of parsley you desperately need to freshen your foul breath. You may threaten all you want but I will not be bullied, coerced or manipulated into helping you use something meant to heal as a weapon. You leave me no choice but to call the constable."

"Don't be daft, woman." He advanced, muscles flexing under his ill-fitting suit coat. "The police would hardly be interested in the ravings of a spinster shop girl. I'll be miles away by the time they arrive anyway. Just give me the herbs I require."

As he reached out to grab her arm, Grace sent the small sachet she'd removed from her pocket flying straight at his eyes, its tie still clutched in her fingers. Fine red dust filled the air and coated Mr. Wiggins' face as she hurriedly backed away, holding a clean handkerchief over her mouth and nose. The hoarse yell the large man let out as he crumpled to his knees and clawed at his streaming eyes reverberated through the shop. The door crashed open and Annie rushed in followed closely by a uniformed constable and a tall, dark-haired man. Annie rushed over, eyes searching her sister's face and frame for injury.

"Are you well, Gracie?" she asked anxiously. "I ran for the constable as soon as I saw Mr. Wiggins enter the shop but I was so worried he would harm you before we returned."

Grace gently disentangled herself from her sister's exuberant embrace.

"I'm fine, Annie. The sachet of cayenne pepper worked just as I hoped it would, as you can see by Mr. Wiggins' obvious discomfort."

She sent a satisfied look at the man still writhing on the floor while the constable attempted to cuff him. She turned to see the dark-haired man watching her with an inscrutable look in his serious grey eyes. Her swift glance scanned him from neatly-trimmed head and impeccably tied cravat to clean, well-shod feet. He murmured something to the constable and he nodded respectfully. The man turned back to study Grace with an intensity that made her want to fidget with her apron, uncomfortably aware of her disheveled appearance. Stiffening her spine, she met his gaze without flinching.

"I do not wish to be rude, sir – particularly to one who has helped remove such a menace from my shop – but who exactly are you?"

3

Ramsey studied the woman standing in front of him, as unruffled by the violent man as if he were nothing more than an irritating fly she had swatted away from her face. The bright intelligence in her warm brown eyes proved she was no fool; yet she had faced the man without fear. Not only that, she had completely disarmed him. Ramsey's respect was difficult to earn, but the woman standing calmly in front of him had done so without even attempting to. In fact, she didn't seem the least bit concerned with engaging his interest. As a result, he was surprised to find, she had done just that.

"I am Detective Inspector Ramsey." He took her hand, bowing over it. "I was interviewing Constable Blackstone here regarding another matter when your sister came running toward us and said we needed to come quickly because a man was attacking her helpless sister."

"Oh, Annie," said Grace with a long-suffering expression. "Really? I had the matter firmly in hand. Mr. Wiggins never had a chance to use his knife."

Ramsey watched as Annie made a face at her sister before sending him a smile designed to stop a man's heart in his chest.

"Well, how was I to know that the pepper sachet would work?

You have to admit, Gracie, that some of your experiments have been much less successful. And others? Outright disasters. Besides, they might not have come if I simply said that a man was bothering you."

She turned back to Ramsey and Constable Blackstone, who had just hauled Mr. Wiggins to his feet. "Would you?" The two policemen exchanged a look.

"I should hope that we would have, Miss..." Ramsey stopped, realizing he didn't know either sister's last name.

"Flynn, Inspector Ramsey. My sister and I run this shop together. I deal with the customers and Grace takes care of preparing all our wares."

"Before you ask," inserted Grace smoothly, "we do not present this shop as an apothecary and it is owned by our brother, James. Though some of the herbs we sell have medicinal properties, we do not carry any actual medicine and certainly never sell anything lethal. That was the basis of Mr. Wiggins' quarrel with me."

The man in question hacked loudly as he tried to speak.

"That's a bloody lie, it is, Inspector, sir. She attacked me for no reason. I was only asking about..." He cast his eyes around the shop, obviously looking for inspiration, "flowers."

"You wanted flowers?"

Ramsey's expression was incredulous. Wiggins colored but held to his assertion.

"That's right," he said firmly, "flowers for my mother, and this harpy threw that powder right in my face."

"Miss Flynn, I am afraid that I need you to accompany me to Scotland Yard to sort this out," Ramsey said, enjoying the incredulous look on Grace's face. "Constable Blackstone, you will see to finding Mr. Wiggins one of our finest cells while we investigate, will you not?"

The younger officer nodded and pulled his prisoner toward the door, ignoring the disgruntled man's curses. Annie held the door open and he smiled his thanks meaningfully enough to make a blush rise in her cheeks.

Grace smiled when she caught Ramsey rolling his eyes at the sight. Obviously the man was not a romantic. Annie's ability to charm young men was as concerning as it was entertaining. Unfortunately, as anything she said about it put them at odds with each other, Grace had long since given up on trying to curb her sister's flirting.

"Annie," she said, remembering the detective was waiting for her, "everything is cleaned up and put away in the back except for Mr. Pinkerton's order. It needs to be transferred to a large glass vial with a cork stopper and labelled clearly. If I am not back in time to close the shop, I will meet you, James, and Papa at The White Stag at seven o' clock." She stopped and tilted her head to the side as a thought struck. "It might be wise to make certain that we both have one of my cayenne pepper sachets on hand at all times. I'll just go fetch a couple of them."

Grace swung the curtain aside and was about to disappear into the back room when she stopped. Her gaze narrowed as she watched Annie's eyes light with as much interest as mischief as she sidled closer to the detective.

"I wonder, Inspector Ramsey, if you would be so kind as to escort my sister to The White Stag once you complete your interview with her? I know my father and brother will wish to thank you for your prompt response to Mr. Wiggins' threat and I would feel so much more at ease if I knew that she was not making the journey by hansom all the way from Scotland Yard alone. We would be delighted to have you dine with us as a token of our gratitude."

The shrewdness in the man's clear grey eyes told Grace that her sister's explanation was not entirely satisfactory to him, but he nodded anyway. It seemed he lived by the code of the honorable gentleman.

Grace hoped, with more bitterness than she wanted to admit, that the Inspector's honor would not make him succumb to Annie's lures.

"As it happens, Miss Flynn, I am without lodgings at the moment and a substantial meal would be very nice. I thank you for your offer and I accept."

Grace felt crimson stain her cheeks, muttering her displeasure as she hurried through the curtain to gather her things. In less than five minutes, she reemerged wearing her cloak and bonnet and holding two sachets. She slipped one into her pocket before holding out the other to Annie.

"I am ready when you are, Inspector Ramsey."

"Then let us be off. Good day, Miss Flynn."

He bowed to Annie before pushing the door open. Grace took his arm as the bell above the door tinkled cheerfully, and they walked together into the late afternoon sun.

Ramsey studied the woman sitting in a chair across from his desk.

In all his years with the force, he had never met anyone so refreshingly candid. Most people tried to phrase their statements so that they appeared in the best possible light. Grace, on the other hand, was utterly transparent about her encounter with Hiram Wiggins. He saw no arrogance in her features, nothing but pragmatism along with mild amusement lighting her eyes every now and then as she recounted the events of the past few hours.

"What is it that you find humorous about Mr. Wiggins' threats, Miss Flynn? I would think that most women would be quite upset over what you say you've experienced."

She laughed, a low throaty chuckle. Ramsey wasn't accustomed to anyone surprising him but this woman managed to do so both frequently and thoroughly. He wasn't at all certain he liked the sensation.

"My apologies, Inspector Ramsey. I was just remembering the way Mr. Wiggins looked after I threw the pepper sachet in his face. I had hoped that it would work but I had no idea it would be so effective. Of course," her eyes grew vaguely unfocused as she fell deeper in thought, "he *was* close enough to get the full dose straight in the eyes and nose. Perhaps I should run some more tests to approximate results at varying distances."

"I beg your pardon, Miss Flynn, but who are you planning to run these tests on?" His tone was dry. "I and my associates would have no problem with you defending yourself against men like Hiram Wiggins, but we do frown upon assault."

"Oh, yes, I know that," her gaze sharpened. "My brother, James, is generally a good sport about such things. He says he would rather suffer some discomfort periodically and have his sisters safe than remain unharmed because we are defenseless."

"A noble sentiment."

"I thought so, particularly since he said that *after* I'd coated his collar with a rather powerful itching powder. He nearly scratched himself raw but he said he was glad to do it if it made London safer for us. Of course, he did require me to swear I'd never do such a thing again without at least trying to use a less potent formulation for testing." She checked the watch pinned to her dress. "Do you have everything you need, Inspector Ramsey? My family will be expecting me to join them for dinner in about thirty minutes and the carriage ride to The White Stag will take nearly that long."

"I believe I do for the time being, Miss Flynn, though I may need to ask you more questions in the future." He placed the notes he had taken in a folder and placed it on top of the stack on his desk before rising. "Come, I will fetch a hansom."

Surprised at the unusual courtesy, Grace followed him from his office to the street in front of the building. She waited in silence while he flagged down a hansom and gave the driver the address. He helped her into the carriage before surprising her a second time and following her inside, settling down across from her. She eyed him curiously.

"Inspector Ramsey? Might I inquire why you agreed to join my family for dinner? I cannot imagine that dining with those you serve in your professional capacity is something you particularly enjoy." She winced, realizing how tactless her words had been. To her relief, he didn't seem to take offense.

"Why do you say that?"

"Annie's explanation of the reasoning behind her invitation was not entirely believable. At least," she clarified, "your expression as she spoke indicated you did not find it so."

"Again," he muttered, looking surprised.

"I beg your pardon?"

"It's nothing." He cleared his throat. "I was merely making an observation to myself. As for dining with your family tonight, my reasoning was simple enough." He paused. "I am hungry."

His simple answer startled her into laughter, the sound reverberating in the clear evening air as the carriage began its progress down the street and into the darkening night.

4

When Grace and Ramsey walked inside The White Stag, a reasonably priced public house near the home where the Flynn siblings boarded, Grace's stomach rumbled in anticipation of food that was both plentiful and tasty. Her father, sister and brother were already seated at a heavy wooden table waiting for them. Seamus waved exuberantly when he spotted them and made Grace smile broadly.

"Gracie. Over here," he called as though she were not already headed in his direction.

"Hello, Papa," she said, kissing his cheek affectionately.

"Papa, James," said Annie as she moved over on the bench to make room for her sister, "may I introduce Detective Inspector Ramsey of Scotland Yard? He and Constable Blackstone came to our rescue this afternoon."

James nodded cordially at Ramsey but Seamus Flynn jumped up and clapped him on the back, nearly sending him face first into the table.

"I cannot thank you enough, Inspector Ramsey, for arresting that foul man who has been bothering my girls for weeks now." He sent a wounded look at his daughters. "I had no idea that they were in trouble as neither saw fit to tell me. Can you imagine, sir, a father's dismay at finding out his daughters have hidden such a thing from him?"

Grace sighed as she dropped down onto the bench beside her sister.

"There was nothing you could do, Papa, and you know it would only worry Mother. We have James at the boarding house, my pepper sachets at the shop and God watching over us always. Annie and I are in no more danger than most women in London. In fact, we are probably in less than a goodly number of them."

Seamus grumbled to himself, oblivious to the fond smiles exchanged by his children at his response.

Ramsey studied the group with interest; the easy affection they showed one another was markedly different from his own experience of family. He rubbed a hand over his chest and cleared his throat.

He hated to cast a shadow over their enjoyment of the meal but their assurance of safety was a false one. "I am afraid I have some bad news." Four pairs of inquisitive eyes turned to rest on his face. "While I wish it were otherwise, I am fairly certain my superiors will not pursue charges against Mr. Wiggins at this time. He will be held for a day or two while I continue to look for evidence against him but it's unlikely I will find enough to try him. Miss Flynn's statement is not enough." He watched Seamus and Annie's faces fall, while James and Grace's features settled into expressions of resignation. "I understand if you no longer wish my company while you dine."

Seamus shook his head and gestured at him to sit down.

"Not your fault, my boy," he said, clapping him on the shoulder. "You still came to my Gracie's aid. I'm sure that if you had enough evidence, you would charge the villain, would you not?"

"Without hesitation."

"Well then, there you are. I had James order the special for us all

– roast beef, potatoes and Yorkshires. I do hope that's acceptable. I wanted to be sure we had time to dine without hurrying. I must travel back to Thatcham yet tonight, you know."

"Not at all. I am very fond of roast beef."

Ramsey wasn't entirely certain where his unusual desire to be congenial was coming from. He knew he was frequently brusque to the point of rudeness, but much to his surprise, he realized that he wanted the Flynn family to like him. He couldn't remember the last time such a thing had occurred and found it unnerving. Best to return his thoughts to the case, he decided, particularly since he still had unanswered questions about Wiggins' motive.

"I wonder, Miss Flynn, could you tell me what types of plants or herbs, readily available, could cause hallucinations or madness even if only temporarily? A case that I am working on in involves such things and I fear I am out of my element."

"Certainly, Inspector Ramsey," she replied, ignoring the exaggerated groans from her siblings and father. "Pay them no heed, sir. They have been forced to listen to my enthusiastic lectures on the properties of plants and herbs for many years and now seek to avoid it whenever possible."

"Please continue, Miss Flynn. Your knowledge may prove quite valuable to me." Ramsey smiled apologetically at the others.

"There are a number that can cause such symptoms but not many are easy to acquire. Do you happen to know when it was ingested and how long it took for the hallucinations to begin?"

"I cannot be certain but I suspect that it was administered in tea, which means that the hallucinations began within an hour or so. Of course, it could have been slipped into something she ate or drank earlier."

He reached into his coat pocket for his notepad and pencil so he could write down the new observation along with any information

Grace had yet to convey. Glancing up, he saw four mirrored expressions of interest. Grace's warm brown gaze was bright with curiosity.

"You do not find the topic offensive to your sensibilities?" he asked.

"Not at all," replied James, his voice a pleasant tenor. "I'm interested to hear about police work and I understand how helpful it is to sort through one's thoughts aloud. Grace and Annie are very understanding when I discuss medical matters with them. My sisters have a keen interest in the world outside those subjects designated fit for female consumption. I fear we've all indulged it."

"Annie enjoys ample opportunity to poke fun at us both for our serious ways," Grace gave a self-deprecating shrug, "but I would be living a half-life if I couldn't pursue the things that interest me most, despite my sex. It's a great blessing to have family who see that."

"Which she never fails to make the most of, the little imp – takes after her mother."

The food arrived as she spoke and all talk gave way to silence as they began to eat. Ramsey once again found himself comparing his own family to the one seated with him. His aunt and uncle had always told him that one must always know the character and family of one's associates before extending an invitation of any kind. They certainly would not deem friendly banter appropriate with mere acquaintances. In fact, they did not consider such familiar behavior proper even between themselves. Pushing the thought, and the lingering resentment that came with it, aside, he turned to Grace once more.

"So there are a few different liquids or powders that could easily be slipped into a lady's tea? Wouldn't she taste it and know something was wrong?"

"Not necessarily." Grace's response was matter-of-fact. "There are combinations that are practically tasteless and the amount required to cause hallucinations without incurring death could be miniscule. Do you know the precise symptoms she exhibited?"

Ramsey flipped open his notebook again and shuffled the pages until he was looking at the notes he'd taken that morning.

"She began to convulse and her pupils grew wide before she suddenly jumped up from her seat and began to scream something about ghosts and specters, tripping over the hem of her gown and falling to the ground, covering her face."

Grace exchanged a glance with James before turning back to Ramsey.

"It sounds like it could have been belladonna. It dilates the pupils and can cause hallucinations in low doses. It is also tasteless, so she would have noticed nothing amiss if someone slipped it into her tea. What do you think, James?"

Her brother raked a hand through his dark auburn hair, forehead furrowing as he thought.

"It's possible, Gracie, and you would know best. But why would somebody want to do such a thing? I mean, outright murder makes a ghastly kind of sense but why this? Would that not only be a delay to whatever conflict prompted the action rather than a final solution?"

Ramsey smiled grimly.

"That is precisely the question I would have asked, had I not known the rest of the story."

"Well tell us, my boy," Seamus said, banging his fork absently on the table as he waved a hand. "Don't leave us guessing."

"I'm afraid I cannot yet, as the matter is still under investigation."

"What? You taunt us with scanty details and then refuse to elaborate?" The older man shook his head in exaggerated disbelief. "Cruel, sir! You are cruel!"

"I do apologize, Mr. Flynn, but I am bound by my profession. You have my word, though, that when it is settled I will write to you with the details myself, if you so desire."

"I'll hold you to that, Inspector Ramsey. Now if I'm going to make it home before dawn, I'd best be off. It's a good thing I can sleep on the way, or I wouldn't be fit for use tomorrow. My carriage can drop you at your residence if it isn't too far. It's the least I can offer for looking after my girls."

The policeman winced as he remembered the morning's events that had left him without housing. Caught up in the case, he'd completely forgotten he had no bed to go to tonight.

"Actually," he said dryly, "I am momentarily homeless. I quit my boarding house this morning and have not yet had a chance to find a new one. I would appreciate sharing your carriage if you are passing any reasonable hotels in which I can find lodgings for the night."

Annie cleared her throat delicately, a flush rising in her cheeks.

"Inspector Ramsey," she said, smiling brightly, "I hope you will not think me presumptuous, but I heard you say this afternoon that you were without lodgings so I sent word to Mrs. Lydiate, our landlady. A room across the hall from James was just vacated and she agreed not to let it until after I returned this evening. I am certain she would be glad to rent it to you if you wish it."

Seamus laughed, pulling her into a warm embrace.

"That's my girl, Annie, always looking out for others. A tender heart and a practical mind, that's what you have. Of course you'll accept, won't you, Inspector? It would set this old man's heart at ease to know that his darling children were living under the same roof as a member of the London Metropolitan Police Force."

Ramsey found it difficult to think of any objections with Seamus pumping his hand so hard that he thought his arm might come loose from his shoulder. He felt strangely touched that anyone at all should be concerned for his well-being. What could it hurt to try the boarding house for a night or two? If it turned out to be less than satisfactory he would be no worse off, that was certain. Lodgings aside, he did still have questions for the elder Miss Flynn and it would be convenient to stay close at hand until he discovered more about Hiram Wiggins and his connection to the Rivers.

"I would be pleased to," he said finally, "and you have my thanks, Miss Flynn, for the trouble you took to arrange the matter."

The charming blush that colored the young woman's cheeks deepened as she smiled. Seamus broke into a lively jig upon Ramsey's acquiescence; a dance so enthusiastic that it sparked applause from the other patrons and laughter from his children as they headed toward the exit. Ramsey followed the family toward the door leading to the street, wondering all the while just what he'd gotten himself into.

5

Louisa Rivers sat on a handsome settee of dark blue brocade in the corner of her husband's office, quietly watching the scene before her. Her husband Elliot met her amused gaze with one of his own before turning back to the man cowering in front of the crime lord's ornate desk, flanked by two large, well-muscled men in the Rivers' employ.

"If I have your story correct, Mr. Fenton," he said, his voice cold, "you were not trying to flee the country on the *S.S. Carthaginian* to avoid paying the debts you incurred at my gaming establishment. You were planning to sail to Africa to mine for diamonds so that you could pay me back with interest."

The man swallowed audibly, nervous sweat glistening on his broad forehead.

"Yes, sir, that's precisely what I was planning. I would never try to cheat you out of your money, Mr. Rivers, sir."

Elliot tapped the tips of his fingers together and stared silently at the man. Louisa watched in rapt fascination as Mr. Fenton curled even further into himself, drops of sweat now sliding down the side of his face. She did so love to watch her husband at work.

"Well, Mr. Fenton," he said after a long moment, "it seems I have two options. I could choose to believe your story and, provided you sign papers declaring you will indeed pay your debt with interest, send you on your merry way. Or, I could choose to make you an example to those who are now contemplating similar ways to escape their own debts."

"Please, Mr. Rivers," he gasped, glancing toward Louisa, as though she might come to his defense. "I will pay my debt to you, I swear it. Have mercy."

Elliot raised a brow and then turned to his wife with a slight smile.

"He begs for mercy, Louisa. I leave it to you. What shall we do with Mr. Fenton? Shall we grant him leniency or not?"

Louisa studied the terrified face before her. That he was from the privileged class was obvious from the cut of his clothing and his well-styled hair, but marks of heavy drinking proclaimed his self-indulgence. His eyes pleaded with her. She turned to her husband.

"Let's make him an example, my love. It does not do to allow sympathy to cloud your judgment. This way, your associates will be certain to tread lightly with you. And if I may, I suggest that your men dispose of poor Mr. Fenton's corpse in a place that makes a statement – perhaps near the dock of the *S.S. Carthaginian?*"

"An excellent notion – Cobb, Jenkins, deal with Mr. Fenton. You may kill him however you wish. Do be discreet, however, when you dispose of his body. We do not wish to draw attention from the police. Afterward, spread the word that Mr. Fenton tried to renege on his debt to me."

The men nodded silently and pulled the now-sobbing man out the door. His cries echoed in the hall, ceasing abruptly as the door shut firmly behind them. Louisa smiled at her husband,

"Oh, Elliot!" she cried. "It's such fun to be part of your business dealings! I've been so frightfully bored lately."

She rose from the settee and walked over to him, kissing him enthusiastically. Cupping her cheek, he observed the excited flush on his wife's face with satisfaction. He was aware of her recent *ennui*. It had worried him, and so he had come up with a scheme that he thought she would find most diverting.

"I wonder, Louisa, if you would consent to give me your opinion. I believe I may have found a lucrative area in which to expand our business. I believe your unique talents, particularly your gift for manipulation, would be quite well-suited to it."

"Really? Oh, Elliot, how thrilling! I do so love making money! What is it?"

"Perhaps," he paused, thinking, "I'd rather show you than simply tell you. Come, let us take a drive together in the carriage. We have some shopping to do."

Louisa cocked her head slightly, two small ringlets of her artfully dressed blonde hair falling softly forward. Her blue eyes gleamed with anticipation.

"Just one thing," she leaned forward and put her mouth next to his ear to whisper, "does it involve murder?"

"Quite possibly."

He wound one of the ringlets around his forefinger, studying her face. A cruel smile crossed her rosy lips.

"How perfect."

Lady Helena Pratt frowned at herself in the oval mirror perched atop her dressing table as her maid put the finishing touches on her hair. Wide blue-green eyes stared back at her with an expression of mingled discontent and boredom – the same look they had held for the past ten years. She barely remembered the days before her marriage at age seventeen, just after her first season in London. She knew that they had been full of anticipation and dreams but her girlish fantasies of love and romance that had died the day she was informed she must accept the proposal offered by Lord Pratt. No amount of tears or pleading could sway her father from his decision. The lure of a title in the family was irresistible to the social-climbing merchant.

So it was that ten years ago, almost to the day, Helena had married a man nearly three times her age. There had been two bright spots in the otherwise bleak years that followed: the births of her daughter, Rosalind, and her son, Winston. She loved them more than words could say, but rarely saw or held them since Wallace decreed that they had nannies for such things and she had responsibilities as his wife.

There was no need for her to waste her time spoiling *his* children since, as he often sneered, her involvement would turn Winston into a sniveling brat instead of a man and Rosalind into a shrew like her mother. Disagreement only risked what little interaction she had with her children, and so Helena hid her growing hatred for the man she'd married. Wallace Pratt was an irascible, pompous man with no interest in anything but himself. Now that he had his legitimate heir in Winston, Helena's husband openly shunned her in favor of his latest mistress. She didn't want his attentions back; no, she was thrilled not to suffer his touch any longer, but the shame of sitting down to tea amid the sympathetic glances of her friends was unbearable.

Overwhelmed by her thoughts she rose and left the sitting room, making her way down the stairs just as the butler came into the hallway bearing a silver tray with a calling card on it. Picking it up, she read the name and her first genuine smile in days appeared.

"Jasper, show Mrs. Rivers into the drawing room and tell Molly to bring us some tea."

After waiting for the butler to depart on his mission, Helena walked through the drawing room door.

"Louisa! What a pleasure to see you. I was dreadfully bored before you arrived."

"I thought you might be, Helena. Goodness knows that Lord Pratt is hardly a scintillating companion when he's here, though I hear that he's away. I wonder if you can be sad about that at all?"

Helena focused on the tea tray the maid had just brought in, dismissing the girl with a wave of her hand. She poured, handing Louisa a steaming cup and settling herself on a chair near the fire with her own cup before answering.

"He is away, yes. It's such a relief when he's gone, Louisa, but I never feel I can breathe easy. His latest companion is the kind of woman that creates a spectacle wherever she goes. She must be quite the fool not to realize he won't put up with that for long, but one outburst is enough for gossip to spread like the plague and land back at my feet. I'm sick of seeing mocking eyes and condescending smiles whenever Lord Pratt is mentioned."

Louisa studied her with a strange smile as she stirred her tea slowly. "I wonder if we can speak frankly."

"Of course — we've known each other since we were girls. There's no friend I trust as much, or whose opinion I value as highly."

"I know that you have little fondness for your husband and he is making your life a misery. Is it too much to say that I believe you would be happier if he were permanently removed from your life?"

"No. You are quite right and yet, what can I do? The law allows me no recourse for unfaithfulness and if I were to leave anyway, he would refuse me access to my children. It is a hopeless state. I was thinking on the matter only this morning and it is enough to depress even the most buoyant of spirits, which you know mine have never been."

She brushed at unbidden tears, annoyed with herself for the display of emotion.

"Perhaps it is, Helena, but perhaps it is not."

"What do you mean?"

Louisa lowered her voice to a whisper as she leaned forward on the edge of her chair.

"What if I told you that there was a way to remove him from this household, still alive, leaving you in control of his fortune and your children? How large a risk would you take for such a gift?"

"I would do anything!" Helena's voice was hushed but emphatic. "But how could such a thing be possible? What would I have to do to achieve a miracle of those proportions?"

"All you need to do is sign a simple document, promising a fee of ten thousand pounds for services rendered once you have access to your husband's fortune. No one but ourselves and my husband will ever see this contract. I can promise you, Helena, that if you sign, within a fortnight your husband will be ensconced at an asylum for the mentally deranged with no hope of escape. There will be no question as to whether or not he belongs there. His actions and speech prior to his entrance into Dr. Wick's care will make that quite clear."

Helena stared at Louisa for a long moment, thoughts whirling. *Freedom.* A whisper-soft voice in the back of her mind uttered a warning. There must be some catch she was not seeing, for it seemed too good to be true. The lure of freedom and fortune, however, silenced it almost before it sounded.

"I agree," she said firmly. "Do you have the contract with you?"

"I do indeed, my dear friend. Your regrettable situation has been such a burden to my heart. I'm so pleased I can give you the opportunity to be released from it."

"I will not be able to thank you enough, Louisa, should this scheme of yours work. Wallace has made my life a nightmare; it is time that he experienced a portion of the helplessness that I have been forced to live through. Come, I'll sign immediately."

She moved swiftly to a small secretary placed against the wall and began to search for pen and ink. With her back turned, she did not see the predatory glint of satisfaction in Louisa's eyes.

"Of course, Helena. I am at your service."

6

Grace hummed to herself as she studied the lavender oil she had just finished distilling. *Perfect*, she thought with satisfaction, *in color, scent and consistency.* Moving to the cupboard on the far wall, she pulled out a tray of small glass vials into which she would pour the oil once it cooled and set it on a shelf next to the cabinet. The bell over the front door tinkled and she listened absently for Annie's cheery greeting before recalling that her sister had gone out to buy some meat pies for lunch. Irritation clouding her face, she whipped her apron over her head and hurriedly smoothed her hair back from her face before pushing through the curtain to the front of the shop. She stopped short at the sight of Detective Inspector Ramsey's broad shouldered form silhouetted against the sunlight pouring in through the wide front window.

Even though he had not had any of his belongings with him at the boarding house the previous night, he somehow still managed to be impeccably groomed. Every hair was in place, his suit clean and unwrinkled—even the tips of his shoes shone. She very much wanted to smudge one just to see his reaction and was immediately ashamed of the petty thought. People who possessed the innate gift of appearing well-turned out in every occasion made her aware that she was a near complete failure in that regard. Unsurprisingly, she was most content when she was alone with her work. Plants, unlike people, were not harsh critics. She wondered what the detective thought of her and then scowled, despising herself because she cared if only for a moment.

"Good day, Inspector Ramsey. May I help you?"

He turned from studying a bouquet of dried feverfew and met her gaze. She had the disconcerting sense that he could read her thoughts and she turned to adjust a sprig of dried parsley unnecessarily in order to compose herself. Her skill with herbs was really the only thing the people she encountered in the shop were interested in. Her work was her sanctuary, a place of order and peace. When the topic of conversation strayed outside that area she floundered, alternating between boredom, while listening to conversation she had no interest in, and irritation with the pitying looks of others at her awkward silences.

"Miss Flynn," his expression was serious but not unfriendly, "I wonder if I might have a few minutes of your time."

"Certainly," said Grace, "but, if you don't mind, I have work to do in the back. Perhaps we could talk while I carry on with it?" She didn't wait for his answer before turning and pulling the curtain to the side and gesturing him through.

He took in the space with interest. Jars, bottles and vials in various sizes gleamed on shelves lining the walls. Everything was spotless — everything except what was obviously Grace's work area. There it appeared that a small explosion had taken place. Dust and bits of plant covered the long wooden table and an apparatus he couldn't identify held an empty flask over an unlit wick. Two more flasks filled almost to the brim with oil of the palest yellow were suspended in holders attached to the apparatus. The smell that hung in the air was strong and sweet with a hint of sharpness. He turned to ask her what was in the flasks but she was already busily knotting the ties of her large apron and moving to a shelf set against the wall. She glanced over her shoulder before picking up something from the shelf.

"It's lavender oil," said Grace in response to his unspoken question as she walked swiftly over to the wooden worktable carrying a small tray holding twelve slim tubes of clear glass. Her wide brown eyes met his for a moment before she focused them on the task in front of her. Picking up a pair of large tongs, she lifted one of the flasks of liquid and began to carefully pour it into the vials.

"What's it used for?" asked Ramsey. "Can anyone purchase those vials? Is it dangerous?"

She shot him an amused look without breaking the rhythm of her movements.

"I recommend it primarily to calm the nerves and relieve headache. It's quite harmless when used properly and applied externally. It's a common remedy, so we try to keep spare vials ready. We also sell lavender-filled pillows for the same purpose that I prepare with Annie. She is hopeless with my herbs and equipment and I don't take pleasure in dainty stitching the way she does, so I dry and prepare the lavender and she sews pretty little sachets to hold it."

Replacing the now-empty flask, she returned to the shelf and retrieved another small tray with twelve more vials and brought it to the table.

"Fascinating." Ramsey's distracted tone belied his words. "Miss Flynn, I have a favor to ask you."

She glanced up with a mildly inquisitive gaze, never ceasing her work. "I didn't think that you were here to pay a social call, Inspector. What do you need?"

"I told you a bit about the case I'm investigating yesterday, if you recall." She nodded as he continued. "The woman who exhibited those symptoms was sent to an asylum just outside London, the

Surrey County Asylum, run by a man named Dr. Mordecai Wick. I believe that he is not the benefactor he appears to be, but is instead guilty of criminal behavior. There may be more victims that I've not heard of. In fact, I'm quite certain that there are. I plan to go to the asylum to see what condition the patients are in and determine if anyone is lucid enough to tell me the sequence of events that brought them there."

"Why not interview the woman you mentioned?" she asked absently, carefully placing cork stoppers in each of the glass vials.

"She was pulled from the Thames about a week ago. She was murdered and her body dumped there to hide the crime."

Grace's face displayed no revulsion at the news, though her eyes grew soft and sad. Her hands stilled for a moment before resuming their task.

"It's heartbreaking what people do to each other, isn't it?" she said quietly. "Was it someone close to her? A member of her family, perhaps?"

Ramsey's gaze sharpened, but he found nothing but pity in every nuance of her features.

"What makes you say that?"

"Well," she responded, setting the final tray of vials aside and wiping her hands on the apron covering her gown of cream, sage and brown striped fabric, "most crimes are committed by someone in the victim's family, aren't they? And understandably so, for we are both the most loving and hateful to those closest to us."

She colored at the expression on his face. His clear grey eyes regarded her with both surprise and curiosity. She felt a quick stab of pain at the sight. Growing up in a boisterous, expressive family had been wonderful but she'd often escaped into her work to preserve her sanity. From that, she'd learned that the behavior of others was far more revealing than their words.

"I owe you an apology, Miss Flynn." Ramsey's mouth tipped up. "I am usually a better judge of character. Your powers of perception are greater than I'd assumed."

"Excuse me?" Grace fiddled with the edge of her apron before catching herself and clasping her hands together.

"From what I've observed, you bridle your tongue and hide your observations more often than not," his eyes were entirely too shrewd for her comfort, "though I cannot understand why. You must have a reason. You don't strike me as a woman overly concerned with being seen as unladylike, particularly given your choice of profession. Indeed, the fact that you have a profession is evidence of your disregard for the dictates of society."

Grace winced at the words and tried to figure out how to answer him without revealing that the candid assessment, though quite accurate, stung. Being completely candid in return made her feel uncomfortably vulnerable, but her conscience would allow nothing less.

"Inspector Ramsey," she sighed, "you met some of my family. The rest of my siblings are very much like my father—endlessly loving, animated, emotional and completely oblivious to the underlying tensions that exist between people. I also grew up in a small village where gossip is a way of life. I would have gone mad had I entered into that constant conversation, even if my intent was to bring clarity while lessening judgment. By choosing to sequester myself with such exacting, methodical work, I have been able to distance myself, somewhat, from the volatility of social interaction. I can still," her eyes brightened with a glint of mischief, "observe unseen when I choose to do so, but I am not mired in it every day."

"Fair enough," he replied after a moment's pause. "This simply confirms that you are precisely the person I wish to ask."

"Ask what, Inspector Ramsey? You still haven't told me why you're here."

"Would you consent to accompany me to the Surrey County Asylum? I suspect some of the inmates are being systematically poisoned and I do not possess the necessary knowledge of the natural world to know whether the so-called remedies are dangerous or not. Now that I've uncovered your secret," he grinned, the expression altering his features so much that she found herself staring at him, "I would also like your impressions of the staff and Dr. Wick himself. Your clear sight would be quite an asset."

Grace turned the request over in her mind. Her gaze took in her workspace: dried herbs, lotions and oils sitting in quiet rows on solid wood shelves. Suddenly, it wasn't quite enough. The adventure might be worth her time, and it didn't hurt that she found Inspector Ramsey a bit of an enigma. Perhaps some time spent in his company alone would uncover the secrets she was certain lurked beneath his calm demeanor. She could hope, anyway.

"I agree to help you, Inspector Ramsey," she met his gaze squarely, "but I'm afraid I cannot simply leave the shop with Annie. She doesn't have the necessary expertise to mix lotions and oils or any of the other tasks I usually take care of here in the back room. We are closed on Sundays and Mondays. However, I could venture to the asylum with you on Monday morning, if that is soon enough."

"Monday would be excellent. That gives me time to gather more information so as to be well-prepared, letting it all simmer in my mind on Sunday."

"Then you may consider me at your service, sir."

He was about to respond when the bell sounded and Annie's cheery greeting floated back to them. Shutters covered Grace's eyes and her face tightened nearly imperceptibly. His innate curiosity flared to life.

The curtain was pulled to one side and Annie hurried through the opening, stopping short at the sight of the detective standing across from her busily working sister.

"Inspector Ramsey," she smiled brightly, "what brings you back to our shop so soon? Do you have more questions regarding Mr. Wiggins?"

"I do, yes," he replied, ignoring the surprise covering Grace's features at his answer, "but I've spoken with your sister and she has agreed to meet with me on Monday to go through the details. I will not interrupt any more of her work than necessary."

"Do you need to ask me any questions?" she asked eagerly, a hopeful look on her fresh young face. Being part of a police investigation appeared to be quite enticing to her.

"I'm afraid there is nothing more that you could tell me about Mr. Wiggins' threats than you already have. It is your sister's knowledge of herbs and their uses that will be most helpful in gathering evidence against the man. I hope to use it to uncover the motivation behind his actions."

"Oh, I see," a slight pout formed on her lips, "but don't you have people working for you who take care of such uninteresting details? Surely a man as important as you shouldn't have to waste your time on that?"

Ramsey smiled politely as some of Grace's guarded behavior was explained. Annie was obviously very much used to being the more admired of the two sisters. Her petulant expression spoke volumes.

"We have doctors that we trust to do post-mortems for us but, sadly, we do not have the resources to pay chemists and other specialists to work on our cases, unless they involve particularly powerful individuals. Your sister already knows what Mr. Wiggins said and possesses the necessary expertise to assist me. She is the ideal candidate."

Annie tilted her head, frowning in thought.

"That makes sense, Inspector Ramsey, and Gracie *is* extremely knowledgeable, even if it pertains to things that most people care little about." She smiled at her sister and lifted the small basket she carried in her right hand. "I have our lunch. I would have been back sooner but Mr. Baskins tried to convince me to allow his son to walk with me in Hyde Park on Sunday afternoon. I had the most difficult time persuading him I was not interested. In fact, it was not until Constable Blackstone happened in to purchase a sandwich that Mr. Baskins ceased his coaxing and I escaped."

The slight coloring in her cheeks gave hint to either embarrassment or excitement over the recollection of the man's admiration. Ramsey suspected the latter, given her coquettish glance in his direction.

"It is most fortuitous that Constable Blackstone happened by then." Grace's voice was dry.

Ramsey grinned in spite of himself, quickly squelching the expression before Annie noticed.

"I will see you on Monday, Miss Flynn," he nodded at Grace. "Good day to you both." He moved to the curtain to depart, but stopped and turned back as a thought crossed his mind. "I beg your pardon for my continued interruption but I meant to ask where you and your brother attend services. The church I have been attending is too far from the boarding house or the Yard."

The stiffening in the shoulders of both women was obvious and their smiles took on the woodenness of suppressed emotion. Grace cleared her throat and answered.

"We all attend early services at St. Jude's Anglican on Sundays, but also I attend a Methodist church that is located only a half mile from our rooms for the mid-morning service. It meets at eleven o' clock in what was formerly an apothecary. I thought that was rather appropriate, given my profession."

She gave another, slightly more genuine half-smile at the statement, but it quickly faded as Annie interjected.

"You'll have to excuse my sister's forwardness, Inspector Ramsey," she sent Grace a scornful glance before turning to him again. "She's foolishly become caught up in the strange teachings of the Methodists and has been causing our family no end of grief over it. To her credit," her condescending tone clearly belied her words, "she continues to attend St. Jude's with us so that we may avoid what small scandal our humble family would incur should she leave the Church of England entirely."

Grace remained silent but the strain of doing so was evident on her face. Ramsey felt a stirring of compassion for both her and the situation she found herself in. It couldn't be at all easy to choose spiritual conviction over family loyalty. Heaven knew it was difficult enough for him to be at odds, spiritually, with his family and he didn't even particularly like them.

"I see. Thank you both. I will not keep you from your lunch any longer."

Pulling the curtain aside, he moved swiftly through the opening and out into the shop. Pushing the door open, he stepped into the sunlit street, his mind already moving to the tasks that awaited him. As intriguing as he found the Flynn family, Grace in particular, there were more important things clamoring for his attention. Murder could not be ignored.

7

The old stone manor that housed the Surrey County Asylum was situated seven miles from the outskirts of London. The main roadway heading out of the city connected with various smaller offshoots, and those with even narrower ones. It was one of these insignificant-looking lanes, halfway obscured by tall bushes, that led the final three miles to the path opening into the courtyard of the asylum. The large wooden door was set firmly in a thick, ivy-encrusted wall of weathered grey stone.

In the two years that he had been operating his institution, Dr. Mordecai Wick had learned a great deal. In the beginning, his fervor to create a name for himself had blinded him to the immense financial strain. Should generous patrons not be found and his institution not be filled to capacity, he would soon find himself in the poorhouse. Sure enough, after eighteen months, he was nearly destitute, with only the income from the families of five private patients to pay the fees he'd incurred with increasingly demanding creditors. He had been on the brink of failure when a man named Nicholas Gosford approached him.

Gosford's correct speech and quality garments immediately identified him as a well-educated, well-paid man of affairs. His eyes, a nearly transparent shade of blue, coupled with the man's white blonde hair, gave him the appearance of some otherworldly creature, wraith-like and ice cold. Wick's thick, unruly dark hair and narrow eyes set deep under thick, bushy brows were a stark contrast. Only his elegant hands bore the mark of refinement.

Gosford had laid a proposition in front of him, a perfectly timed gift from above, of that he was certain. "My employer is an unusual man, Dr. Wick," Gosford said coolly, folding his hands in his lap, "and your vision for an institution that promotes innovative, unconventional treatment of the mentally deranged has caught his attention. He is impressed by your plans, but being a businessman himself, is aware that such schemes require a good deal of capital to progress."

"They do, indeed." Dr. Wick didn't bother to dispute the fact. "In truth, I am without the necessary resources to make my asylum into what I envision. I had hoped that once my methods were made public, the families of those suffering from mental distress would show their generosity. Unfortunately, there are a number of my colleagues who would prefer that things remain as they are, and have been most vocal in their opposition. As a result, I will be forced to close my establishment before the new year." He'd clenched his fists, fighting to keep calm. "I don't understand how my idea can be cast aside as having little merit when the York Retreat and their moral treatment foolishness is well-funded and growing. Say what you will about the piety of those confounded Quakers, they must be liars, for no one could have the success they speak of without the use of restraints and medication. It's ridiculous. Given half a chance, my asylum would put them all to shame."

"My employer wishes me to make you an offer," Gosford unclasped his hands and leaned forward, withdrawing a large sheaf of bank notes from his breast coat pocket. He placed them face down on the table. "He knows of a number of ladies, and a few gentlemen as well, who suffer from a variety of maladies. They share two things in common: a propensity for delusions and family members who do not wish to be embarrassed by their antics. The proposition is thus—you will hire a matron selected by my employer to oversee the everyday care of these individuals and admit them to your institution. Once here, they are yours to treat as you see fit and you will receive five hundred pounds a year for your trouble."

Dr. Wick did not consider himself a stupid man. He was well aware that there was probably something he was currently unaware of connected to the man's offer but he could see no other way to stay solvent. The thought of his name on the lips of influential men as the most esteemed doctor in all England was motivation enough to accept. His fists clenched in fury as memories of his colleagues calling him a quack rang in his ears.

Three days after Gosford's visit and Dr. Wick's acceptance of his employer's terms, Matron Green arrived to oversee the women's wing. She brought with her two women suffering from hysteria and paranoia. Dr. Wick had gone straight to work on both of them and by the end of the week, he could hardly remember what it had been like to scrape for funds with the constant fear that his dream would die. In the nine months since, he'd experienced not one iota of regret.

Staring out the window of his office, Dr. Wick smiled and sighed with contentment. The folder in front of him was nearly complete; a final accounting of the days just prior to Georgiana Kingsley's escape and untimely death. He felt no remorse over the woman's difficult end. She was little more than a case study to him; an experiment gone wrong and a particularly troublesome one at that. She'd been unusually resistant to the treatments he employed: immersion in ice water to revive the mind, electrical shock to the head and limbs and metal restraints to limit self-harm. When he had instructed Matron

Green to hold Lady Kingsley down while he placed the burning end of a cigar to the bottom of her feet in order to re-center her mind, she had bitten her lip, keeping silent until she could no longer stifle her scream of pain. As he had opened the door to leave after applying his expertise, she had shrieked that she would do the same to him once her husband finally rescued her.

Those eyes had been empty of life only three days later. Not his fault, he thought complacently, as he wrote down the date her body had been pulled from the Thames. He followed that entry with the date, two weeks later, that he had finally been called in to give evidence at the inquest held in regard to her death. Her mind had been very troubled; he had declared forcefully. Her behavior was erratic and occasionally violent. No, he'd said sorrowfully, he was not surprised to hear that she'd met an unfortunate end and he agreed with the doctor in charge that she had been strangled. He saw no reason to share his methods with the public until he could present his patients before them, fully cured, so he claimed that the burns and bruises on her body were certainly self-inflicted during one of her hysterical episodes. To say otherwise would only serve to confuse weak minds unable to grasp the complexity of his work. He also neglected to say that as soon as he had been informed Lady Kingsley had escaped, he had panicked and sent word to Mr. Gosford. A one sentence missive had been the reply: *It's been taken care of.*

A slight shiver touched his spine and he straightened, trying to ignore the sensation. He did good work, necessary work. People were going to be helped by what he learned and in every medical advance, there were casualties. Besides, the woman had been completely unreasonable. No wonder her husband had committed her to the institution. From what Dr. Wick had read in the society column of the London paper, Lord Kingsley's new fiancée was very young, beautiful, sweet-tempered, and titled. He was better off and the asylum was benefiting from an extra bit of generosity as a gesture of his gratitude for his late wife's care.

He closed the folder on his desk and sat back, steepling his fingers under his chin. A new patient was due to arrive at precisely one o'clock this afternoon, the first man to be admitted into his specialized treatment program. He could hardly wait to begin.

Lord Wallace Pratt was titled and well-respected. Mr. Gosford assured him that Lady Helena Pratt, Lord Pratt's wife, had documented her husband's clear slide into insanity. Delusions, hallucinations, convulsions and violent outbursts were only the beginning of his decline. According to Mr. Gosford, the man was now nearly catatonic most of the time, only rousing to shout at specters. Rubbing his palms together, Dr. Wick glanced out the window at the bare lane leading to the manor. He pulled out his watch, flipping it open. At three minutes to twelve, he had just over an hour to wait.

Rising, he picked up the closed folder and carried it over to the large mahogany cabinet standing against the wall. Unlocking the bottom drawer with the key he kept on a chain around his neck, he slid the folder into the appropriate slot, then closed and locked the drawer once more. He had just enough time to have a bite to eat before Lady Pratt was due to arrive with her husband. He could hardly wait to try his methods on the stronger sex and document the results. The thousand pounds that the asylum was receiving for Lord Pratt's keep would allow Wicks to travel to London and Paris to inspect the very latest in electrical shock devices—as well as replenish his supply of opium and expensive brandy. The thought made him almost giddy with anticipation. Perhaps his association with Mr. Gosford was not entirely above board but it no longer mattered. The science was everything. Nothing could be allowed in the way of that, not while he was learning so much about the human capacity for pain. His eyes glittered as he pulled the door open. His patients were waiting.

8

Grace listened absently to the resonant voice of the priest as he uttered the final prayer of Sunday's morning service. The words were so familiar that she could recite them with ease but they still evoked a sense of awe and reverence in her heart. The Amen sounded and she crossed herself before opening her eyes, rising from the kneeler and settling down once more on the pew. Beside her, Annie slipped her handkerchief into her reticule, having occupied herself during the lengthy sermon by tracing the embroidered initials and flowers in the top right corner. Grace smiled somewhat bitterly as she considered her sister's outrage over Grace's desire to fully join with the Methodist movement. The younger woman only tolerated Sunday morning services of any kind because they were a chance to see and be seen.

Light streamed in through the stained-glass windows, coating the parishioners in gold-tinged red, blue, and green. The low hum of voices filled the church as people gathered prayer books and reticules and then filed out of their pews. In their own pew, James rose, stepped out and then turned back to wait for his sisters. Offering an arm to each of them, he escorted Grace and Annie out of the church and into the mild morning air.

"I don't know about you two," he said, "but I think today would be a lovely day for a walk and picnic in the park. For once, I am not needed at the hospital so we have the whole day together. I'm certain that if we asked nicely enough, Mrs. Lydiate would pack us a lunch basket."

Annie's eyes sparkled at the thought.

"Oh, what a wonderful idea, James. We need only go back to the boarding house to change into our walking dresses and then we can be on our way."

Grace shifted uncomfortably.

"I'm afraid I cannot go right away, Annie. The Methodist service starts in a quarter hour and I need to hurry if I am going to make it on time. I think a picnic would be a very nice way to spend our Sunday afternoon, though. Perhaps I can meet you in the park once the service is done?"

Annie's face clouded with irritation.

"Gracie!" There was a whining edge to her voice. "Forget your other service this once. I don't see why you insist on going every Sunday anyway. Surely God does not expect such devotion from a mere shopkeeper. Mama and Papa are already very displeased with your insistence on attending there since the Church of England is the only church that God is truly pleased with."

Grace tried to gentle her voice and posture even as her sister's stinging derision hit its mark.

"Annie, you know we do not agree on matters of faith. It is pointless for us to discuss this again. I have already explained the Methodist church on Slate Street preaches the same God we worship at St. Jude's. They also teach much more about Jesus and encourage all of us to study our Bibles on our own. My going has little to do with piety and everything to do with becoming better acquainted with the Bible and Christ Himself."

James was clearly uncomfortable with the topic, shifting from foot to foot as Annie frowned in annoyed disappointment.

"Fine. If you insist on having your way, go, regardless of my feelings. James and I will be in the park in between the fountain and the especially large willow. I hope you can find us without too much trouble."

Turning with the kind of offended swish of the skirt that only a truly skilled woman can manage, Annie stalked off in the direction of the boarding house. James was forced to jog to catch up, casting an apologetic glance over his shoulder at Grace as he followed his youngest sister. She stood for a moment, struggling to suppress her hurt. All she wanted was to make it to the welcoming arms of the little Methodist congregation. A time of studying Scripture and worshipping with people who, to her constant surprise, had genuine affection for her would do much to settle her soul so that she could simply enjoy the afternoon with James and Annie. She did love them, but it was not always an easy relationship.

Breathing a sigh of relief that she'd made it on time, Grace slipped quietly into the little room and sat down on one of the hard, wooden chairs. Glancing up, she smiled and waved at her friend and customer, Alice Fairchild, who sat near to the front with her husband and three children. She smothered a giggle when Alice's youngest, three-year-old Johnny, turned and shouted her name, waving frantically. She was still fighting her chuckles when a shadow fell across the chair next to her and the weight of someone sitting down caused it to creak. She looked over to find Inspector Ramsey's grey eyes assessing her. A tiny smile quirked his lips and she felt color in her cheeks. Trying to ignore her sudden nervousness, she nodded politely.

"Good day, Inspector Ramsey. I wasn't expecting to see you here."

"I thought I'd join you this morning, if you don't mind. I knew some fellows in university who were devout Methodists and found we shared very similar views and habits, despite my Church of England raising. It simply never occurred to me to search out a Methodist congregation until you mentioned this one the other day."

"I hope it's not a disappointment to you, Inspector. I'm very fond of the people here and the preaching is quite inspiring, I find."

"I can't imagine that I would find anything amiss, then." He paused. "Miss Flynn, why is it that you attend both this service and St. Jude's?"

Grace's eyes darkened and she looked away. "I'm afraid it's rather complicated, sir."

"I don't mind complications. They make life interesting. Go on, if you do not mind." His clear gaze invited her to trust him.

"As you wish, but don't say I didn't warn you it was complicated." Her expression grew wistful. "My family came to England from Ireland when I was five years old. My father and his brother felt that there were better opportunities here and a brighter future. They brought their wives and children and were fortunate enough to find good employment in the same village. That wasn't the only reason they left. They were Irish Protestants and the tensions between them and the Roman Catholics were becoming increasingly volatile. So they emigrated here and raised us in the faith they themselves had been raised."

"That makes perfect sense and explains the first service you attended this morning."

She raised a brow at his interruption and he smiled his apology, gesturing for her to continue.

"When I came to London eight years ago with James and Annie, we began attending St. Jude's together. We were terribly busy getting settled and established and Sundays became a respite from work. I think James felt that most strongly since his studies were so heavy. After about six months, however, I began to feel as though something was missing. We had a Bible at home that my mother used to teach each of us to read and I loved reading the Psalms. The psalmist always spoke directly to God himself, not through a priest, and that thought warmed my heart. I wanted to do that too but I didn't know if it was possible."

She chuckled softly to herself, eyes faraway with memory.

"The look on Father O'Reilly's face when I asked him my questions was priceless."

"What did he say?"

"That a young woman should not question traditions set out by the church and tested by men much more intelligent and able to comprehend deep theological truths than she would ever be."

Ramsey's mouth tipped up further in a sardonic smile.

"I imagine you found such an explanation most helpful and immediately stopped questioning anything."

"Naturally," her eyes flashed with mischief. "No, by the time I left home I was already questioning the church — not God, but the man-made institution and the rituals added over the years. I could find no evidence of most of them when I read Luke's account in the Book of Acts of the early church. It was terribly confusing, truth be told."

"What then?" asked Ramsey, clearly intrigued. Grace wondered if he'd known others interested enough in the truth about God that they searched diligently for answers. She hadn't encountered many men *or* women, for that matter, who did so outside of the small congregation she was now sitting amidst. She looked at the people sitting around her with a swell of affection in her heart before continuing.

"About a month after the shop opened, a woman came in looking for something to treat her frequent headaches. Annie was out running an errand, much to my consternation, so I waited on her. She was very easy to talk to and I discovered that she was the wife of Mr. Markham, the man who preaches here. When she invited me to attend a service, I decided to try it for a Sunday and see if I could find any answers. The first sermon I heard was a straightforward exposition on the third chapter of Romans that cut me to my heart. I went home and told James and Annie. It caused such a row that I decided it was simply better for me to continue attending St. Jude's as well as coming here. I've been doing so ever since."

"Eight years and your sister still holds that against you?"

His voice was soft. She smiled, but it was tinged with sadness even though her voice was matter-of-fact.

"She has never questioned her faith the way I did. While she has no real interest in God at the moment, she sees my leaving the Church of England as demeaning our family's history while hurting her chances at a good match in the process. My actions make her uncomfortable and that makes her lash out. I understand her fear and that lessens the pain."

"But it still hurts, does it not?"

She raised her eyes to meet his, strangely discomfited by the understanding there.

"Yes," she replied quietly as the organ signalled the start of the service. "Yes, it does."

By the close of the service, Grace seemed to have found a measure of peace. Ramsey stayed by her side, content to observe her interactions with the other members of the small congregation. He found the ease with which she laughed and smiled at them such a marked contrast to the reserved attempts at connection he'd seen her make toward her family. It intrigued him, yet another element of her character that did so. He'd never considered joining his life to anyone and he wasn't quite sure what, if anything, he wanted to do about it.

He fell into step next to Grace as she gathered her things and made her way swiftly to the door.

"Don't you wish to stay longer?" he asked as he pushed the door open for her. "You were clearly enjoying yourself, and I'm not in any hurry."

She looked up, blinking in the bright sunshine flooding through the opening.

"I wish I could but I've arranged to meet James and Annie for a picnic in the park. They will be there waiting already so I must hurry back to Mrs. Lydiate's to change my gown."

"It would be ungentlemanly of me not to escort you home, but perhaps you would allow me to escort you to the park as well?"

Her face registered surprise, and he wondered if his did as well. He wasn't quite sure he could explain, even to himself, why he wished to spend more time in her company. Suddenly uncomfortable, he retreated to the safety of work as they stepped out into the light of the midday sun.

"I have some questions that I was hoping to ask you before we go to visit the asylum tomorrow. There are a number of plants I've heard of recently, the properties of which I'm quite unfamiliar."

"Which plants?"

"Belladonna and bleeding heart are foremost on my mind. That's what Hiram Wiggins wanted from you, is it not?"

Grace thought for a moment before answering, her brow wrinkling in concentration.

"It still doesn't make much sense to me why he wanted large quantities of belladonna if all he wanted was to cause hallucinations or convulsions. If he was even a little off in his measurements, whomever he slipped the belladonna to would die a very painful death. The crushed leaves and roots of bleeding heart, however, wreak havoc with the nervous system. They would be most effective if one wished to cause mental instability."

"If my guess is correct, Wiggins and his employer receive payment for providing the means and motivation for removal from London to the asylum. If the victim dies after being taken there, it is not as though they have not made a profit. If, however, the victim is a long-term resident of Dr. Wick's facility, ongoing payments are required from their families. I wonder," he paused as a thought took shape, "whether they wanted the belladonna to use when they have extracted all the money they can and have no reason to maintain the expense of keeping the inmate alive."

"How horrible," Grace's voice was low and filled with pity. "No wonder you are so determined to stop them. Do you know who is behind such a thing?"

Ramsey's fists clenched automatically and he forced himself to relax his fingers.

"I have a strong suspicion, yes." He took a deep breath, fighting to reign in his rising fury. Her look was piercing and he realized that she had seen more of his internal struggle than he desired. "For over two years, I have been hunting a couple by the name of Elliott and Louisa Rivers with the goal of dismantling their part of London's criminal underworld by bringing them to justice. A man named William Sanders was, at one time, the most powerful member of London's criminal network, the head of it you might say. About two and a half years ago, he was betrayed and killed by his right hand man, Elliott Rivers. I am certain that Rivers was assisted in that endeavor by the woman who is now his wife. Unfortunately, I could not find enough evidence to charge either of them with the deaths, let alone any of the crimes I believe they have instigated. About a year ago, I found out through a friend, a private investigator named Jonathan Hayes, that the Rivers had turned their attentions to forcing destitute young ladies of good breeding into prostitution, ensconcing the ruined girls in a number of their many brothels. Since that is not technically illegal, I could do nothing. Again, innocent lives were lost and I could not find the evidence to convict. This time I mean to have them."

Warm approval shone in Grace's eyes. "I will do whatever I can to help you, Inspector Ramsey, though I know there is little I *can* do. At the very least, I will offer you greater knowledge of the plants we discussed just now if you do not mind waiting while I change my gown and collect my natural encyclopedia." She hesitated for a moment and then forged on somewhat nervously. "Why don't you join me for a picnic lunch in the park instead of merely escorting me there? We can talk further and better prepare ourselves for tomorrow."

The warm sensation in Ramsey's chest strengthened at the invitation. He appreciated the frankness that was too often lacking, because of the dictates of society rather than those of personality, in other women her age.

"Thank you, Miss Flynn, that would be very pleasant," he said and a brief, genuine smile altered his features from formidable to almost friendly — well, almost. The sharpness of his gaze would never allow him to be truly at ease, a cost he'd accepted the moment he chose to become a member of London's police force. Fighting the darkness and despair that lurked throughout the city left an indelible mark, one that could never be removed.

He'd never questioned if it was worth it. Ridding the streets of crime and providing a greater measure of safety for innocent people was his strongest desire. Until this moment, that is, when walking down the street with a lovely, intriguing woman on his arm gave him a glimpse of a different life, one of quiet and normalcy. Twin sensations of anxiety and anticipation filled Ramsey as they turned down the street that led to the boarding house. *God help me. I'm so far out of my depth and I do believe I'm actually considering matrimony.*

9

Ramsey wondered what he was getting himself into as he paced the small, sparsely furnished parlor of Mrs. Lydiate's boarding house the next day. He had long ago made it a practice not to work on the Sabbath if possible and habitually spent the day alone. In fact, he thought dryly, he spent every day he was not working alone and rather preferred it that way. Yet, when Grace had invited him to join her and her siblings for their picnic in the park the previous day, he'd surprised himself by accepting immediately. To his amazement, he'd enjoyed the afternoon immensely. Certainly the younger Miss Flynn had occasioned a few awkward moments with her coquettish behavior, but he'd been so intrigued by the elder Miss Flynn that even that hadn't detracted from the outing.

Occasionally Jonathan Hayes and his wife, Verity, took pity on him and invited him to dine, usually as part of a dinner party including their friends, Thomas and Charlotte Brooke, and Jonathan's father, Matthew. Ramsey had served with the elder Mr. Hayes for two years in the police force before Matthew had retired to work in private investigation alongside his son. Outside of that small group, he really had nobody who was more than a passing acquaintance. He sometimes wondered if anyone would grieve over him long if he happened to be killed in the line of duty, and the thought exposed an emptiness in his life that concerned him.

He heard the sound of swift footsteps and swishing skirts in the hallway and turned to the door. Grace appeared in the opening dressed in a simple plaid gown of blue, brown and cream trimmed with dark blue satin banding at the wrists and hem. A bit of ivory lace lay in pleasing, elegant folds to form a loose collar, making her dark auburn hair gleam with copper lights that matched the flecks in her brown eyes. It took him a moment to realize that he was staring, a fact that only dawned on him when he noticed the self-conscious way she tugged at her sleeves, straightening the wristbands.

"Is something amiss, sir?"

"Not at all – I'm afraid my mind was just wandering a bit. Come, we had best get started if we wish to return to London by nightfall. Do you have your natural encyclopedia with you? It might be helpful to have it on hand."

"It's in my satchel, along with a small selection of lavender pillows, a bottle of witch hazel, smelling salts, three hairbrushes and some mint-flavored paste for cleaning teeth. I thought that even if this asylum does not turn out to be involved in anything criminal, the residents probably still suffer from lack of attention to their basic needs. I've heard of nowhere but the York Retreat that treats the mad as more than animals. I hope to give them something to make them feel a bit more human."

Ramsey smiled as he reached to take the satchel from her, admiration and respect growing with every word she spoke.

"Your soft heart does you credit, Miss Flynn."

A flush suffused her cheeks and she turned away. "It is not a soft heart so much as a practical mind, Inspector Ramsey. The poor souls have nothing of their own and are treated with little attempt to preserve their dignity. If I can alleviate even a small portion of their suffering to show them God's love, I must do so."

Quick footsteps sounded in the hallway and Annie peeked through the doorway.

"Detective Inspector Ramsey. I wondered if I would see you before you and Grace headed out on your mission," she rolled her eyes drolly as a dimple winked in her cheek. "You should have seen her packing her satchel this morning. I told her that no madwoman is going to have any use for a hairbrush or lavender pillow but there was no dissuading her. I hope you're not too embarrassed by her plan, well intentioned as she is."

She fluttered her eyelashes as she smiled up at Ramsey. He caught the stiffening of Grace's shoulders from the corner of his eye and saw her deliberately relax them. He spoke before she could say anything in response.

"Actually, I was quite impressed with her foresight and her compassion. If we can come up with no other way to gain entrance, I can introduce her as a benefactress who prevailed upon me to escort her for safety's sake. Scotland Yard is not immune to the pressures of society and we are occasionally called on to serve those with influence in the hopes of garnering their favor." He paused and lifted a brow quizzically. "I am surprised that a bright young woman such as yourself would not have seen the cleverness and compassion of your sister's actions. Perhaps you are overtired?"

Annie's face flushed crimson and her eyes shot sparks of fury at Grace, who appeared to be trying desperately to pretend that she hadn't heard his reply. The younger woman was not used to men criticizing anything she said. Ramsey mused that most fell under the spell of her vivacious personality and striking appearance immediately and he had no doubt that she used her assets to their full potential. Many men of his acquaintance were simply unable to resist the thrill of a young, pretty woman who flattered them with a witty turn of phrase. He wondered if her thoughtless cruelty mattered at all to Annie or her admirers.

"We had best be going," he said, offering his arm to Grace. "It is a two hour journey each way and our business with Dr. Wick will take some time. I bid you good day, Miss Flynn."

Not allowing Grace time for anything more than a quick farewell of her own, Ramsey piloted her down the hallway and out the door into the early morning light. A nondescript black carriage harnessed to a mismatched pair of bays was waiting for them. The coachman greeted Ramsey by name and lifted his hat to Grace as the inspector opened the carriage door, helping her inside. She settled herself, arranging her skirts and lifting a hand to check her hair without really paying attention. Ramsey felt his spirits rise in anticipation. A journey out of London was a rare and pleasant thing, indeed.

The carriage bounced as he climbed in and sat down across from Grace, shutting the door behind him. He knocked on the roof to signal the driver and, with the groan of wheels and creaking of the leather harness, the vehicle began to move. The boarding house faded from view and they headed away from the center of London, toward its outskirts and the countryside beyond.

Digging in her satchel, Grace pulled out her natural encyclopedia and Ramsey read the page on belladonna listing the various forms the plant could be administered in and what they looked like. If they came across anything like that in the asylum, they would be able to recognize it — well, at least, Grace would. Ramsey didn't quite trust his brief study of the single page with its delicate sketch of the plant to give him the expertise he needed, otherwise he would have left Grace in London where she would be out of danger. She'd also shown him the pages containing information on opium and the poppies it was derived from, bleeding heart, yew, and monkshood. She'd also read through a monograph describing the uses of laudanum and morphine, belladonna and other substances for treatment of various diseases.

His forehead creased as he recalled a story Grace had told him the day before, chronicling the long, harrowing weaning process she had gone through with two women in her neighborhood, one a cook and the other a seamstress, as they struggled to stop taking even small amounts of laudanum on an hourly basis for the constant pain they suffered. The doctor had diagnosed them with neuralgia, a nerve pain that was unrelenting and often caused emotional breakdowns by its ceaseless wearing on the body.

Laudanum had helped both in the beginning but soon, neither woman could function without it, even though they were far from able to afford the drug. It had taken months of consultation with James while she encouraged them to wean themselves from the drug while mixing compositions of lavender and feverfew to manage the symptoms instead. Ramsey's internal conflict over his growing attraction to her had become increasingly intense as she'd described the situation with both candor and humility — particularly when he observed the cost of both in the face of Annie's derisive comments.

Ramsey studied Grace as she studied her book. If Annie were there, she would no doubt be chiding Grace for ignoring him, while herself chattering away and doing her best to charm him. He was uncommonly grateful it was the elder sister who was his companion this day. If her frank and gentle spirit weren't attractive enough, she had the added draw of form and features that he found lovely. Her eyes were golden brown and warm, her skin smooth and clear but for the freckles sprinkled across her straight nose and her russet hair was thick and healthy. She was not in the first blush of youth, but at nearly thirty, she had a maturity and self-knowledge that simply enhanced everything else.

She must have felt his eyes on her because she lowered the book to her lap and glanced up. "How much longer do you think it will be before we arrive? I rather lost track of time while I was reading," she smiled self-deprecatingly. "I'm a poor traveling companion, I know."

"Not at all," he said with a nod toward the book. "Are you still reading about the herbs we discussed yesterday?"

"This section deals with the effects of laudanum and morphine. It is often used to treat nervous disorders and I wanted to be as prepared as possible for the poor souls we may encounter while at the asylum. If I can at least recognize what they are being treated with, perhaps you will be able to charge Dr. Wick with something, some crime of abuse or neglect?"

Ramsey sighed, absently rubbing a hand across his eyes.

"I would like nothing better than to lock that man up and throw away the key, preferably in his own asylum so he can experience everything he's done to his patients. Sadly, I don't see how it's possible. None of the witnesses could be declared of sound mind in a court of law, as their families will all too readily testify."

He turned his gaze to the passing countryside, the gathering clouds a pleasing contrast to the vibrant green of the fields. His features tightened at the thought of the residents, the horror he believed they faced daily at odds with the asylum's bucolic setting.

"Inspector Ramsey," Grace said tentatively, breaking into his thoughts, "I believe I may have a way to discover what Dr. Wick is truly doing at the asylum. It would also allow me access to the patients so I could determine whether or not they are the victims of ongoing poisoning."

He studied her nervous expression, his own gaze darkening with resignation. Despite his plea for forgiveness for allowing obsession to rule his actions, he knew that he'd be unable to resist if her plan would gain them entrance into the asylum.

"I'm not going to like this, am I?"

"It is a good plan, sir, and perhaps the only way to accomplish anything tangible."

"You did not answer my question. Am I going to like this idea of yours?"

She shifted, fidgeting, then clasping her hands loosely on top of the book on her lap to still their movement.

"Probably not – but it is our best chance at putting Dr. Wick in prison. Will you at least hear me out?"

Ramsey met her gaze steadily, eyes intent on hers, then he sighed and leaned back against the padded seat.

"I suppose I must. You have my attention. Convince me."

10

The weather-beaten stone manor of the Surrey County Asylum loomed at the end of the narrow lane, its air of worn nobility belying the potential perversity within. Ramsey hated Grace's idea but he'd been right. He wasn't able to resist the lure of gaining entrance and finding evidence. The closer the carriage drew to their destination, the tighter the knot in his stomach became. It was a dangerous plan, clearly formed on impulse, but too brilliant to refuse regardless of the risk. If it were only his safety at stake, but the possibility of harm to Grace had him torn. However, no argument would sway her, and, he admitted, he hadn't argued long.

He slid his gaze sideways and, despite his anxiety, he couldn't help the amused twitch of his lips at Grace's altered appearance. Her formerly neatly-arranged hair was untidily pulled back into a haphazard bun with locks straggling out, one cuff was nearly severed from her gown, hanging by only a few threads, and dusty bare feet peeked from beneath her skirts. A smudge of dirt across the bridge of her nose and one on her cheek completed the transformation she had accomplished in a matter of minutes when they stopped at the side of the road before turning down the rutted lane that led to the asylum.

Ramsey prayed that both their acting skills would be convincing.

They would present themselves as brother and sister, a Mr. and Miss Barrett, he having just inherited a respectable fortune at the death of their father and wary of having his chances at an advantageous marriage ruined by the taint of insanity in the blood. Her "illness" would mirror the unfortunates they had already discussed as closely as possible without being obvious imitations. Hereditary madness, through the mother's side, was their consensus. Ramsey would assure Dr. Wick she was no danger to herself or others with the hope that she would be left unshackled long enough to find evidence of criminal activity. She would have only an hour before Ramsey came back for her as a detective inspector of Scotland Yard. Even that was far more time under Dr. Wick's power than he was comfortable with but the lure of discovering something was so strong, and the likelihood of advancing the case so slim otherwise, that he had agreed.

The carriage slowed and then stopped, rocking back and forth as it settled. Ramsey wondered if he should make one final attempt to change Grace's mind. He wanted to protect her, to shield her from the despair and vulgarity he knew she would encounter inside. However, seeing the determined gleam in her eyes, he closed his mouth without uttering a word. The glimpse of such strength of will where he had predominantly seen a soft heart previously gave him that increasingly familiar feeling of warmth in his chest again. He rubbed his knuckles over his breastbone.

"Are you ready for this, Miss Flynn?"

Though her eyes were calm and steady, the excited flush in her cheeks and impatient tapping of her toes on the carriage floor told of her suppressed excitement. She removed two miniature cloth bags from her satchel, slipping them into a pocket he had not noticed along the side seam of her full skirt. She took a deep breath and then gave him a brilliant smile that transformed her habitually reserved expression into one so open and free that he felt himself struggling for breath once more. He rubbed the heel of his hand hard against his chest, trying to assuage the odd ache. He would perhaps have to ask her about his symptoms once they were on their way back to London.

"To tell you the truth, Inspector Ramsey, I can hardly wait. An hour from now, I will hopefully have the information we need and you will be back to save me from Dr. Wick's clutches."

She chuckled, looking uncommonly confident. She was only playing a part, but it appeared the role of the madwoman was giving her a tempting taste of what it felt like to throw off the encumbrances of propriety. She would have to be very careful indeed, or she might find herself behaving with more abandon than was wise once the guise was shed. After studying her for a long moment, Ramsey pushed open the carriage door, climbed out, and then extended a hand to help her down. Ignoring his outstretched hand, she gathered her skirts and leapt from the vehicle, landing lightly on the balls of her feet. Spinning around, she grinned at him.

"Don't worry," she whispered to him as he took her arm and tugged her toward the large wooden door. "I'm not without resources of my own, should I find myself in trouble."

He rapped the old iron knocker three times in quick succession.

"I don't even want to know," he muttered as the door swung open on groaning hinges and a gaunt-faced old butler invited them in. There was no turning back now, even if he wanted to.

Dr. Wick looked up from his paperwork as the butler tapped discreetly on the doorframe.

"Yes, Percival, what is it?"

"A Mr. Barrett to see you, sir," the man's voice was low and rasping, "and he's brought his sister with him. He wishes to install Miss Barrett here under your care and he desires an audience with you."

The doctor set the papers aside, interest piqued. "Tell him I'll be there directly, Percival, thank you."

The butler nodded and backed out of the room, shutting the door softly. Dr. Wick rubbed his hands together in anticipation. A new patient, he thought giddily, and one that was not brought to him courtesy of his employer. He was truly living a charmed life. He no longer worried about finances and, someday soon, his name would be known far and wide for his revolutionary methods. This case sparked his interest more than anything in months, simply because the likelihood that Miss Barrett's mental derangement was organic, rather than chemically-induced like those individuals his benefactor had sent to him. As much as he enjoyed testing the limits of minds under the influence of who knew what combination of chemicals or herbs, there was nothing he loved more than trying his latest ideas and treatments on a naturally unstable mind.

He rose, adjusting his suit coat as he walked to the door. It took only minutes to make his way to the spotless, well-furnished drawing room, so it was essential to give the families of patients the impression of quiet competence and subdued good taste. As long as the part of the manor they saw was well-kept and tastefully decorated, they could pretend that the patients lived in the same conditions. He discreetly cleared his throat to announce his presence, eagerness increasing exponentially at the sight before him.

Lively brown eyes flicked toward him and then back to the window before returning to fix their gaze on his face. Their owner tipped her head slightly and gave him a sweet half-smile as she twisted her fingers together and rubbed one bare foot over the top of the other. He didn't even notice the room's other occupant, so intent was his gaze on the woman, until a fastidiously-dressed man laid his hands over hers, forcing them to still.

"Jenny," said the dark-haired gentleman, "can you say good day to the doctor?"

She frowned at her brother before smiling wistfully at Dr. Wick.

"I'm not stupid, Robert, no matter what Papa told you, and am quite aware of the dictates of propriety. One should always offer a cordial greeting, particularly when one is a guest in another's home. Good day, Dr. Wick, it's a pleasure to meet you." Her voice was childlike and petulant. She cocked her head slightly, as though listening. "Oh, yes, you're quite right, Sarah. Robert should know me far better by now, but in his defence, he *has* been gone from home for some seven years and who knows what Papa wrote to him."

From the painfully embarrassed expression on Robert Barrett's face, it was obvious it would be easy to convince the young man to not only leave his sister at the asylum, but to keep his visits few and far between. She was clearly delusional, a perfect specimen for his methods. He had to stop himself from rubbing his hands together in anticipation when he thought of how his electroshock machine might affect her. Perhaps ice water treatments would help strengthen her grip on reality. At the very least, they would make for an entertaining spectacle.

"Welcome to my home, Miss Barrett," he said. "I do hope that your brother has informed you how much I and my staff would like to have you stay here for a while."

"He has said nothing to me, Dr. Wick, but that he cannot leave me alone at our estate in the country while he is in London. I told him that I have Sarah to keep me company but he says that I must stay somewhere safer, that," she lowered her voice to imitate that of a man's and rounded her tones to exude pompousness, "Sarah is *your* friend, Jenny, but she has no other acquaintances and cannot be trusted with your well-being." Her voice returned to its original pitch. "Well, why not, I ask you? She is as respectable a lady as anyone I've ever met. Certainly she's a good sight more respectable than some of Papa's lady friends."

Robert Barrett looked distinctly uncomfortable as he faced Dr. Wick.

"I would have sent Jenny to an aunt or uncle but we have no close relations and I cannot bring her to London. The city is far too dangerous for her."

What he meant, thought Dr. Wick, was that it was far too dangerous for *him* because someone might realize that his sister was unbalanced and ruin his chances of marrying well.

"I would be most pleased to have you stay here, Miss Barrett, and there are plenty of other young women to keep you company. Why don't you say goodbye to your brother and I'll have my housekeeper show you to your room while he and I discuss some matters of business?"

She turned obediently to the man standing next to her and nodded her head regally.

"Goodbye, Robert. Do visit soon, will you? Papa would not have approved of your leaving me here, but you must do what you deem best. I cannot blame you for following in Papa's footsteps, I suppose."

He patted her shoulder awkwardly and gave her a crooked smile as he slid his eyes away.

"I hope you find your stay here pleasant, Jenny. I will write to you once I'm settled in London."

Jenny's brown eyes darted around the room as she cocked her head once more.

"Of course, Sarah, you're absolutely correct. I will ask directly." Her gaze focused on Dr. Wick. "I assume that this home is chaperoned by a respectable woman, sir? Neither Sarah nor I would care to live in a place that was not governed by the rules of propriety. We have our reputations to consider, you know."

"Naturally, Miss Barrett, my housekeeper is in residence and a very respectable spinster occupies a room very close to the one you will be given. Sarah was very wise to ask such a candid question."

He only hoped his face did not betray his growing enchantment with his new patient. Until the matter was settled with a transfer of funds and the brother departed, he must remain the calm, detached professional. He walked to the wall and pulled the thick, braided cord hanging unobtrusively against the dark wood panelling. Moments later, Percival stepped into the room.

"Percival, please show Miss Barrett to Matron Green's sitting room and tell her I will join them shortly to give our guest a personal tour of the manor. I will see Mr. Barrett out myself once our business is concluded."

The butler nodded and then gestured the woman to the open door leading to the hallway. Without a backward glance at her brother, she picked up a satchel that he had not noticed on the floor next to her and moved across the parlor and through the open door. Percival stepped out behind her and closed the door. Dr. Wick turned to Mr. Barrett and saw the man heave a sigh of relief.

"You will keep her here indefinitely?" asked the younger man, his face betraying a hint of uncertainty. "I would not wish to move her to another facility if she becomes too erratic for your staff and residents."

The doctor barely kept his smirk in check at the thought of his other patients. If only Mr. Barrett knew what his sister was going to face...but that was the beauty of his work. Privacy and discretion were essential for the clients, as well as for him.

"She will be welcome here for as long as you wish it, sir," he replied deferentially, "and for as long as her fees are paid."

An embarrassed flush worked its way up from the younger man's collar and his eyes darkened with anger.

"They will be paid, sir! How much do you require?"

Both his voice and posture were stiff. Wick eyed the man's good-quality coat, well-cut hair and finely sewn trousers. His cravat was spotless and tied in an elegant style that was neither outdated nor the latest fashion. Everything about him gave evidence to quiet affluence without excessive wealth. A calculating gleam entered the doctor's cold eyes.

"Room and board equal a thousand pounds a year." He held up a hand as the younger man's mouth opened to protest the exorbitant amount. "Your sister requires very specialized care, Mr. Barrett, as I'm certain you are aware. Her treatment is not inexpensive. You want what is best for her, do you not?"

Barrett blew out a breath and nodded.

"I do not have such a large amount here. I will need to go to my bank in London to withdraw the funds and send them to you."

"See that you do it promptly, Mr. Barrett," replied Wick evenly, "or you will find yourself beset by an emissary of mine in a very public place. I would be required, I am afraid, to send your sister along with him as well."

The dark-haired man gave another tight nod as his lips thinned in anger.

"You have my word."

"Good – then you have mine, as well."

11

Grace studied the room around her with undisguised interest. Percival had shown her into the sitting room before leaving to find Matron Green. She not only needed to stay in character, she also needed to have her wits about her. *I am Jenny Barrett.* It would be a difficult task, particularly given the inhumane conditions that were the norm in institutions of this kind. Neglect would have to be most severe, causing death or dismemberment, in order for the courts to prosecute. Still, prosecution might be possible. Dr. Wick had not done anything overtly untoward when she was in his presence but something in his eyes made her wary. She was certain that whatever he was involved in was not only illegal, but evil, and must be stopped at any cost.

Footsteps sounded in the hallway, the sharp slap of shoe on stone echoing. The door swung open, groaning on ancient hinges as it reluctantly gave way. Grace fixed a bright smile on her face and tipped her head slightly. The woman who entered the room behind Percival looked, at first glance, to be her mother's age but was, upon closer inspection, perhaps only ten years older than herself. Hard eyes and a face set in dour lines made her look shrewish and discontented.

"Matron Green," announced the butler before stepping back and pulling the door shut. The matron's smile of welcome was so obviously forced that its effect was quite the opposite.

"Good day, Miss Barrett. It is a pleasure to meet you. May I call you Jenny?"

Grace let her gaze stray for a moment and cocked her head further as though listening to someone on her left before focusing on the woman again and smiling politely.

"You may, Matron Green, but Sarah would prefer that you address her as Miss Shaw until she knows you better."

The woman looked confused for a second before recovering her composure.

"Is Sarah a close friend of yours? Have you known each other for a very long time?"

"Oh, for ages, Miss Green – why, I cannot recall a time when we have not been the most intimate confidantes! I tell her everything and she always gives the best advice. She is quieter and more reserved than I am but we find that our differences just make us better friends."

The woman's lips curved upward again, but no light entered her eyes.

"How nice for you both." her tone was that of someone speaking to a child. "It would be a shame for differences of opinion to separate you from such a close friend. Shall I ring for tea while we wait for Dr. Wick to finish his business with your brother?"

"If you wish," Grace shrugged nonchalantly. "To be honest, I would rather explore the manor and grounds. If I'm to stay here, I would like to know what kind of place I will be living in."

Matron Green's smile disappeared. Grace deliberately relaxed her shoulders and looked around the room, tipping her head back to study the chandelier. She muttered to herself, giggling periodically. She had just emerged from exploring behind the heavy curtains draping the windows when the door opened and Dr. Wick stepped into the room. She couldn't help the shiver of apprehension that traveled up and down her spine at the sight of him. When he raked his eyes over her from top to bottom, she had the sinking feeling that he thought of her as a new toy to play with until she either broke or he grew tired and threw her away.

"Oh, hello again, Dr. Wick," she said in a sing-song voice. "I was just asking Matron Green to show me the manor and grounds. I'd love to see them and Sarah wants to know where our room is. She's a bit weary from the journey. Have you any hidden passages? I do so love secrets."

The man's eyes assessed her with interest.

"I would be delighted to give you a tour of the manor myself, Miss Barrett. I shall introduce you to your housemates and show you the common rooms and gardens. Matron Green can show you your quarters once we return."

"How wonderful! You are certain you do not mind?"

"Not at all, Miss Barrett; it will be my pleasure."

He held out an arm to her expectantly. Quelling her aversion to touching him, she placed a hand lightly on his forearm and gave him her most ingenuous smile. He nodded sharply at Matron Green and, without another word, led Grace out the door and into the cool, dank hallway.

Ramsey looked down at the ground below him and fought the urge to curse. He'd never been fond of heights, thus finding himself hanging from an ancient trellis covered with thick ivy twenty feet above the grassy earth gave him ample reason for bad temper. Breathing hard, he felt a trickle of sweat make its way down his temple as he reached up, using his upper body strength to pull himself closer to the stone ledge he'd spotted upon his return to the manor. He'd left the carriage safely hidden off the rutted road in the shade of a small, leafy glen with the coachman, Hobbs, standing guard. Ramsey had briefly considered returning as Robert Barrett, saying he'd had a change of heart regarding his sister to gain more opportunity to interview the doctor himself but it was clear by the time Dr. Wick had ushered him to the door that coming back as a concerned brother rather than an inspector with the authority of Scotland Yard behind him would be a mistake. He would gain nothing through further conversation, if the doctor's manner remained as closed as it had been during their first encounter, and every minute he spent digging for information was one more minute Grace spent alone in an insane asylum. Although he'd promised to give Grace an hour to search for what evidence she could find, he did not wish to wait the hour and then seek entrance to the manor. It would serve them both best, he concluded, if he found entrance into the manor, hid himself in some inconspicuous place, and stayed there until the promised hour was up.

With a grunt he heaved himself upward, fingers closing around the weathered stone ledge as his feet scrabbled for purchase on the trellis slats. He rested a moment and then pulled himself up again until he was able to see through the ancient, warped glass of the large window above the ledge from which he hung. The room was empty, the dusty shelves with bedpans and scrub brushes lined up in neat rows appearing to be the contents of a storage closet. Propping his elbows on the wide ledge, he reached into his coat pocket for his handkerchief and carefully wrapped it around his right hand. Wincing as he looked down, inadvertently reminding himself of the precariousness of his position, he forced himself to study the area below until he was certain there was no one else around. In one swift move, he pulled his arm back and slammed his covered fist into the window.

The fragile glass shattered easily beneath the force of the blow. He grimaced at the sound, hoping that there was nobody close enough to the room to hear it. He swept his cloth-covered hand across the breadth of the ledge to remove most of the glass shards before heaving himself into the dark, musty space. He landed softly on the balls of his feet and circled the room, relieved to see that he was indeed alone. Unwrapping the handkerchief from his right hand, he shook it out and dabbed the sweat from his forehead and neck before folding it and tucking it back into his pocket. The pistol in his right coat pocket bumped his thigh as he stepped toward the door. He had best be armed, he thought grimly, before leaving the safety of the storage room. He removed the gun from his pocket and held it close to his side as he moved toward the door.

Carefully unlatching it, he tugged it slowly open and slid stealthily into the passageway. The shadowy hall was sparsely lit by flickering lanterns placed intermittently along the walls. Six feet ahead to his right was a thick wooden door and another lay six feet beyond that on the left. Though the hinges were blackened iron, the locks were shiny and new. The sound of a man's wracking sobs filled the air, loud even through stone and solid wood. Tucking his pistol into the crook of his arm, muzzle pointed at the floor, he reached into his left coat pocket and retrieved the slim leather holder containing a set of lock picks given to him by Jonathan Hayes the previous Christmas. The gift had been meant in fun, a jest at his stickling for rules and regulations. He'd never been one to ignore either but over the past couple of years, his encounters with the Rivers and their unscrupulous behavior had caused him to rethink some of his methods. While he couldn't countenance breaking the law, he had come to terms with occasionally skirting around the edges of it. A foray or two to the brink of legality were worth it if he had a chance at finally breaking the Rivers' empire to pieces.

He started as a loud clanging sound filled the hall with the echo of metal on stone. Coupled with the sobbing, now increasing in volume, the din should have brought someone running to check on the inmate. Ramsey stayed where he was, well within reach of the storage room door should anyone appear and make it necessary for him to hide. One minute passed, then two, and then three. Just as he pulled out a lock pick, he heard footsteps approaching. He quickly slipped back inside the storage room, leaving the door open just enough for him to hear what was happening in the hallway. Two sets of footsteps were now distinguishable along with the low murmur of voices.

"I told you he needed more than a few sips of laudanum to keep him docile!"

The voice was young, male, and unfamiliar to Ramsey.

"How was I to know that you actually wanted me to give him an extra dose, Endicott? Your comment sounded like a mere observation, not an order. Besides, any more laudanum and he'll spend his days unconscious and his nights the same. Dr. Wick wants him lucid enough for accurate results from the electro-shock machine."

"I didn't say he needed more laudanum, Ripley." The second man's tone was condescending. "I said he needed something to keep him docile."

"What do you suggest we do then, Endicott?" The first voice sharpened in frustration. "Tie him up and muzzle him? Oh wait, he's already bound and chained to the wall. If you're so concerned about keeping him docile, you're going to have to figure something else out yourself."

"Why do you think I'm carrying this tea tray, Ripley? Last time I checked, I was not attired as a parlor maid, nor," sarcasm dripped from his words, "do I hold that station. I've laced the tea with valerian root. It should calm him quickly once he drinks it and I'm certain he will drink it. He's had nothing to assuage his thirst for at least a day."

"You mean," Ripley snickered loudly, "nothing unless you count all the water he must have swallowed during his last ice water treatment. You would think our poor idiots would learn to keep their mouths shut instead of shrieking pointlessly."

His companion chuckled.

"The fool never did grasp that screaming would only get him a lungful of water, not a reprieve from our tender ministrations. Now, unlock the door for me, Endicott. Let us see if I can persuade the esteemed Lord Pratt to take his medicine like a good lad."

The sound of a key turning in its lock was followed by the harsh squeal of rusty hinges. Weeping turned to pleading as Ramsey waited, silently grieving the fact that Lord Pratt would likely suffer a good deal more torment before there would be a chance to free him. The heavy wooden door thudded shut and Ramsey took the risk of pushing the storage room door open a bit farther and sneaking a glance around. The passageway was deserted and he could hear the low murmur of voices amid Lord Pratt's renewed sobbing. This was his best chance, he thought, and slipped into the hall, shutting the door softly behind him. Moving swiftly, he headed toward the far end of the passage toward stairs leading up to the third level. Logic told him that wherever they were conducting their experiments would be as far out of earshot of any visitors as possible. His intuition told him he'd better hurry before Grace faced something more dangerous than either of them had anticipated.

12

Ramsey's steps were soft and measured as he climbed the staircase lit dimly by a flickering torch. The stone beneath him was cracked and worn from countless feet climbing for hundreds of years past. He emerged at the top into a passageway even more dark and damp than the one below. He crept closer to the nearest room, light gleaming from beneath the heavy door. He heard a strange crackling sound and a chill went through him as he recognized the excited voice of Dr. Wick.

"Come, my dear Miss Barrett, why don't you sit down in this special chair so Matron Green can use those metal bands she's holding to measure your head for a brand new hat? Don't you want a brand new hat?"

"Oh yes, I'd love one!" He heard Grace answer brightly. "But I can't get a new hat if Sarah doesn't get one. It wouldn't be fair."

"Naturally," Dr. Wick soothed, "but I wonder if you know that Matron Green and I cannot actually see your friend Sarah?"

"Well, why ever not, Dr. Wick?" Ramsey could just imagine her eyes widening innocently and he cursed himself for allowing her to put herself at risk. "She's standing right next to you."

"I'm certain that you think so, Miss Barrett," continued the doctor, "but in reality, she is locked inside your head. You are the only person who can see or hear her."

"You're lying."

The exclamation was that of a petulant child.

"No, Miss Barrett, I fear I am not; but I have good news for you! There is a way that we can rescue her from your mind. It is a simple procedure called trepanation and can be done right here at the manor."

"But she's *not* in my mind, Dr. Wick." The sound of a foot stomping punctuated the declaration. "Indeed, she is standing right next to you. It's not my fault if you have something wrong with your eyesight. I will not stay here if you and Matron Green insist on being so disagreeable."

"I'm afraid that won't be possible, Miss Barrett. You see, your brother has paid my institution a good deal of money to keep you hidden away. He'll not be back for you and you no longer have a home outside these walls. You are now one of my special patients and I have some very particular plans for you."

"What do you mean? What kinds of plans?"

The fear in Grace's voice was genuine and Ramsey prayed that the door was unlocked. The time it would take to pick the lock might be enough for Dr. Wick and his assistant to do serious harm. He gripped the pick he'd removed earlier tightly and listened intently.

"Ordinarily, with a new patient, I would begin with a treatment of herbs and chemicals to see if that affected your interactions with your friend Sarah. After that, I might try some ice water sessions, leaving you mostly submerged for a few hours or submerging you and pulling you out in quick succession, multiple times. You, however, are so intriguing a conundrum that I am going to introduce you to my electrical machine before trying anything else. It's a very special machine. An associate of mine invented it. My machine does not just create electricity. It transfers it through those metal bands Matron Green is so eager to fit around your head."

"Why would you want to transfer electricity to my head? What purpose could that possibly serve other than hurting me? You want to hurt me?" Grace's words cut Ramsey's heart even as he heard the doctor chuckle.

"The amount of screaming that emanates from this room during treatments would suggest that I do not find my patients' pain off-putting, or even a consideration in their treatment. I am still examining the results of the electroshock sessions but the participants do seem more docile, if a bit twitchy. I am willing to offer you a second option, as you are, my dear Miss Barrett, an excellent candidate for trepanation."

"What if I do not wish to have either done to me? Neither sounds at all pleasant."

Ramsey leaned closer as another female voice began to speak, and he strained to hear Matron Green's first comment while working the lock with his pick, praying he would soon hear the click that indicated success.

"It does not particularly matter if you *want* to have it done to you, Jenny. You *will* have it done if we decide those are the methods Dr. Wick most wishes to use. The procedure itself is rather simple. We will tie you down so that you cannot fight us and then the good doctor will bore a hole through your skull so that Sarah can exit."

Ramsey's stomach clenched. While Dr. Wick's enthusiasm was unsettling, Matron Green's indifferent tone while uttering such a horrific statement was downright frightening. He had not realized that the doctor had a close associate, and a dangerous one at that. Her presence, and that of the two men he had overheard earlier, complicated things a good deal more than he had anticipated. The lock gave way with a quiet click and he quickly tucked his pick back into its holder. He slipped it back into his pocket and took firm hold of his pistol in his right hand. *God,* he prayed silently, *we are in desperate need. Help me to bring Grace out of here unharmed.*

"What do you mean 'exit'? I told you that you're wrong about Sarah."

Grace sounded slightly hysterical and Ramsey didn't blame her. Gripping his pistol tighter, he laid a hand on the door latch.

"No, Miss Barrett, it is you who are mistaken." Dr. Wick's voice shook with excitement. "I have studied cases like yours, dating back hundreds of years. The voice you hear belongs to an evil spirit that has taken up residence in your head. By boring a hole through your skull, I will give it a way out! Just imagine, after a lifetime of suffering from delusions and hallucinations, it will take me less than one day to free you of them. When I follow that treatment up with my electroshock machine, you will become a shining example of what my methods can accomplish. The world will bow to my genius."

"I do not want to be freed of anything. You have no right to do such a thing to me if I tell you I do not want it. What you suggest is not genius, it's ludicrous."

"Ludicrous? You are the fool, Miss Barrett. My methods are, as my weak-willed colleagues have said, 'irregular' but they will be widely accepted soon enough, as soon as I have enough research and documentation compiled from experimenting on subjects like you."

"Subjects like me?"

"Yes, Miss Barrett. People nobody wants and nobody will miss. People with no value to society or their families. People just like you."

It was time to intervene. Ramsey pushed gently at the latch, relieved when it slid easily and silently back. The door was just swinging open when screams erupted alongside a loud crash. Throwing the door wide, he charged into the room, pistol at the ready as he prayed he wasn't too late.

13

Pushing back a large swatch of hair that had fallen out of her chignon, Grace wiped the sheen of nervous sweat from her brow and sent her would-be rescuer a weak grin. Doctor Wick was writhing on the floor about two feet from the crooked hem of her skirt while Matron Green appeared to be unconscious, lying slumped against the electroshock machine that was still emitting a loud crackling noise and intermittent sparks. A thin trickle of blood trailed down her cheek from a small gash on her temple. The metal bands she'd been holding as she advanced on Grace lay in a harmless heap on the floor beside her, her right hand still gripping them loosely.

"Did they hurt you?"

The low-voiced question and gentle hand on her arm almost broke her composure. She'd protected herself without a qualm but the concerned relief in Ramsey's serious grey eyes and feeling his soft touch brought a curious weakness to her limbs. She shook her head, afraid to examine the sensation.

"No, they didn't have the chance. Did you hear much of what was said before you came to my rescue? I must say, you have impeccable timing and my thanks for it."

"You're quite welcome, though it appears you had things well in hand. Is the good doctor," he quirked a brow in irony, "suffering the same effects Mr. Wiggins experienced only a few days ago?"

A grin flashed across her face.

"Dr. Wick did indeed receive a faceful of cayenne pepper," she waved a square of white linen about half the size of a handkerchief, "and Matron Green had an unfortunate collision with the electroshock machine after Dr. Wick's flailing knocked her off balance. I really had nothing to do with putting her out of commission, so I don't feel I should take credit for it."

"I can see how that might happen." Ramsey nimbly dodged the whimpering man's wildly kicking foot. "Perhaps I should secure him before he causes himself further damage."

"That does seem wise."

In a matter of minutes, Dr. Wick was restrained and propped against the wall. Grace rose from where she'd knelt next to Matron Green, checking the woman's breathing as she tried to staunch the steady flow of blood from her minor head wound. It had slowed to a trickle but the fact that Matron Green had not yet regained consciousness concerned Grace.

"What are we going to do with them?" A terrible thought struck and she turned her worried gaze on Ramsey. "Have I ruined your case against Dr. Wick by defending myself? Oh, Ramsey, I'm so sorry. This is all my fault."

"Do not blame yourself." His voice was steady and calm. "We may be able to convince these two to testify against the Rivers in exchange for leniency in the charges against them. If they will say nothing in regard to that case, what has just occurred is ample cause to lock these two up on charges of assault."

The concern in Grace's gaze dimmed only slightly. A deep sense of guilt over the prospect of failure had already taken root. She patted

Matron Green's cheek gently, trying to rouse her. The woman's eyes flickered open and she groaned. Grace held up two fingers.

"Can you tell me how many fingers you see, Matron Green?" she asked, ignoring the hatred in the woman's gaze. "I need to ascertain whether or not you are concussed."

"Two fingers, carroty hair and muddy brown eyes." The older woman smirked. "Your pasty complexion could use some color. Allow me to assist you."

The muscles in her shoulders bunched as she swung the iron bands still grasped in her right hand upward while raking the nails of her left across Grace's face. Grace threw herself backward to avoid the heavy blow aimed at her head, narrowly escaping it. The momentum of the swing carried the woman's arm across her body, the metal bands landing next to her with a clatter. Before either had a chance to regroup, Ramsey stepped between the two women and casually cocked the pistol in his hand. He pointed it at Matron Green.

"Are you through, madam?"

With only the slightest hesitation, she nodded, holding out her hands with palms down and wrists together. Grace sat up carefully, wincing as she brushed her fingertips across the bloody crevasses on her cheek and listening with half an ear as Matron Green's increasingly colorful expletives accompanied Ramsey's movements as he tied her hands behind her back with a length of rope he'd produced from his pocket. She was fumbling for a handkerchief when Ramsey laid a hand on her shoulder.

"Here, allow me," he said, crouching in front of her with a square of clean white linen. "Do you have anything to disinfect the scratches? I hear the claws of a wild beast can be quite filthy."

Grace's lips twitched in amusement even as another slew of curses erupted from the matron. He cupped her chin lightly and dabbed carefully at the droplets of blood trickling down her cheek. Grace could feel her face heating at the intimacy of his touch and tried to appear unaffected. His palms were calloused and rough, but the sensation was not at all unpleasant. She found herself wanting to lean her face against his hand and revel in its strength. The awareness that she was about to do just that made her jerk back in embarrassment.

"Did I hurt you?"

"What?"

Grace struggled to gain a hold on her thoughts.

"I must have hurt you, Grace. I'm sorry."

"No, no," she rushed to reassure him lest the distance of guilt replace the warm concern in his gaze, "it was just a delayed reaction to the stress of the situation."

Her heart skipped at the sound of her Christian name on her lips. It was ridiculous, she thought, to be so affected by the familiarity of the address. She sincerely hoped she didn't look as stupid as she felt. Ramsey didn't act as though he saw anything amiss, but the man was abnormally perceptive. She tried to smile but it turned into a wince as her cheek pulled painfully.

"Do you have any salve or balm that would be beneficial for your wounds with you? Where is your satchel?"

"I'm afraid I was forced to leave it in the matron's sitting room, one floor below us. If you wouldn't mind helping me to my feet, I'll go and collect it."

"Nonsense. You sit here and rest while I fetch it for you. Don't move. I'll be back in just a minute."

Without waiting for a response, Ramsey strode to the door and disappeared into the hallway. Grace watched him go, still holding his handkerchief to her cheek.

"It appears that he's not your brother after all, is he?" Grace started at the sound of Dr. Wick's voice, turning to find him staring at her with undisguised malice. "Or if he is, your obvious feelings for him are quite inappropriate."

She flushed, disgust rising in her throat at the man's insinuation. His eyes were still streaming and his face blotchy and covered with fine, reddish dust, but she found little pity in her heart for him.

"You are clearly addled from your recent infusion of cayenne," she said coldly. "You cannot trust yourself to see anything accurately until your eyes stop tearing. Besides, you are hardly qualified to speak about appropriate relations given your abusive history with your patients."

"You foolish woman. My treatment would have changed you a great deal, for the better." His mocking gaze was replaced with dark fury. "No one seems to understand that. My genius is without parallel and yet I do not receive the recognition I deserve."

Grace was spared a reply by Ramsey's return. He entered the room carrying her satchel in his left hand, right hand still holding his pistol.

"I found it just where you said I would, Grace. Do you need my assistance finding what you require?"

"Thank you, Inspector," she couldn't help the formality that crept into her tone. Dr. Wick's comment had made her uncomfortably aware of the detective as a man, "but I can manage. I'm fairly certain I remembered to bring a few vials of aloe extract which will soothe the cuts and help speed healing."

Ignoring her unspoken dismissal, Ramsey crouched in front of her, holding the bag open for her as she rummaged through its contents and pulled out the vial she was searching for. He took it from her, removing the cork stopper. The viscous liquid inside slowly oozed out to coat the tips of Ramsey's fingers as he tipped it upside down. He smoothed it over the shallow scratches, making Grace's cheek tingle. The cool aloe immediately soothed her wounds and she sighed in relief even though her nervousness grew at the breach of propriety.

"Thank you, Inspector. That feels much better."

"I've no doubt it does," the doctor sneered as Matron Green laughed scornfully.

"May I have my handkerchief back, please?" Ramsey asked, stretching out his hand.

Grace's eyes slid shut in embarrassment as she handed it to him, but she made herself open them again. She watched as he stood and strode over to his two captives. Without a word, he shoved the soiled piece of linen into Dr. Wick's mouth. Turning to Matron Green, he raised a brow. She glared at him mutinously, but remained silent. Apparently deciding it wasn't worth the risk, he pulled a second handkerchief from his pocket, forcing it into the woman's mouth when she opened it to protest.

Satisfied that both captives were, if uncomfortable, at least able to breathe freely, he returned to kneel in front of Grace. He picked up the vial from the floor, replaced the stopper and placed it back in her satchel before helping her to her feet. Grace wished she knew if it was her imagination or if he really did squeeze her fingers a little longer than necessary before releasing her hand. *Stop it,* she told herself firmly. *This is no time to behave like a flighty schoolgirl.*

"How are we going to get out of here with these two? Without getting caught, that is? I saw a young man on our way to this room and there may be others."

Ramsey grinned, the expression surprisingly boyish. Her heart tripped and she gave herself a mental shake. *Did you not hear what I just said, Grace? You're smarter than this.*

"We shouldn't have too much trouble as long as we avoid the main staircase. Only servants use the back stairs and there are no servants here so loyal that a few shillings will not buy their silence. I overheard two men, orderlies rather than servants, I should think, on my way to find you, but they are busy at the moment. As long as we gag both our prisoners good and proper, we shouldn't have a problem."

Grace's eyes were dark with concern.

"I hate to leave the other inmates here, Ramsey. It is not exaggeration to say their treatment is close to torture. We cannot just walk away."

"We won't. Once we get these two outside and into the carriage with Hobbs, I'll tell you what I have in mind for this place." His lips quirked. "I think you'll find the idea quite intriguing. However, the wait will be payback for the anxiety this scheme of yours caused me. Not," he said, holding up a hand to forestall her defence, "that coming here was your idea. I suppose. Ultimately, the culpability is mine."

"As long as you recognize that," she said tartly, feeling more herself, "I can wait for your explanation."

"You may give me your evaluation once we're free of this place. I look forward to watching your mind at work." He smiled over his shoulder as he pulled Matron Green to her feet. "It's quite fascinating."

Grace stared at his back as he hauled Dr. Wick to his feet, guiding the man to stand next to Matron Green. Her mind was, indeed, always working. This was the first time in many years that she'd had trouble comprehending something. Ramsey turned toward her with a smile and outstretched hand, and her stomach fluttered. *I think I'm in trouble, Father. Or if I'm not, my heart is.*

14

Transporting two bound and gagged prisoners down the servants' staircase without being seen was easier than Grace had anticipated. Though neither captive was cooperative, the glint of the pistol that Ramsey kept trained on them was enough to ensure their compliance. Stealthy reconnaissance of the kitchen, performed while Ramsey remained in the staircase with the prisoners, showed that whatever cook ruled that space was missing in action. By the number of empty gin bottles that lined the counter, it was a good guess that she was in the pantry sleeping off the effects while a large pot of something that could only charitably be described as soup simmered sulkily on the stovetop.

Grace slipped silently through the kitchen to confirm her suspicions. One glance through the lead glass pantry door inset was enough to show a distorted figure slumped against the wall with her chin on her chest, her faint snores clearly audible. Grace pitied the woman, despite the temptation to laugh at the sight and sound.

She hurried to the back door and unbolted it, then ran back to the servants' stairs. She tugged open the door, signalling Ramsey that all was clear. Dr. Wick walked out, followed closely by Matron Green, with Ramsey bringing up the rear. Ignoring the glares directed her way, she slipped past them to fetch her satchel, still sitting just where she'd left it next to the stairwell door. Picking it up, she turned and followed Ramsey and the others across the kitchen and out the door. Once outside, the waiting Hobbs led the way to a large wagon neatly hidden behind a wall of hedges. Grace looked around for the carriage in confusion. A rough-hewn man leapt down from the wagon seat and took hold of Dr. Wick's left arm as Hobbs grabbed the right. In less than two minutes, both prisoners were safely, albeit unhappily, seated on the floor of the wagon.

"John Blake, Inspector, sir," said the stranger, shaking Ramsey's hand and nodding respectfully to Grace, "Miss. Let me tell you, it's a right pleasure to be carting these two off to prison. Once my Mary gets through spreading the word in the village, I've no doubt you'll be hearing the cheers for miles."

Ramsey slanted a glance at Hobbs, eyebrows raised.

"I didn't think it would hurt for the villagers to know that they have no further need to fear these two." Hobbs jerked a thumb at the two sullen-faced captives in the wagon. "It seems that Dr. Wick decided that Mr. Blake's village was there for his personal amusement. He practiced his experiments on the villagers whenever he could."

"Why didn't you just say no?" blurted Grace before she could stop herself. She cringed, wishing she'd at least phrased her question more tactfully. To her relief, the man took no offence.

"We couldn't." His fists clenched and he glared at the doctor. "We are a poor village. Our income comes from working the land that belongs to the manor. When Dr. Wick bought the manor, the land was included. My father came to collect our wages after harvest last year and was told that the only way any of us would receive what was owed was to send two men, two women, and two children to be examined by him. When asked why, he said that too many people were afraid of doctors and he wanted to help us by making sure that the villagers were healthy."

"And you agreed because you had no choice."

Ramsey stared flint-eyed at the doctor.

"Exactly. He kept each of them for three days. None have been the same since. The little ones haven't spoken a word in six months. The only noise they make is when they wake up shrieking from night terrors. Then their screams are loud enough to wake the dead."

Bile rose in Grace's throat. She could imagine what those children had suffered. Given the events of the past two hours, she had a clear picture of how he would experiment, given the opportunity. Righteous fury filled her, blazing brighter at the doctor's remorseless stare. To keep from leaping into the wagon and planting her fist in his smug face, she turned her mind to the problem the man had described.

"Mr. Blake," she said, rummaging in her satchel, "I have a couple of items in my satchel that may soothe the children that this charlatan abused. Lavender oil and lavender-infused pillows should help calm them and encourage a deep, natural sleep. If you and the rest of the villagers agree, perhaps I could come to visit soon to see if there is anything more I can do to help? I will not know without seeing the poor souls myself which other herbs may be of benefit to them. If you are amenable, I will also bring my brother. He is a physician, and a fine one at that."

The big man's eyes grew suspiciously damp as he grasped the items she had retrieved from her bag. He tried to speak, cleared his throat and then tried again.

"Thank you, miss. I would be pleased to introduce you to my neighbors. I know they will be most grateful for your gifts."

"That's settled, then."

"I'd best be off, sir," Blake turned to Ramsey. "I'll be right behind your carriage with these two all the way to London."

"You have my deepest thanks for your willingness to transport them, Mr. Blake. I realize it's a long journey for you and I can't offer much, if anything, by way of remuneration."

"Oh, just seeing these two tossed in prison is payment enough. If you could make those prison cells dark, damp, and cold, I'd be in your debt, sir."

"I can't make any promises, I'm afraid," said Ramsey, "but I will do everything in my power to see that justice is served. I should think, though," he turned a flinty stare on the pair in the wagon bed, "that the probability of extreme discomfort is quite high."

"That'll have to do, then."

Blake climbed back onto the driver's seat of the wagon, reins held firmly in his calloused hands. The large, shaggy horses hitched to the vehicle stamped their feet, anxious to be on their way.

"The carriage is right where we left it, Inspector, sir," Hobbs gestured to a cluster of trees about twenty feet ahead of them.

"Then let's be off. I'd like to have this journey over and those two behind bars as soon as possible." He offered his arm to Grace. "Are you ready, Miss Flynn?"

"Yes, of course." She placed her hand in the crook of his elbow and allowed him to lead her to the carriage. Hobbs hurried to pull the carriage door open.

As Grace lifted her skirts slightly to climb in, she suddenly realized that she was still attired as a madwoman. She blushed brightly as a wave of embarrassment flowed through her. It was one thing for Ramsey to see her in such a state while she was playing a part, but riding in close quarters back to London made the situation entirely different.

"If you don't mind giving me a moment of privacy, sir," she began, ignoring the heat searing her cheeks as she turned back to the men, "I need to make some alterations to my appearance before I can be seen in London. I am not appropriately attired to travel in the company of a man, no matter how respectable he is."

"But of course, Miss Flynn," Ramsey's gaze lit with comprehension. He was gentlemanly enough not to look at her uncovered ankles, but those steady, watchful eyes meeting hers made her feel exposed nonetheless. "Just rap on the door when you're ready. Hobbs and I will wait outside until you give the signal."

Nodding, Grace stepped into the carriage and dropped down to the padded bench. The faint murmur of the men's voices provided a soothing background as she dug around in her satchel for her sewing implements. Leaning down, Grace gently tugged at the hem of her skirt and carefully snipped the loose stitches she'd put in place earlier. To her relief, her skirts settled naturally into the even, straight edge they'd been before her alterations. She retrieved her boots from where she'd stowed them in the corner of the carriage. Her stockings were sadly soiled and needed darning, but that could not be fixed until she was back at the boardinghouse. She slid her feet into the boots and used the boot hook she carried in her satchel to pull the buttons through their tiny openings.

Satisfied that the lower half of her attire was restored to propriety, she sat up and went to work on her sleeves. She couldn't sew the cuff back into place without removing the gown, but she could pin it in place easily enough. Rummaging through her bag, she found the small packet of John James pins in their black and yellow paper packet. She swiftly tucked the cuff in place, securing it with the pin she held and then selected another and continued the process. Satisfied that her dress was as neat as she could make it with the tools at hand, she began tucking the loose locks of hair she'd pulled free back into the chignon she wore at the nape of her neck.

Thankful she'd never had the patience to arrange her hair in the sausage curls that were so fashionable, she smoothed her hands over her hair in a final check for loose locks. She licked the corner of her handkerchief and rubbed at the smudges on her face. She didn't relish Ramsey seeing her complexion after such a vigorous scrubbing, but there was no help for it. *Why should I care so much what he thinks of me?* She gave herself a mental shake and rapped on the carriage wall.

The door opened immediately. Ramsey said something she couldn't quite make out to the wagon driver and then nodded to Hobbs. The carriage bounced as Hobbs took his place at the reins and Ramsey climbed inside. A quick rap on the roof signalled Hobbs and the carriage jerked forward, settling easily into a smooth swaying motion. The detective studied her, lips curving upward in what she imagined was amusement over the drastic change. Grace tried to smile in return but the day's events rushed in on her at once, stealing the semblance of calm she'd found while making repairs to her appearance. They sat in silence as the carriage made its way down the lane and turned onto the main road. Ramsey turned from gazing out the window to face her.

"You're very quiet, Miss Flynn. Are you quite well?"

Grace was unsure how to respond. The oddest mixture of melancholy and hysteria seemed intent on spilling out of her, and she fought to suppress it. She tried to speak but was startled when she emitted a strangled laugh instead. Despite her attempts to gain control, she found herself laughing harder with each breath she took. She was relieved to see, when she finally managed to calm herself, that the detective was watching her with amusement rather than consternation. She sheepishly took the handkerchief he offered and dabbed at her streaming eyes, fervently hoping that she did not look as unhinged as she felt.

"I apologize," she managed after trying and failing more than once to speak clearly. "I fear the strain of the day has caught up with me."

"I do not blame you," replied Ramsey, bemusement marking his features, "but I should have thought a fit of tears would be more likely than a fit of laughter."

"Perhaps, and I may yet indulge in that as well, but I'm ashamed to say that my sense of humor is rather macabre."

"I don't understand. What has that to do with your nerves being affected by the strain of recent events?"

"If you must know, just as you asked if I was quite well, the memory of Dr. Wick flailing like a dying fish while Matron Green sagged against the wall like a sack of potatoes filled my mind. I fear the image was so ludicrous that it made me slightly hysterical."

Ramsey's lips twitched at the mental image her words evoked. "I suppose if I had not been so focused on assuring myself you were unharmed I should have seen the humor the moment I opened the door on that particular tableau. Now it will reappear in my head during the most inopportune moments, such as while I am reporting to my superiors. Laughing in the face of my superintendent is an excellent way to volunteer for a demotion."

"Do you know this from personal experience, sir?" A glimmer of fun lingered in her warm brown eyes.

"It would not be to my benefit to comment on that," he responded swiftly, "lest you decide I make a habit of insubordination and cease to trust me."

"From what I have seen, sir, it would take a good deal more than that to make me cease trusting you." Grace bit her lip nervously, surprised at herself for revealing so much of what she felt. She quickly redirected her comment. "That is, you have been the epitome of the experienced professional in every circumstance. How could I help believing that you would always and only act for the sake of what is good and right?"

Ramsey absently rubbed his fist against the persistent ache near his breastbone. *I must ask James about this confounded pain in my chest. Strange I've never noticed it before.* He studied the woman across from him as she occupied herself by watching the countryside go by. She wasn't conventionally beautiful, but there was something about her that drew the eye and held it. She was witty, compassionate and brave but more than anything it was her warmth that drew people to her. Spending time near her made him feel settled somehow, even as he tried to figure her out. She was quite complex, indeed, but the pieces which comprised her made such an appealing whole.

"Will you tell me now what you have planned for the Surrey County Asylum, Inspector? You *will* do something to set things right, will you not?"

"As far as I can. I must admit, I would dearly love a round or two of fisticuffs with whomever is the source of this horrific scheme. If it is not Elliott Rivers, I will be shocked beyond measure, but until I have evidence of that fact, I must investigate every avenue fully."

"And I would dearly love a round or two of fisticuffs with his wife, if she is as vile a creature as he. From the state of affairs in the asylum, if the Rivers are the instigators of what we saw, I am inclined to think she is." She paused, her eyes growing serious. "Fisticuffs or not, you are indeed fighting already. I see the fire burning in your eyes when you talk about innocent men and women victimized by the powerful. You fight for those who cannot fight for themselves. It is a calling, much more than the need to earn your way in the world."

"I agree," he replied slowly, "though such an assertion makes me sound entirely too noble. I've not always managed to conduct my investigations in a way that achieved justice. Sometimes it is impossible to put things to right; one can only expose the wrong."

"I suspect you carry the burden of that with you constantly."

"The burden would be far heavier if I did not trust that God will deal with evildoers as the ultimate judge. He is far better equipped to dispense justice than I, and will do so in his time and his way." His lips quirked as he met her gaze once more. "I do, however, frequently pray that his way and time include my hunting down and caging those willfully harming others for the duration of their sorry lives. That would be my preference."

Grace gave a burst of surprised laughter, revealing a row of endearingly crooked teeth.

"Your candor is most refreshing. I, too, often find myself wanting to play judge and jury. It is comforting to hear that I am not the only one who must be reminded that such things are God's responsibility. I admit, I do occasionally wish that I could deal with things precisely as I saw fit."

"A fault we share, Miss Flynn, though perhaps it is not so much a fault as an overzealous desire to reflect God's heart for the oppressed. It's not a bad inclination to have in my profession and, I suspect, comes in rather handy in yours."

"It does if I can temper it with compassion and good sense. And," she added thoughtfully, "recognize that God's purposes are both deeper and more committed to redemption than mine. Too often I simply want to punish the wrongdoer when the best outcome would be to see them repent and change."

"Quite so. But while God extends grace and forgiveness, we humans have a need to see justice done and forget that God is more just than we can imagine being. It's complicated." Ramsey couldn't help the intensity of his gaze on Grace. The passion in her voice was visible in the very way she held herself, her bright, burning spirit somehow constrained, not unnecessarily, by her body. "I hope that you will agree that my tentative plan for the Surrey County Asylum shows both compassion and good sense. If not, we shall have to work together to find the solution."

"What do you have in mind? There must be something that can be done, despite the limitations of legalities and funding."

"I believe there is. How do you think your brother James is getting along in London? Does he enjoy his work at the hospital?"

Comprehension lit her gaze and she began to smile.

"That," she murmured slowly, "may be the most brilliant notion I've ever heard. James is quite capable of overseeing and restructuring an institution while he works with the patients. I believe he would relish the challenge. If I tell you again it is a brilliant notion," she eyed him warily, "just how much larger will your ego grow?"

Ramsey drummed his fingers against his thigh, considering.

"No more than twice its current size," he decided, "so have no fear; we shall both still fit comfortably in this carriage for the remainder of the journey."

Grace snorted derisively. She managed to sound so incongruously ladylike that Ramsey couldn't help chuckling.

"Just barely, I'll wager," she murmured.

The sound of their mingled laughter echoed amid the rumbling of the carriage wheels as the lumbering vehicle made its way slowly down the road toward the city.

15

The cell was dark, damp, and infused with the fetid smell of unwashed bodies. For the first hour of his imprisonment, Dr. Wick paced the length of his prison, pausing every few minutes to pound on the door and demand at the top of his lungs that he be released. By the second hour, he'd given in to his weary muscles and perched on the edge of a rotting wooden bench next to the wall. It was uncomfortable but it took the weight off legs already aching from the journey to the city, bound and cramped in the wagon bed next to Matron Green.

The driver had covered Matron Green and him with blankets before they started on their way but the cool breeze had sharpened to an icy wind as daylight faded. Early along the way, one of Matron Green's hairpins dislodged from her chignon and poked into the side of his face. His already dark mood had him envisioning wrapping his fingers around the woman's throat, the mildly cheering thought alleviating only a small portion of his fury.

By the time they arrived in London, his face bled from a number of shallow scratches and the matron's hair straggled around her shoulders in oily hanks. Detective Inspector Ramsey had begun questioning him immediately, but Dr. Wick had refused to answer any of the policeman's questions. He had, however, shouted that his credentials — a medical degree obtained at a university in France — and work should have made him a hero in his field. Instead Ramsay treated him as a common criminal and only promised more questions the following day. The doctor's lips thinned as he studied the cell's dirt floor with its scattering of straw, the rivulets of water running down the worn stone walls creating a muddy trail toward the heavy wooden door with its iron bars.

Somehow, he would have Detective Inspector Ramsey thrown out on the street for the trouble he had caused him. *When his superiors find out who I am and with whom I am connected, he will be fortunate to escape coming up on charges himself. The Rivers may be responsible for my present situation, but they wield a great deal of power. They'll get me out of here soon. They have to.* He reached up to scratch his cheek and cursed, wincing as his nails broke open the cuts left by the matron's hairpins. His fingers were stiff and cold and they helped numb the painfully throbbing gouge.

Reaching into his breast coat pocket, he tugged out his handkerchief and wiped his bloody fingertips on it. True to habit, he refolded the square of linen in precise quarters before setting it next to him on the stone bench. He did not want to stain his coat with blood. Shifting, he cursed again as he realized that the bench was more wet than damp and had soaked through his trousers. He stood, brushing the backs of his pant legs ineffectually with the folded handkerchief while swearing viciously. *That bastard Ramsey will pay for every indignity I suffer. Just wait until I get out of this pit...*

The screech of the bolt being drawn back pulled Dr. Wick from his musings. He dropped the handkerchief onto the bench and faced the slowly opening door. The sneer he had affixed to his face disappeared at the sight of the man following the prison keeper into his cell.

"You have as much time as you need with your client, Mr. Gosford." The keeper's respectful tone and posture were a stark contrast to the way he had shoved Dr. Wick into the cell.

"Thank you, Mr. Owens. I will knock on the door to let you know when I am ready to leave."

The door clanged shut, the sound echoing in the dimly lit cell. The barred window high above Dr. Wick's head let in only a minute amount of sunlight, leaving both men's faces in shadow. It did not matter. Dr. Wick had recognized his visitor's voice the minute he had begun speaking. His hands fisted by his sides.

"What took you so long?" He hissed, glaring at the impeccably attired man. "I have to get out of here. Can you even imagine what my colleagues will say if they hear I've been arrested?"

His guest simply stared at him, eyes glinting in the semi-darkness, face impassive.

"What are you looking at?" Crimson suffused Dr. Wick's cheeks. "You don't think this is *my* fault, do you? Certainly, *I* did nothing to draw the eye of the police. I had no trouble until you and your employers entered the scene."

Still saying nothing, the other man pulled his gloves off, one finger at a time. The silence stretched between them for what seemed to Dr. Wick like ages. Finally, his visitor spoke.

"Surely you are not suggesting that either I or my employers are responsible for your troubles? That would be quite unkind of you, Dr. Wick, after all we've done for you."

His voice was mild but something in his tone sent a shiver down Dr. Wick's spine.

"No, no, of course not," he tried to smooth the matter over, "I only meant that I had nothing to do with it. It must have been one of the family members of a patient, or perhaps someone from the nearby village."

"I see. Well, suppose you tell me everything that Detective Inspector Ramsey has discovered and everything you've said so that I can formulate the best way to argue for your release."

Dr. Wick was more than happy to comply.

"I swear to you, Gosford, I never said a word about you or the Rivers. I know from whence my bread is buttered and beyond that, confidentiality is essential in my profession," he hastened to assure the man, well aware that their assistance depended upon his convincing Gosford he was trustworthy. "You would not believe what that uncouth policeman did to my electroshock machine. It's going to take me ages to repair, not to mention the cost of replacement parts. All of the files on the treatments I've performed are compromised now. That inspector and the stupid cow he brought with him have ruined years of my work in one day."

When he paused for air, the other man put a hand on his arm.

"Calm down, Wick, and breathe. It will be taken care of, I promise you. Detective Inspector Ramsey will get what he has coming. Tell me though, who did he bring with him? Surely the London Metropolitan Police Force is not stretched so thin that they are accepting *women* now?"

"No, of course not," snapped Dr. Wick. "And don't tell me to calm down. Do you not see where I am?" He waved an arm, gesturing broadly at the cell that held him. "I don't know who the woman was, but she deserves to feel the effects of my wrath. Lying, vile creature, and the damage she did to my machine."

His voice trailed off in a pathetic whine and his lip trembled.

"Come," Gosford reached into his coat pocket and produced a small flask, "have a drink of brandy. It will brace you up until you are able to leave this place. I brought this from my personal stock."

Dr. Wick's hands shook as he reached for the flask and lifted it to his lips, taking a long swallow. The liquid burned down his throat, warming his belly even though the air remained cool on his skin. He handed it back to Mr. Gosford, murmuring his thanks. He felt his muscles relaxing and he rolled his shoulders to loosen them further.

"Keep this," Gosford held out the flask. "It will help keep you comfortable and I can always retrieve it later." He glanced around as Dr. Wick's fingers closed over the metal container. "You had best conceal it until after I am escorted out or the prison keeper will confiscate it. That far corner may work. They would not expect you to go near those iron shackles hanging from the wall."

"Excellent idea, Gosford," replied Dr. Wick, turning so quickly to hide the flask that he missed the glint of torchlight reflecting off the object his companion stealthily pulled from his pocket. "I'll just tuck it into the shadows here. Then I can tuck in when I feel the need." He chuckled at his own joke, rising from his crouched position.

A whisper of air brushed the back of his neck as sudden pressure constricted his windpipe. He clawed at his throat, dimly registering the feel of wire beneath his fingertips as pain sang through his nerve endings. He gagged, seeking breath that was impossible to find. Helpless, he felt his legs give out and he dropped to his knees. Darkness encroached on his vision as a voice whispered in his ear.

"It's a pity you have to die, doctor, but it is necessary. There is simply too much at stake for my employers to leave you alive and able to speak. My sincerest apologies. I do mean that."

The fingers that had been clawing frantically relaxed, dropping to reveal long, bloody furrows in the tender skin of the doctor's neck. His nails had scored his own flesh trying to dislodge the garrotte but it had not made a difference. The heavy weight of his body and his sightless, bulging eyes told his attacker that the pompous physician was no longer a threat to the Rivers' peace of mind.

Gosford let the body drop face first into the dirt floor of the cell before crouching and using a clean handkerchief to pick up the flask and stood. He tucked it into his pocket after he had wiped it free of straw and dirt and, with a final, unpitying glance at the man lying in an undignified sprawl in the shadows, he walked to the cell door and knocked briskly. It opened immediately.

"Have you completed your business then, sir?" asked the prison keeper, not bothering to cover his gaping mouth as he yawned.

"Yes," murmured Gosford, "I believe we are quite finished."

He stepped through the door, pausing as it clanged shut after him. He turned, reached into his pocket, and withdrew his billfold. He removed a small wad of notes, folded them and slipped them to the burly man.

"Mr. Rivers sends his regards."

The keeper's eyes were hard as he took the money, tucking it into his coat pocket.

"Safe travels, sir." He tipped his head to side. "Shall I give the good doctor any message from you when he gets his bread and water?"

Gosford met the man's eyes, appreciating the cruelty in them.

"No," he replied smoothly, "I believe I got my message across quite nicely, thank you. Anything more would be superfluous."

With that, he turned and walked down the long, narrow corridor, his tuneless whistle echoing eerily in the clammy prison air.

The back room of the shop was heavy with scent as Grace busily checked flames and flasks before turning to her mortar and pestle to grind the dried herbs into the fine dust necessary for pastes and plasters. Enveloped in her much-abused apron, she worked away, revelling in the scents and sounds around her. She was so engrossed in the tasks at hand, murmuring to herself and humming snatches of songs wandering through her mind, that she didn't heard her sister push the curtain aside and call her name.

"Grace? Grace!"

"Hmm? Did you say something, Annie?" Grace glanced over her shoulder, still busily grinding the herbs in the ceramic bowl into a fine powder.

Annie stared at her in exasperation, hands planted on her hips.

"I've been trying to get your attention for the past five minutes. Honestly, Gracie, I don't know what to do with you. I've been waiting all morning to hear how your journey with Inspector Ramsey went yesterday. I know you told me last night when you arrived home that you were too tired to speak of it, but you've had a night's sleep to recover and I've had too many hours to speculate without a smidgen of information from you. It's not fair."

Grace kept her movements steady, wishing she could calm her volatile sister as easily as she could turn powders into lotions. Annie's eyes were bright, with as much irritation as excitement. With a sigh, Grace set the bowl aside and turned around.

"There's honestly not much I can tell you, Annie. Inspector Ramsey instructed me not to talk about what happened at the asylum with anyone. There is a trial ahead and I may be called as a witness. If I speak of what happened beforehand, I may become less clear about what actually occurred. Besides, I should not feel right talking about the sad misfortunes of the inmates. They are not there for our entertainment. They are to be pitied."

"Nonsense." Annie's lips slid into a pout. "It's just me, Gracie. Why can you not tell your sister? If you had taken me along, as you should have, I wouldn't need to press you for details."

"It was not my decision, Annie. You know that."

"It was too your decision," retorted the younger woman. "You knew Inspector Ramsey fancied me and you couldn't stand it. I think it was cruel and downright selfish for you to exclude me that way. I can't help it," she reached up and patted her shining copper hair with a sniff, "if men find me more attractive than you. You needn't let jealousy turn you into a vindictive shrew."

"Annie," Grace forced herself to speak calmly as her temper flared, "that had nothing to do with the matter. The inspector needed a particular form of knowledge, which I happened to possess. However," her voice cooled further, "you may want to refrain from flaunting your many charms in the presence of decent men, or declaring your popularity with gentlemen at all. It is behavior unbecoming to a lady. Father would be horrified to hear you speak so."

"Father is delighted that he has one daughter whose face and form are pleasing to look on," retorted Annie, the barb striking home painfully. "I'm leaving early today. I have no wish to spend the rest of the afternoon with a harpy of a spinster whose obvious interest in a certain inspector is laughable. Besides," she tossed the words over her shoulder as she swept the curtain aside, "I have an engagement with a new customer — a gentleman, and a handsome one at that. You can tell Inspector Ramsey, if he should happen to stop by, that he will have to work quite hard to win my favor after the abominable way he's acted thus far."

Grace stood silent and unmoving as the door opened, then slammed shut. Slowly, she turned back to the table, mechanically picked up the mortar and pestle and returned to her work. Tears slid down her cheeks unheeded as she stared unseeingly at the table in front of her. *Oh Lord,* she breathed hard, fighting a swell of emotion. *What a mess. She hates me...and, Lord help me, I'm trying not to hate her. But I fear I'm not succeeding.*

Shoving the bowl and pestle aside with a clatter, Grace laid her head on her arms and wept.

16

Ramsey stared at his desk with eyes that were bleary and red-rimmed from constant rubbing. He was fighting exhaustion but feared that he was losing the battle. The words on the paper in front of him bled together — an unintelligible greyish mess from which he was somehow supposed to glean enough information to solve a murder. He sighed, forcing himself to lower the hand he'd just lifted to rub at his eyes again. The pressure around murder investigations was always intense, but that surrounding the death of Dr. Wick in his prison cell had brought an unforeseen amount of scrutiny. He was determined to find the killer and prosecute him to the full extent of the law. Perhaps, he thought morosely, that would assuage his feeling of responsibility. A knock sounded at the door, the sound startling him into dropping his pencil.

"Come in," he called, hoping his voice would carry through the thick wooden door. Just the thought of rising from his desk exhausted him.

The door opened, revealing the greying hair and taut features of his superior officer. The older man walked into the office, shutting the door behind him. He was neither tall nor broad; in fact, Superintendent Norris appeared deceptively slight. His wiry frame, however, was all lean, hard muscle. Ramsey had watched the man subdue criminals much larger than himself and knew that wherever the man had learned to fight, it had not been a place that respected the gentleman's code of honor.

His quick movements and habitually bunched shoulders gave the impression of tightly coiled springs that would burst forth under the slightest provocation. Ramsey's experience was that it did not take much more to provoke Superintendent Norris than a difference of opinion. He had once, as a young constable, made the mistake of stating that the amusements found in the gentlemen's clubs of his social betters were a waste of time. When Norris had called him a fool for speaking about something he clearly didn't understand, Ramsey had said that whether or not he understood the habits of gentlemen was hardly relevant since neither of them had been born one. He hadn't realized then that the superintendent harbored a deep desire to better himself in the eyes of society. Ramsey had spent the next month patrolling the dangerous, filth-ridden streets in Seven Dials from dusk until dawn as punishment for his comments.

"Ramsey," Norris' eyes flicked over the office, taking in the uncustomary disorder on his desk. Setting down the pencil he hadn't realized he still held in his grasp, Ramsey braced himself. "I'm here about the matter of Dr. Wick's death. It was on your watch that the man was killed."

"I am aware of that, sir. You have my word that I do not intend to rest until I find the man who took his life and have gathered enough evidence to hang him with it."

"Your *determination*," the superintendent uttered the word as though it tasted sour, "is admirable, but you need not concern yourself with this any longer. I've looked at the report you wrote regarding the asylum. The man was clearly delusional and criminal in his actions; we would have hanged him anyway, so justice is done.

Close the book on this and move on to something more worthy of your time."

Ramsey couldn't stop disbelief from etching itself across his features. The directive was ludicrous. Ignoring a crime was a corruption of justice; ignoring a murder was unthinkable.

"Sir," he said, praying that his tone was a good deal more respectful than he felt, "a crime has been committed practically within our walls. We must at least find out how the killer entered Dr. Wick's cell without catching the prison keeper's attention. If, and I pray this is not the case, but the question must be asked, the man *did* know that something was amiss, it is crucial that we discover just how much a prison keeper's honour is worth! He was bribed, and our attempts at implementing justice are a mockery if we do not root out such corruption."

"Your penchant for melodrama is unseemly and unnecessary, Ramsey," Norris' condescending tone made Ramsey's blood boil. "Surely you can see that nothing would be gained by finding Dr. Wick's killer. It's just as likely that the man killed himself. He had to be depressed at the realization that his career was over. He was unimportant in life, he is unimportant in death, and that's my final decision on the matter. I need your attention focused elsewhere. The Waverly case is far more crucial to the interests of the Yard and you've shown disappointingly little progress."

"The Waverly case?" Ramsey knew his anger was visible, and he tried to calm himself. "Sir, the Waverly case is a ridiculous misuse of our time and resources. Lady Waverly lost her lapdog. That is hardly a matter worthy of our attention at the best of times, let alone when we have a corpse on our hands. Dr. Wick, whatever he was in life, still deserves justice in death."

"Perhaps you misheard me, Inspector; I wasn't implying you had a choice." The superintendent's voice was cold. "You will close this case. You will declare Dr. Wick's death a tragic accident and that will be the end of it. You will focus your time and energy on finding Lord and Lady Waverly's beloved pet because that is what I, your superior in every way, am telling you. Do you hear me?"

Ramsey slammed a fist against his thigh, unseen under his desk, as he hissed out a breath through clenched teeth.

"Are you certain you wish to proceed in this manner, sir? You are perilously close to misusing your authority by covering up a murder."

"And you are perilously close to losing your job. Do not test me, Ramsey, or I will turn you out on your ear this very day. You will do what I have commanded and that is the end of it. If you refuse, you will feel the full weight of my authority, and my displeasure, have no doubt of that. Do you hear me?"

Ramsey fought for control. If he resisted any further, he would lose his position. He'd seen men cut loose for less under the man's purview. The time might yet come to break from the force, but not yet. He'd made his argument and, despite the risk, would attempt to investigate Dr. Wick's death on his own time.

"I hear you. I will do as you ask, but I respectfully request your permission to investigate the events surrounding Dr. Wick's demise when I am not working."

"I cannot control your activities during your personal time," Norris scowled, "though I would advise you to seriously reconsider that notion. If you hope to advance in the force, you will have to display both respect for your superiors *and* the wisdom to know when to let a case go. Carry on with the Waverly case. I don't want to hear another word about Dr. Wick cross your lips. I expect to see a completed report closing that case by the end of today. Is that understood?"

"Yes, sir. You'll have it by the end of today."

Without another word, Superintendent Norris strode out of the office, leaving the door open behind him. Ramsey wanted to plant his fist through the wall to vent the wave of fury that threatened to overwhelm him. *With my luck,* he thought irascibly, *I'd break my hand and then have to deal with that along with the hole in my wall.* The superintendent was so concerned with pursuit of power that he could not see past his own nose. His directives had rankled in the past, but this was a new and disturbing low. If he did not feel so strongly that God had placed him on the force to expose and challenge injustice, within the structure that already existed, Ramsey would have left years ago. As it was, he felt no sense of release from that call, even now. Frustrated that he could not pursue the investigation full–time himself, he threw his pencil down and stood, pacing the length of the room. He stopped suddenly, a thought striking. *But I do,* he realized, a wave of hope coursing through him, *know someone who can.*

The offices of Hayes & Associates were on the second floor of an inauspicious building near the heart of London. As Ramsey climbed the stairs, he thought back to the first time he'd met the proprietor, Jonathan Hayes, a man who possessed one of the keenest minds he'd ever met. It had been a murder case, Ramsey's first. Ten years ago, he had been a freshly hired constable, young and eager to make his mark. While on night patrol in a Seven Dials alley, he had stumbled across the body of a young woman, dress torn, bloody and stained with a week's worth of filth. It was clear from these factors that she was a streetwalker — or so he thought.

Ramsey shook his head, dispelling memories, as he opened the door and stepped into the outer office. The desk, crowded with pens, ink and stacks of paper, was empty and the door to Jonathan's office was slightly ajar. He could hear the sound of voices, soft and low, as he moved closer. He tucked his hat under his arm, smoothed a hand over his hair before brushing a minute speck of lint from his coat pocket, and prepared to plead his case to the private investigator. After ten years of friendship and intersecting investigations, he knew without doubt that Jonathan Hayes could be trusted, even to the death. He only hoped that such debt of trust would never be required of either of them.

17

Grace flinched as the curtain separating her workroom from the rest of the shop parted. Things had been tense with Annie ever since their argument, and the passage of time did not appear to be lessening her sister's anger. Every subsequent encounter had high emotion and harsh words on both parts, much to Grace's chagrin. One glance at Annie's reddened cheeks and narrowed gaze told Grace that today would be no different.

"You have a visitor."

Grace set down the tongs she'd been using to transfer small vials of oil bubbling over open flame to cool in a tray by the window and wiped her hands on her apron.

"Who is it, Annie?"

"It's your *gentleman friend*," Annie smirked as Grace's face flushed with embarrassment. "Oh, don't be such a prig, Gracie! You're only spending time with Inspector Ramsey to help his investigation, isn't that right? So you keep telling me. Why should you be embarrassed by my teasing? Oh," she affected a look of distress, "you really are throwing yourself at the poor man, aren't you?"

"Why are you being so cruel? I've done nothing to deserve your scorn, have I?"

Annie shrugged laconically, not looking the least bit contrite.

"I'm only teasing you, as any sister would. We both know that he's not interested in you that way, so I don't see why you should be upset. I thought you realized long ago that you were not the kind of woman men admire. It cannot matter to you any longer," she pointed a finger at her sister, "after so many years of them choosing me over you, can it? Honestly, Gracie, you must learn to accept your limitations. You are not accustomed to interacting with men, after all. I suppose you cannot help your awkwardness. Now, will you come out to the front? I have an engagement and I need to return to the boarding house to change my gown."

"If those words are your idea of sisterly affection," Grace could feel her face flushing darker, this time from anger, "then you have a great deal to learn on the subject. Besides," she said, drawing a deep breath and fighting for calm, "the shop doesn't close for another hour and I have orders to fill. What am I supposed to do while you go off and leave the front unattended? I cannot do both your work and mine."

"You will manage quite well. You always do. That's all I was trying to say, that you are so terribly self-sufficient. Sadly, men do not admire such traits in the fairer sex. Why do you look so put out? Hardly anybody comes to the shop the hour before we close and this was the only time that Mr. Gosford had free for three whole days. I couldn't make him wait, not such a handsome man as he!"

Annie whisked the curtain aside and hurried through the opening. Grace pushed through the curtain after her.

"Wait a minute, Annie. You cannot just go off with a man that neither I nor James knows anything about. It's neither safe nor wise."

"Oh hush, Grace. I will go wherever I please, with whomever I please. I'm twenty-one years old, not a dried-up spinster like you. I want to have fun. Mr. Gosford is a man of business and he kindly invited me to go for a drive with him in the park. That's a perfectly respectable outing, and you know it. Now, I'm leaving so I can put on a gown more appropriate to the occasion and nothing you say will stop me. I'll see you this evening."

Grabbing her shawl from behind the front counter, Annie strode to the door, pushed it open and hurried out into the street. Grace could hear the rapid beating of her heart roaring in her ears in the silence that followed. She took a step toward the door and then stopped. Going after Annie would only escalate the argument and she couldn't leave the shop unattended. She rubbed the heel of her palm across her brow, trying to suppress the throbbing pain that had begun.

"Do you need to sit down, Grace? You don't look well."

Grace started at the sound of Ramsey's voice. She hadn't even noticed him standing near the front window to her right. Mortification filled her as she realized that he must have heard the entire exchange.

"No, Inspector Ramsey, I'm fine. I'm afraid," she tried to smile, her lips stiff and unyielding despite the effort, "that your arrival sparked one more argument in a long series of disagreements with my sister. My apologies for anything untoward you may have overheard."

"It was of no consequence to me," Ramsey lifted a shoulder in a dismissive gesture, "but your sister seems to relish reasons to malign your character. It was quite clear from what I heard that she has little understanding of you at all. Has she always behaved with such self-centeredness? Perhaps all young ladies go through such a phase and I, lacking experience with the species, am simply unaware it is so."

"It's difficult to answer that, sir. When Annie came of marriageable age and her pastimes grew to include," she cleared her throat delicately, "a broader range of interests, it seemed we were always at odds. My dedication to my work and lack of social ambition, or savvy, for that matter, seem to bother her a great deal. I've never understood why. I truly don't think she understands how unkind she can be, though I suppose that is not much of a defense at all, is it?"

"Not in my estimation. She was cruel to you, Grace, and untruthful. You are not a prig," he said matter-of-factly, "nor are you a dried-up spinster. You are a warm, compassionate woman who loves her work and her family. Just because you are not as vivacious as Annie does not mean you are less of a woman. You are highly individual, Grace Flynn, and that makes you most intriguing."

Grace's face flamed as a deeply suppressed longing unfurled inside her, fighting for space next to lingering shame. *He must have heard her taunting me about courtship,* she thought, a fresh wave of humiliation overwhelming her, *and now feels he must say something kind to show his pity.*

"You needn't pity me, sir," she fought back unexpected tears. "I realize you must have heard Annie speaking of you as my gentleman friend, but I never said such a thing to her, I swear it. I know that you are only interested in my help with your investigation. Please don't feel that you need to offer sympathetic phrases to ease wounded feelings. I know myself. I've never had throngs of callers at my door and I don't expect them. I would hate to think that you felt obligated to handle me carefully because of a potential misunderstanding. I do not break so easily."

Ramsey's face was unreadable. Grace's trepidation increased with every second that passed in silence. To her utter shock, he stepped closer and took her hand in his.

"I was not offering platitudes, Grace. I hadn't intended to ask you just yet, but I believe the time is right. I wish to declare my intention to court you, if you're amenable to the idea despite," his lips quirked, "not having had 'throngs of callers at your door' before this point."

"Your intentions to what?" Her mouth dropped open in shock.

"To court you, Grace. I would be honored if you would allow me to call upon you as," he grinned slyly, "your *gentleman friend*."

"You want to court *me*?" Grace's eyes widened and she blurted out the first thing that crossed her mind. "Why on earth would you want to do that?"

Ramsey laughed softly and squeezed her hand. The sensation warmed her even as her confusion grew.

"That response is one of the reasons, Grace. You are such a unique woman. I've never met anyone like you and the more time I spend with you, the more things I find that win my admiration. I'd settled long ago that marriage was something I was unlikely to experience, for a variety of reasons, not the least being the all-consuming nature of my work. You've made me hope that perhaps I was wrong in my assumption."

She shook her head in disbelief. "Are you very sure? You are not simply trying to raise my spirits out of some sense of pity?"

"I am, indeed. My feelings surprised me, but only because I hadn't expected to feel this way about anyone. I rather thought that I was the kind of man who would be unable to win a wife, to be truthful, and I didn't particularly want one of the kind of women that I've come across until now. When I met you, I saw for the first time what a blessing it would be to have a strong, gentle woman at my side. I am quite determined to follow the matter through, providing you are amenable. We need not hurry. I would prefer that we take our time to know one another well before, should this endeavor unfold as I hope and pray it shall, we arrive at the altar."

"Naturally," Grace knew her voice was weak but her grasp on her faculties was returning. True, she had never honestly considered the prospect of a beau but that did not mean she could not think the matter over, did it? It could be an experiment. She was good at experiments, and once she had conclusive data on the matter she could make a decision about the next step. "You certainly took me by surprise, Inspector Ramsey, but I find that I am indeed amenable to the concept." She paused, her lips curving upward in her first true smile of the day. "Given our recent experience at the Surrey County Asylum, however, I must ask you one thing."

"Certainly." Ramsey squeezed her hand once more, a broad grin breaking out on his face. "You may ask me anything."

"Are you quite certain that you're not insane?"

He laughed, releasing her hand.

"Fairly certain, yes," he managed, "but I may not be the best authority on the matter."

Grace studied the man, a new question forming. How was she to address him? As her beau? Her gentleman caller? What was appropriate? Perhaps she should simply continue to call him Inspector Ramsey. Or, perhaps, his Christian name, but then she didn't even know his Christian name.

"What should I call you?"

Ramsey looked at her in confusion, brow knitting. "I beg your pardon?"

"What should I call you? Now," she hurried on, "that we are becoming better acquainted, I was wondering what I should call you. Addressing you as Inspector Ramsey seems a bit incongruous for the change in our relationship." She paused, feeling foolish. "Do you understand what I mean?"

"I do, yes. I believe it would be very nice to hear you using my Christian name. I have not had the pleasure of being called Jack for many years, but if you find that too intimate you may simply address me as Ramsey. I leave it you to decide."

"You have already begun to address me as Grace, so it only seems fair that I call you Jack, but this needs some getting used to. I've only ever thought of you as Inspector Ramsey."

"Quite understandable, though I'm sad to hear it." She felt her face flush again and he grinned. She shook herself free from self-recriminations as he continued. "It will take time for both of us to become accustomed to the change in the nature of our relationship. I confess, the prospect of escorting the woman I am courting to her home is somewhat abnormal."

"It is rather discomfiting. I wonder if I will ever be as confident as Annie is in your presence."

"I prefer you to be as you are, Grace. Annie may be confident, but it is your warmth and kindness I am drawn to."

"Indeed?" Grace blushed, wondering if she would ever become accustomed to hearing herself praised. She cleared her throat, flustered once more. "It's all very interesting, from a scientific standpoint."

"A scientific standpoint?" Ramsey raised a brow. "My dear Grace, you are not using me for research, are you? Perhaps conducting an experiment to see what affections grow between a man and woman somewhat at odds with what our society demands?"

"You should be so fortunate, Jack," she replied, a grin flashing across her face as she uttered the quick retort.

"Quite right. Research or not, I count myself very fortunate indeed."

"How convenient," murmured Grace, watching his face light with amusement and feeling a lovely warmth settle near her heart, "so do I."

18

Nine bells announced the hour as the clock in the boarding house drawing room chimed. Grace looked down at the handkerchief knotted in her hands and smoothed it out again. She had repeated the process countless times over the course of the past two hours and the square of linen was hopelessly wrinkled. When her sister failed to appear in time to take dinner at the boarding house, Grace had been certain that wherever Annie was, it was nowhere she should be. Coming into the drawing room after dinner to await Annie's return, she hoped against hope that the younger woman had some plausible reason her long absence.

No amount of warning made a difference when it came to Annie's enthrallment with romance. She steadfastly refused to believe that her flirtatious behavior would lead to anything other than gentlemanly attentions. Grace feared that while she had willingly gone driving with this Mr. Gosford, the situation may have progressed to the sort that ruined reputations and lives.

"You have no idea where she could be, Gracie?" James asked, not for the first time. His fatigue after a long day at the hospital was evident, but he refused to sleep until Annie was safely home.

"None, James. She and Mr. Gosford were taking a drive through the park, but that was hours ago. I've no inkling where she could be now. Knowing our sister, if Mr. Gosford spoke flatteringly enough, she would have gone without another thought. Please," she pleaded as he rubbed a hand over his weary features, "go to bed and get some rest. I will wait up for her. You may to speak with her first thing in the morning."

"I will not leave this matter for you to deal with, Grace," James' jaw clenched in anger. "It was foolhardy of Annie to go off with a man we know nothing about. If she does not return within the hour, I will alert the police so they can begin to search for her."

"Oh James, she will never forgive us for embarrassing her, even if she is in a precarious situation. I simply don't know what to do. She's so angry with me all the time. Yet I must try to keep her from harm. Tell me, how can we possibly convince her that she must give more thought to her own reputation, if not to that of her family?"

"I wish I knew, Gracie." He sat down and patted her hand in an awkward attempt at comfort. "I can't ever remember a time when Annie was interested in anything that did not directly affect her. She is such an engaging creature that it is easy to forgive such a flaw, but she has never experienced the consequences to her actions. I fear for her, Grace. You make her angry because you force her to face herself and I suspect she does not enjoy what she sees. And thus, she runs farther and faster than before."

"Gentlemen have paid her attention since she was but fourteen years old." Grace sighed. "She has always been so confident and I've not heard an uncharitable word spoken of her, though I admit I've thought one or two myself."

"You truly have the oddest distortion of perception with regard to our sister," James said wryly. "Annie has been trying to measure up to your intelligence and your ambition since she was a child. As much as you have been envious of her vivacity and beauty, she has resented your clear direction, settled heart and bright mind. You complement each other wonderfully when you are able to get along."

"I'd never realized…" Grace broke off. "I thought I was the only one who was jealous. I've felt so foolish over it. It never occurred to me that Annie had anything to be envious of in me."

"She does, Gracie. Your actions to her have always been much kinder than hers toward you." He paused, looking at the clock again. "We must do something. I cannot wait another hour to see if she will come traipsing in, safe and sound, when she may be in trouble. I will go to Scotland Yard and see what can be done."

"Wait, James. I believe Inspector Ramsey is upstairs. He told me that he would not be present at dinner but did not expect to be out late this evening. We can ask him what he thinks we should do. If he had known the situation, I'm certain he would have offered his professional assistance already. If you will be so kind as to go up his room and fetch him, I've no doubt he will come down immediately and help us."

"Why should he get involved? He's not on duty and I would hate to bother a man with whom we are not well acquainted." James turned a puzzled gaze toward his sister. Understanding dawned as he took in the blush that colored her cheeks as she studiously smoothed her handkerchief again. "Grace? Is there something you wish to tell me?"

Grace was trying to frame her response when a voice spoke from the doorway.

"James, I should have sought you out directly after I arrived but I had some notes to go over relating to my latest case and was rather distracted. I offer my apologies for not coming to you right away. This afternoon, I declared my intentions to your sister and she," Ramsey's usually formidable expression softened with a smile, "has accepted my suit. I wish to ask for your blessing. I will write to your father as well, naturally."

"I say," James looked completely nonplussed, "how did I miss this unfolding? Does Annie know?"

"You've been working so hard, James. Besides, I must admit that Inspector Ramsey's declaration was a surprise to me as well. Annie doesn't know yet, but I'm afraid she was rather put out with me because she felt that I was trying to compete with her for his attentions. We argued about it just before she left for her ride in the park. Oh, Jack, we must do something. I have the strongest sense that something is terribly wrong."

"In that case," Ramsey walked across the room and laid a hand on her arm, "allow me to be of assistance. James, you can accompany me to file a report with the desk sergeant on duty at the Yard. I have a few ideas of where a man with less than honorable intentions might take a naive young lady, but I'm afraid that none of them make intervention easy. Grace, now is the time for prayer."

"Of course," Grace placed her hand on his, "and I will continue to do so as we search."

"I will send messages with our progress as frequently as I can, but I'm afraid you may not hear anything for some time if she is not at the first places we look. You must try to get some rest. We will bring her back as quickly and safely as possible."

"No, you won't." She removed her hand from his and walked toward the door.

"What do you mean, Grace?" His eyes flickered with both surprise and hurt, though his face remained impassive. "I promise you, we will find her eventually and I pray it will be in time to prevent any real harm from coming to her. Do you doubt that?"

"Of course not," she replied calmly, "but you will not bring her back to me because I am going with you to fetch her."

"Of all the fool ideas!" James burst in, his face flushing. "I am not going in search of one sister in who knows what kinds of sordid places while bringing another along with me. You must be mad to think I would allow such a thing."

"You do not *allow* me," Grace's eyes narrowed as she enunciated each word, "to do anything, James. I am a grown woman, fully capable of making my own decisions. I am not waiting here while you go after Annie simply because you think I need to be shielded from the darker side of human nature. I am as aware of depravity as you are, possibly more so given the poor souls I see in my shop and on the streets every day."

"Grace, you must reconsider. Don't you see that I will be distracted by your presence because of my concern for your safety?"

Ramsey may have hoped that his argument would appeal to her logic, but Grace levelled a quelling look at him.

"Inspector Ramsey," the formality of her address was deliberate. "Have I, in any of our past encounters with danger, proven unable to protect myself? I am an intelligent, capable human being. You are more likely to have to protect James, who has never fought a day in his life, than worry that I will not be able to, at the very least, incapacitate any attacker with my cayenne sachets long enough for me to run away."

"I don't like this one bit, Grace," Ramsey's voice was low, "and I would stop you if I thought I could."

"I'm not anticipating it with much pleasure myself," she said, clasping her hands tightly in front of her as she stared at him, eyes dark with worry, "but I need to do this. Please, don't be angry with me, Jack."

"I can't promise that right now," he frowned, rubbing a hand over his jaw, "but I will try. Enough arguing. We must be off."

"Yes, of course."

Without another word, the three would-be saviors headed out into the night.

Grace watched Ramsey clench and unclench his jaw in the dim light of the carriage. He hadn't said a word since they'd made a report with the desk sergeant at Scotland Yard and seen James off in a separate carriage to enlist Jonathan Hayes' help.

"You're still angry with me, aren't you? Please, just say so and let us be honest with each other." She clamped her fingers tightly together in her lap, trying not to fidget nervously while waiting for his response.

"I'm not angry with you, Grace," Ramsey said, after a long moment. "I admit, I do not relish bringing you into gambling dens and the other equally sordid places we may be forced to search, but I am not angry with you."

"If that is so, then why have you been so silent?"

"You are a distraction," Ramsey said bluntly, "and that adds to the danger of what we're undertaking. I need you to promise me something and I've been trying to figure out the best way to present my request."

"You need only ask. I may not agree to it," she said dryly, "but you can ask anything."

"Very well. Will you promise me that if things go badly, you will run for help immediately? If Jonathan, James or I are injured, you must not try to help us but take Annie and flee for safety."

Grace closed her eyes. Images flashed through her mind—James, his face white and drawn with pain, and Ramsey lying motionless in a pool of crimson blood on the scarred floor of a crowded, smoky room. How could she leave either one behind? And yet, what good would it do to stay? Her medical knowledge was hardly sufficient to heal grievous wounds and her pepper sachets were nowhere near able to incapacitate two or three men at a time. Ramsey's request was more than fair.

"Of course. You have my word."

Ramsey briefly cupped her cheek, eyes holding hers, before dropping his hand and settling back into his seat.

"I know what that promise cost you, Grace. I won't forget it. I wouldn't have asked if it wasn't absolutely necessary in the unfortunate event that things go awry."

"I know that. I will run for help if it comes to that but until that point, I will do whatever I must. I will not purposefully endanger myself, but neither will I shy away from peril."

"Understood. You will do what you must and I will do what I must."

"Then we are agreed?"

"We are. And," Ramsey's expression darkened as the carriage rolled to a stop, "we are here."

Grace looked out the window. They were halted in front of a large building with a name she could not make out inscribed over the arch of the doorway. Ramsey had instructed the coachman to take them to one of London's most popular gaming establishments. This must be it.

"God help us, Jack."

He opened the door, stepped lightly to the cobblestone street and turned to help her down.

"That's what I've been praying for since this all began, Grace."

She glanced up, meeting his gaze as her feet touched the ground.

"We are going to need it," she murmured, studying the building in front of her. Hazy lights filtered through heavily leaded glass windows with shadowy forms barely visible within. Tinny music and raucous laughter filled the air, spilling out of the door along with three disheveled gentlemen. They stumbled out with their arms draped over each other's shoulders, singing ribald songs loudly and off-key as they wove down the street. She gripped Ramsey's arm more firmly and stepped toward the entrance.

"God help us, indeed," whispered Ramsey as they neared the door. Taking hold of the handle, he tugged it open and they stepped through the portal into another world.

19

The room was large but so filled with smoke and noise that the air was stifling. Every breath seemed to settle a heavy grittiness in Grace's lungs as she strained to see in the dim light. A woman laughed, the sound unnaturally bright amid the low murmurs of men at the card tables. Gripping Ramsey's arm tightly, Grace held her skirts close to her legs in an effort to move more easily through the crowded tables. A crash sounded, followed by violent cursing. She watched with morbid fascination as two burly men lifted a pale, puffy-faced man away from one of the tables and escorted him to a door nearly hidden in a recess near the back of the room. One of the men knocked sharply and the three of them disappeared from sight through the door. Grace had a horrible suspicion that the patron would never emerge —or rather, he would never emerge alive.

"There! She is at that table near the east wall, amid that throng of men."

She turned to look in the direction Ramsey indicated. Annie sat, face flushed with excitement, holding her cards tightly as she slid a note toward the pile of paper in the center of the table. The man sitting next to her wore the expression of ennui on his face that was typical of gentlemen of leisure but there was a sharpness in his pale blue eyes that belied the facade. The man was playing a part, of that Grace was certain. Her fear grew stronger with each step she took.

"Be careful, Ramsey," she whispered as they approached the table.

"I beg your pardon for the interruption, gentlemen," he said, smoothly angling his body so that Grace was largely shielded from view but still able to see their faces. "I wonder if you would permit me to borrow Miss Flynn. I have a matter of some urgency to discuss with her."

Annie looked up from her cards, eyes widening at the sight of Grace and Ramsey standing before her. Her cheeks flushed a deeper crimson, whether from embarrassment or anger Grace couldn't tell, and her gaze narrowed.

"I am in the middle of a hand, Ramsey," she said shortly, "and I'm not interested in hearing anything you or my sister have to say." She picked up another note from the table and laid it on pile lying in the middle of the table.

"Annie!" Grace exclaimed. "What are you doing making wagers? You haven't the funds to pay if you lose. Come with me before you ruin yourself entirely."

"How dare you." Annie threw down her cards, shoving her chair back and rising in one fluid motion. "How dare you speak so indiscreetly of my personal affairs in front of these gentlemen? And you call yourself a lady. I'll have you know that I've been quite successful. Isn't that so, Mr. Gosford? It seems I have a gift for the game of Faro."

"It's true," murmured the man next to her, reclining casually with one leg crossed over the other, "that you've done quite well. Until now."

"What do you mean? Look at my hand. I've won five rounds straight and with these cards, I cannot lose."

"That is the bit of amusement I've been waiting for," he said, uncrossing his legs to rise, unhurriedly adjusting his jacket, "if Mr. Hanover would be so obliging as to display his hand." A weak-chinned man with the reddened eyes and nose of a habitual drinker obediently laid down his cards. Gosford pointed to the table. "Now, Miss Flynn, you will see that you've lost the sixth round quite spectacularly. You've lost everything you made as well and it appears you've also written a promissory note for another two hundred pounds."

Annie's face went white and her hand went to her throat. Grace inhaled sharply. It would take the shop nearly six months to make two hundred pounds, and that was excluding the expenses every business incurred. It was an astonishing amount, one neither she nor Annie had any hope of acquiring.

"Very well," Annie smoothed her skirts and sat down, "I will play another round or two and make up my losses."

"Annie," Ramsey spoke quietly, laying a hand on her shoulder, "you will not recoup your losses. The men at this table have been toying with you. I would wager," he smiled sardonically at the play on words, "that they have been aware all along that you have no money of your own. The deeper into debt you go, the steeper the payment they will require. I would not be at all surprised if they desire something much more rare than pound notes from you."

Annie paled further but refused to move. She glanced up at her companion, uncertainty filling her gaze.

"Mr. Gosford? Is that true? You would not lead me to believe I was successful when you planned to trick me, would you? Surely a gentleman such as yourself would never do something so despicable! Not when you said that you," she colored again, the brief reddening of her cheeks only emphasizing the unnatural pallor fear had cast over her skin, "were enchanted by me and could not bear to spend a single moment apart. A gentleman would not make a mockery of the woman he loves, would he?"

"It appears you took my words far more literally than I intended. You were a pleasant diversion, nothing more." Shocked pain covered her face and his cruel smile broadened at the sight. "Inspector Ramsey is quite correct. My employers were displeased with your sister's interference into their affairs. They instructed me to cause her a great deal of pain in a way that would last for the rest of her life. You are an attractive young woman, so it was no hardship to pay court to you while intending to ruin your reputation and that of your family. I would have pursued your sister herself to the same end but I quickly perceived that she was entirely too sensible to be taken in. You, on the other hand, were wonderfully naïve."

"Your employers?" Annie's eyes glinted with moisture, but she refused to give way to tears just yet. "Who would command such a thing? And what kind of man would agree to it?"

"Elliott and Louisa Rivers would, and they would do so with pleasure," a new voice spoke and Grace turned to find the source. A tall, dark-haired man was striding toward them, flanked by a well-dressed woman near her own age. Her deceptively simple gown of dark blue wool revealed a slim build while accenting thick, mahogany hair and dark grey eyes. The impression of strength and competence the newcomers carried with them was palpable.

"Mr. Hayes," Gosford's expression registered his distaste, "I believe you have been told quite clearly that neither you nor your wife," his gaze flicked dismissively over the woman, "are welcome here. My employers do not wish to have you anywhere near their business. I must ask you to leave at once. If you refuse, I shall be forced to call Smith and Percival to escort you out, and you'll not find that a pleasant experience."

"We have no plans to stay, Mr. Gosford," the woman replied

calmly. "We are simply here to offer the use of our carriage and escort the two young ladies home. Shall we depart?" Her gaze encompassed Grace and Annie before resting on Ramsey.

"I am quite ready to leave," said Annie, lifting her chin in an attempt to reclaim her dignity, "but I never want to see you again, Mr. Gosford. You are a cad, sir, and I shall never forgive you."

Gosford caught her arm.

"I'm afraid I cannot let you leave without paying your debts, Miss Flynn. Give me the two hundred pounds you owe and you may do as you please."

Grace's stomach churned as she watched uncertainty and fear play over Annie's face. She wanted to do something, even promise to pay the debt herself, but there was simply no money. Ramsey reached out, breaking Gosford's grip on Annie's arm and guiding her to stand behind him, next to Grace.

"We are leaving, Gosford. You cannot stop us."

"I can, indeed, sir." Gosford's eyes flashed. "The woman owes two hundred pounds and cannot pay. She has two options: pay the money or work off her debt. If she is inclined to choose the second, I know of a well-run establishment looking for gentle ladies to cater to their gentlemen clients. She'll be quite at home with the other tarts, of that I've no doubt."

"How dare you." Grace stepped forward. "My sister is a respectable woman, and you would do well to remember it."

He smiled patronizingly.

"Call me what you wish, but you know I speak the truth. My employers run some very successful businesses that cater to a gentleman's most intimate needs. There is always a place for a young, fresh-faced woman. Annie would be quite popular, at least in the beginning, and should be able to work off her debt in, say, a year, perhaps a bit longer. If her manner with me is any indication, your sister has a great deal in common with the women in The Dove's Cry."

Annie swayed and would have fallen had Jonathan Hayes' wife not stepped forward and caught her. Grace lunged at Gosford, fury blinding her. A strong arm gripped her waist, holding her back. It felt like a band of steel, unbreakable regardless of how hard she struggled. Jonathan stepped between her and Gosford as Ramsey pulled her further back.

"She will not be entering your employment, Gosford. We are leaving now and you will not stop us."

"I don't think so, Hayes. The law is on my side. Just ask your friend, Inspector Ramsey. She owes a debt and it must be paid."

Grace sagged in Ramsey's hold, fear clawing at her. There had to be a way out. Annie did not deserve what Gosford had in mind for her, no matter what she'd done.

"I will not contest that she owes a debt to you," said Ramsey. Gosford's eyes gleamed but the spark of triumph died as the detective continued. "How fortunate for you that you have a member of the London Metropolitan Police Force here to enforce the law. Miss Flynn," he turned to Annie, "I regret to inform you that you are under arrest for defaulting on your debts. You will come with me to Scotland Yard, from whence you will be transferred to Newgate Prison to work off what you owe. This way, please."

"You cannot..." Annie's cry was cut short as Ramsey and Jonathan each took an arm, pulling her toward the door. Gosford's expression was murderous, but he made no attempt to stop their progress.

"You will regret interfering, Ramsey," he shouted as they headed toward the door, "and you too, Hayes. Don't even imagine that the Rivers will forget this."

"Come, Miss Flynn," Verity Hayes took Grace's arm, prodding

her to follow the men. "We don't want to stay here and have these *gentlemen* decide to hold us in Annie's place."

Grace followed her, moving swiftly. "They wouldn't dare do such a thing, would they? I have some pepper sachets that might temporarily blind them, but I doubt that would hold such a crowd as this at bay."

"I wondered if you and I might be women of similar mettle." Humor flashed in her grey-blue eyes. "And in answer to your questions, they could try, but they wouldn't get far."

"Because your husband and Ramsey would defend our honor?"

"Certainly they would, but it would hardly be necessary. I am quite able to defend our honor myself."

Flicking her skirts, the woman exposed just enough of her ankle for Grace to see that a blade was strapped to her calf. Gaping, Grace stared, nearly tripping over her own feet before tearing her gaze away. They reached the door, emerging into the chilly evening air. As her eyes adjusted to the darkness, Grace saw Jonathan Hayes next to an unfamiliar carriage, holding the door open for them. He helped his wife inside and then assisted Grace who settled herself next to Annie. The younger woman stared out the window. Ramsey, on Annie's other side, smiled reassuringly at Grace over the top of her sister's head. Jonathan climbed in and rapped sharply on the roof. The carriage jerked, and started forward. He turned to his wife and smiled, taking her hand.

"Did you introduce yourself, my love, or simply show off your knives?"

"Knives? You have more than one?" The question slipped out before Grace could stop it.

"I do. I did indeed forget to introduce myself. Thank you for pointing that out, Jonathan. I am Verity Hayes, Miss Flynn, and it is a pleasure to meet you." She shook Grace's gloved hand firmly.

Releasing it, she slid her left sleeve up to her elbow, exposing the leather sheath strapped to her forearm. "One simply never knows what one will come across in places such as this. It's best to be prepared, don't you think?"

"Naturally," Grace admired the knife and Verity's ingenuity. "One never knows." She turned to Ramsey, an inscrutable smile forming on her lips. "I believe that your friends and I shall get along quite nicely."

"I was rather afraid of that." Ramsey's look was wary. "What are you thinking now? I can almost see your brain working."

"Given the situation we just left," Grace said matter-of-factly, "I find myself wondering if it would be wise to have other methods of defending myself rather than simply relying on my pepper sachets. Perhaps," she turned to Verity Hayes, "you would be kind enough to teach me how to protect myself with a small blade? As a precautionary measure?"

"I should be glad to," replied the other woman promptly, ignoring Ramsey's frown. "Oh, Jonathan," she turned to her husband, swatting his arm at the sight of the wide smile on his face, "do try to show Ramsey some sympathy. I recall it was not so very long ago that you were less than pleased at my determination to defend myself. Taunting him is quite unbecoming."

"I said nothing." The private detective held up his hands in a gesture of innocence.

"You didn't have to," growled Ramsey, "and you don't have to now. I see I'm outnumbered. That does not mean," he continued, brows lowering over his clear grey eyes, "that I have to like it. However, Grace is a determined woman and I will not stand in her way, particularly since the danger around her is my doing."

"Don't think that." Grace laid a gloved hand on his arm. "If anything, you've gone to great lengths to protect me, and I am grateful for it."

"You are?" He covered her hand with his, apparently forgetting the others in the carriage. "Perhaps, once we have sorted this mess, we can discuss your gratitude further."

"We shall see."

A derisive snort sounded and Grace turned to see Annie's pretty mouth twisted in a scowl. The younger woman muttered something under her breath, too quietly for Grace to make out the words. She suspected she didn't want to know anyway. The warmth of Verity's conversation and Ramsey's teasing were lost in the presence of Annie's scorn. Silence fell as black streets rolled by, illuminated only by the flickering light of street lamps. The world was cloaked in darkness and so, Grace thought as heaviness settled in her heart once more, was her sister.

20

The journey to the headquarters of the London Metropolitan Police Force at 4 Whitehall Place had seemed interminable to Grace. Her head pounded from excitement and fatigue. Annie hadn't spoken a word, but her eyes, flickering periodically toward Grace, had been hard with anger. Ramsey escorted both sisters inside when they arrived while Jonathan and Verity went off with a constable to give their accounts of the night's events. Sighing, Grace shifted on the hard wooden chair, trying to relieve the ache in the small of her back as she waited for Ramsey and a constable to finish questioning Annie. A long day in the shop bent over her worktable followed by the stress of the evening left her feeling sore and worn.

"Grace, you must be exhausted." Ramsey spoke from the doorway. "I apologize for my protracted absence. I should have insisted that you return to the boarding house to get some rest while I do my job."

"It's nothing." She straightened her shoulders. "I want to wait until I know what will happen to Annie." Tears threatened as she met his gaze, nearly spilling over at the compassion she saw there. "I'm afraid I don't see how this can possibly turn out well for any of us. I have no way to stop Mr. Gosford from pursuing the matter in the courts if he so chooses, and I don't see how you can do anything either.

He tricked Annie, it is true, but her choices up to that moment had already damaged her reputation, and our family's, beyond repair. I fear, however that leaving her to rot in a debtor's prison will not be enough for him — or the Rivers."

"I knew you blamed me for Mr. Gosford's lies." Grace winced at Annie's shrill voice. She hadn't realized that her sister was standing in the hall beside Ramsey, just out of her line of sight. The younger woman pushed past the detective to face her sister. "How dare you, Grace. How dare you. I have done nothing wrong. You are as selfish as ever, blaming me for being a victim of his deceitfulness. You *want* me to go to prison because you are tired of living in my shadow. No man looks twice at you when I'm around and you hate me for that!"

She tossed her head, pride and anger evident. Grace drew her breath in sharply, color flooding her cheeks as she avoided looking at Ramsey.

"Annie," she began, fighting back tears of hurt and anger, "what has happened to you? You were once a charming woman who was occasionally heedless of the effects of your words, but now you are wilfully cruel. I came after you tonight because I love you, but I cannot sit here and not say anything while you lie to yourself and others. You made the choice to go off with Mr. Gosford. You chose to follow him into a club that was obviously not a suitable place for respectable women. And, you chose to wager money you did not have."

"How can you say such things, Grace?" Annie's eyes glittered with angry tears. "You have always been jealous of me and now you're destroying my future. I could have made the money back, given enough time. If not, I'm certain I could have found a gentleman at the table willing to cover my debts in exchange for my companionship. They were most attentive to me. In fact, one of them did offer to help me, if I agreed to accompany him to dinner at his residence. I had the situation under control."

"Enough." Verity Hayes stepped through the doorway, her voice whipping through the air like a lash. "You clearly have no interest in hearing the truth from your sister, Annie, but I have nothing to lose in shattering your illusions...or rather, your delusions, for that is what they are."

Grace stared at her in shock, barely noticing when Ramsey covered her hand with his.

"How dare you? You know nothing about me," Annie's face went crimson with rage.

"Oh, I know you well, Annie, likely better than you know yourself." Verity's face softened with pity but her voice was firm. "I have known your kind before. You are not an original. Do you not realize that your solution would have turned you into a prostitute?"

"It would not. I would never have compromised my honor with one of those men. I have always been able to make gentlemen do what I wish and this would have been no different."

Verity's voice was flat when she looked at Annie, "Had Grace and Ramsey not come after you, you would have found yourself ruined and alone. The Rivers are quite capable of binding you to them so firmly that you would never break free of their hold."

Annie's face went white, even as she shook her head in denial.

"You're wrong. Any one of the gentlemen I was playing cards with would have covered my debt. Why, you should have heard them offering me jewelry and gowns and outings before you arrived. Had I accepted only a few of those gifts, I would have had more than enough money. Besides, I would have won the next hand, I know it."

"Don't be a fool, Annie. They were making you a jest. Every man there knew that you were Gosford's companion and that meant one of two things—either you had already traded your favors for money or you soon would. I wouldn't be surprised if Gosford had informed them in advance that you were new merchandise from his employers for them to look over, promising that one fortunate man would be playing more than cards with you before the night was over. Didn't you notice that not a one of them was surprised when Gosford offered to let you work off your debts in that capacity?"

"But they were gentlemen." Annie insisted. "How would they even know about such things? They were all high-born, wealthy, and honorable men! They were most solicitous to me. You're trying to confuse me."

Verity laid a hand on Annie's arm. The younger woman shrugged it off, jerking away from the unexpected gesture of sympathy as though it were an act of offence.

"Noble birth is no guarantee that a man is a gentleman. You may trust me on that." The look on her face told Grace that there was experience behind the statement, but Verity did not elaborate. "Some of the worst offenders that Ramsey and Jonathan expose in their work are those who have every advantage in the world. Those *gentlemen* you were gaming with are so bored with their lives that they constantly seek more thrilling ways to entertain themselves. More than one young woman has been robbed of her virtue by those same men, and I would wager that they wouldn't stop at murder if they thought it necessary."

"You're lying."

Annie whispered the words but her voice no longer held conviction.

"No, Annie, I'm not. From the way you treat your sister, I can see I am likely one of the first people to tell you the unvarnished truth. Grace cares far too much for your feelings to do so."

Grace felt a pang in her heart at the statement. Indeed, it *was* easier to just let Annie have her way and, as frustrating as it was for Grace, it had not seemed to matter a great deal. Tonight showed her just how wrong she'd been.

"Verity is right, Annie," she gathered her courage. "I have never spoken to you so plainly because I didn't want to fight or hurt your feelings. I've not loved you as I ought."

"So your way of *loving* me is to humiliate me in public and allow your policeman beau to cart me off to prison? What kind of love is that?"

"No, Annie," she spoke quietly, "my way of loving you will be to tell you the truth and bear with you whatever comes afterward."

"And what do you think will happen to me in prison, Grace?" Annie's features tightened. "All that awaits me is exactly what you say was in store for me with Mr. Gosford."

Grace looked helplessly at the others. She wanted to assure Annie that she would be safe in prison, but she couldn't. Ramsey squeezed her hand gently.

"There I can offer you some reassurance, Annie," he said. "While you will not find Newgate Prison pleasant, and your life will indeed hold difficulties you are not accustomed to, I will do everything in my power to make certain you are shielded from any real harm. I am sorry that I cannot do more."

Annie's face crumpled as the reality of her situation finally sank in.

"Is there truly nothing you can do to stop this?"

Grace's heart broke at the pitiful whisper. She reached over to grasp her sister's hand.

"I will come and see you every day, if they allow it. You will not be alone, Annie, and I will pray constantly that God will watch over you, even when you feel as though you are."

Tears slid down her own cheeks as Annie began to weep. She touched Annie's cheek, her thumb smoothing away the tears as quickly as they fell.

"I'm afraid it is time for Annie to be taken to her cell, Grace." Ramsey gently pulled her away from her sister, nodding to his waiting constable to take hold of Annie. The sober-faced man did so with a gentleness Grace hadn't anticipated, and it made her tears fall harder as Ramsey spoke again. "She will have as much protection as I can manage. You have my word."

With Ramsey and Jonathan leading the way, the constable guided Annie out of the office and down the hall. Verity took Grace's arm and led her toward the front door.

"Don't fear, Grace," Verity said reassuringly. "God has not abandoned you, nor has He abandoned Annie. There is yet hope. You must know that Ramsey will do everything in his power to make certain Annie is treated as kindly as possible."

"I cannot see room for hope anywhere in this," Grace's voice shook with emotion. "I must trust that God knows what He is doing, yet how can I not grieve over Annie's fate?"

"Grieve over what has been lost," Verity spoke softly, "but know that it can be found again. God is able to redeem even the most hopeless circumstances, and draw the most distant hearts to Himself."

"You pray that will be so, Verity," Grace said bleakly, "because I'm not certain I can believe it at the moment."

"You have my word."

21

Grace rubbed her neck, grimacing at the grinding of knotted muscles under her fingertips as she slowly sat up. Climbing stiffly from her bed, she had washed her face in cold water and re-pinned her hair into a semblance of order before heading downstairs to breakfast. After hurriedly downing a cup of tea and piece of toast, she walked to the shop. As much as she dreaded seeing anyone, the events of the previous night still foremost in her mind, she could hardly afford to lose revenue by staying closed.

"Gracie? You look as though your mind is a thousand miles away. Tell me you're not still wasting your energy thinking about Annie."

Grace frowned at her brother. James had been silent at the breakfast table and turned up at the shop, still not saying a word, just after she'd opened for the day. His relief at seeing Annie alive and well the night before when they'd brought her to Scotland Yard, where he'd gone to wait after sending Jonathan and Verity to assist Ramsey and Grace, had swiftly been followed by fury. The row that followed was loud, long, and did full credit to James and Annie's Irish tempers. James had left the police station when Annie was taken away for questioning, saying he did not wish to hear any more from or about his younger sister.

"I'm just a bit stiff, James. It was a long night and it's turning into a long day on top of that. I can't help wondering," she said slowly, "how much we have contributed to the circumstances that led to Annie's fate."

"Surely you can't think that we are remotely responsible for her folly." James protested. "She was clearly enamored with this man, Gosford, and her attachment to him led her astray. That's not our fault. Our parents taught her better than this. I fear the news of her imprisonment will cause them irreparable damage. How can you reconcile yourself to having a sister who has behaved so scandalously? I find it impossible. Can you imagine what my colleagues will think, to say nothing of what this will do to your chances of marriage? Her selfishness knows no bounds."

"I know you're angry, James, but don't you wonder if we made it easier for her to be led astray? Why shouldn't she believe whatever lies Gosford fed her if it's been made clear that her only value is her pretty face. None of us ever expected anything else from her, that is certain."

"What were we supposed to do? Should we have praised her intellect?" James looked incredulous. "I don't see how we could have. She's not like you, Gracie. Annie has only ever wanted to be fawned over and flirted with and all her energy, mental or otherwise, was expended to that end."

"That's what I'm saying, James! We taught her that was all she was capable of — maybe not in so many words, but certainly by our actions. In our desire to keep her happy, we hindered her from becoming a woman of character. Why are we surprised that she encourages the attentions of any handsome man who crosses her path?"

James sighed, rubbing his forehead.

"Perhaps so, Gracie, but it's too late now. She's on her way to prison. Prison. How are we supposed to explain that to our family, let alone society? Nothing more can be done for her. We must cut our losses and forget we ever had a sister." He held up a hand as Grace opened her mouth to speak, "Do you really think that anyone in polite society will accept her after this? Certainly no honorable man will offer for her hand. Even if I wanted to, I'm not certain I could bring myself to visit her."

"No one is ever so lost that God cannot find them," Grace said quietly.

"I hardly think that he is all that pleased with our sister at the moment, either, Grace. If I cannot forgive her for the shame she's brought on our family, I doubt God can do so."

"God does what we cannot. He can forgive her—that is, if she repents."

James snorted.

"No amount of penance will fix the mess she's made, Grace. She's a hopeless cause. Just another ruined life."

"It's not about fixing the mess she's made. Of course she cannot make things right herself. Oh Jamie," the words were a sigh, "this isn't about us. It's about what Annie needs, and what she needs is grace, not our condemnation."

"Say what you will, Grace. I cannot forgive her for this disgrace and, what's more, I don't wish to."

"Answer me one question, James," she placed a hand on his arm, waiting for him to meet her gaze. "Have you never done something you deeply regretted?"

James frowned, but any reply was cut off at the sound of the bell chiming as the door opened. Grace dropped her hand as Ramsey entered the shop, shutting the door firmly behind him.

"Jack! What can you tell me about Annie this morning?" Grace hurried over to him. "Is she well? How was her first night in prison?

Oh, what kind of question is that? How could her first night be anything but dreadful?"

Ramsey held up hand to stem her outpouring of words.

"Slow down, Grace. I can't tell you much." He rubbed a hand over features marked with exhaustion. "I'm doing everything I can to make certain Annie is safe while we continue our investigation. She was taken to Newgate Prison early this morning. She will be allowed to receive visitors by tomorrow afternoon. Elizabeth Fry and the British Ladies' Society for Promoting the Reformation of Female Prisoners have made accommodations much more humane than they used to be but it will be difficult and Annie will suffer. However, she will be fed and allowed visitors who may bring her food and other gifts to help meet her basic needs."

"That is all we can ask for, at the moment," Grace forced a smile. "Thank you for everything, Jack. I can never repay you for all you've done."

"You will receive no thanks from me for your intervention, Ramsey," James' face tightened as he struggled to control his anger. "If Annie could not be brought back with her reputation intact, you should have left her to rot where she was. At least we could have pretended was respectably dead."

"James. Stop. You can't mean that." Grace clapped her hands over her ears, trying to block out the harsh words.

"I do mean it, Grace. It would have been easier to tell our parents that Annie was dead than disgraced and imprisoned. If you two are going to continue talking about her, I'm leaving." He walked stiffly to the door. Turning, he gave Grace a long look. "You might think twice about trying to help Annie, Grace. Even if she does see the error of her ways, her reputation is in tatters. If you associate with her, yours will be too. Cut your losses. I have." His footsteps echoed across the wooden floor as the door swung shut behind him.

"Grace? What can I do?" Ramsey laid a hand on her arm, the heat of his palm through the fabric of her gown combating the cold despair left in James' wake. "There must be something that will give you comfort. You have only to ask."

"The only thing that you could do to comfort me right now is to hold me," Grace turned toward him, face pale and strained, "but I cannot ask you to do something so improper." A sad smile crossed her face. "Even if I am ruined along with my sister."

Without hesitation, Ramsey enfolded her in his arms, cradling her head against his chest as her tears began to flow in earnest.

"I will hold you as long as you need me to, Grace, despite what anyone might say. In fact, if you asked me to, I would hold you forever. But," he placed a finger on her lips as she raised her head and tried to speak, waiting until she relaxed again before removing it, "that is a discussion for another day. Let yourself rest with me, and I will bear this burden with you."

22

"I beg your pardon?" Ramsey shook his head, certain he hadn't heard the desk sergeant correctly.

"I said there's a Mr. Morris Ramsey to see you, sir." The sergeant's broad forehead furrowed, his gaze clouding with confusion. "He spoke as though you would see him without delay. I thought perhaps you had arranged to meet with him. Would you prefer I take his information and send him away?"

"No," Ramsey shook his head again, "no, send him in please, Sergeant. I will speak with the man."

The sergeant retreated, closing the door to Ramsey's office behind him. Ramsey looked down at the tidy pile of notes sitting in the open file on his desk and sighed. He closed the file and set it parallel to the edge of the desk, carefully aligning his pencil with it and adjusted the cuffs of his shirt and straightened his collar and smoothed his hair before realizing what he was doing.

A knock sounded at the door, pulling him from his thoughts.

"Come in," he called, rising from his chair and moving around the desk to greet his visitor. The door opened and the sergeant walked in, followed by a tall, thin-lipped man. The dour lines that marked his face, indicative of a fractious nature prone to pessimism and discontent, were more deeply etched than they had been when Ramsey had last seen his uncle five years ago.

"Mr. Morris Ramsey," the sergeant announced before reluctantly retreating, curiosity apparent on his face, and shutting the door once more.

"Uncle Morris," Ramsey extended a hand, "it's good to see you. What brings you to London? Surely you and Aunt Martha haven't moved back to the city?"

"Certainly not," Morris' lips thinned, nearly disappearing, in displeasure. "Nothing could induce us to move back to this cesspool of sin and filth. We are quite happy," Ramsey valiantly fought a smirk at the incongruity between expression and statement, "with our home in Buckinghamshire. I would certainly not leave my post as headmaster at Eton, for I can imagine no greater opportunity to train up young men to live exemplary lives. I have been quite successful," he sniffed haughtily, "in my attempts, so much so that Mr. John Shaw, Jr has recently completed his designs for our expansion."

"Congratulations, Uncle," Ramsey swallowed down a wave of resentment. He was entirely too familiar with his uncle's methods to appreciate them, having experienced both the shame and pain of a skillfully wielded switch more times than he could count. "I wish you and your pupils all the best. Perhaps you would care to tell me what does bring you to London — and to Scotland Yard?"

"I will not draw the matter out, Jack," the older man paused, displeasure morphing into a look of pure disgust. "Your mother is dead. I received word three days ago of my sister's demise and have come to London to settle her accounts and see that she has a decent burial, though heaven knows she doesn't deserve it. Still, I am her brother and must do my duty," he paused again, "as must you."

Ramsey sat silent. He wasn't sure what, if anything, he was feeling at the announcement of his mother's death. Should he feel grief? The woman had deposited him on her brother's doorstep when he was only days old, declaring him an unwanted encumbrance — a fact of which his uncle had never failed to remind him whenever he did not meet Morris Ramsey's exacting standards.

"Well?" Irritation filled Morris' voice. "You will do your duty, won't you, boy? I will pay for the burial but I expect you to contribute. After your mother abandoned you, expecting that I would raise you regardless of cost and inconvenience, which I did, I should think that you would own some obligation to me. God knows that I could have used the money raising you cost me, to say nothing of the time."

"Since you put it so graciously," Ramsey fought to keep his tone level, "I will certainly contribute to my mother's funeral expenses. Do you happen to know," he swallowed his pride to ask the question burning in his heart, "if she left anything for me? A letter, perhaps?"

"You're a fool, Jack." Morris' voice dripped with derision. "You still hope, after all these years, that my sister had regrets over giving you up, don't you?"

Ramsey said nothing, pain slicing through him. He hadn't realized it until that moment, but such a hope had indeed been lingering, unseen, in the depths of his soul.

"Your very existence brought shame on my household, and my sister thought nothing of it." Morris' face contorted with an anger all too familiar to his nephew. "Mistress to a man she refused to name, pregnant with his bastard son and, as though that weren't selfish enough, Philippa cast you upon me like a millstone, knowing that I couldn't refuse to do my Christian duty even as she went running back to her married lover!"

"Yes," Ramsey's grey eyes were icy, "you certainly did your idea of 'Christian duty' by me, Uncle, though I've found nowhere in the

Scriptures that condones starving and beating a child in the hopes of eradicating the 'taint of wickedness' you told me that I carried."

"I did what I had to, boy, to keep you from bringing even more shame on my family, and it worked, didn't it? At least, it worked until you threw everything away to work here," he flung an arm out, gesturing at the office, "at Scotland Yard, where you are daily surrounded by the very dregs of society! And you wonder why neither I nor my wife seeks to acknowledge our connection to you."

"And you still wonder," Ramsey spoke slowly, "why I chose this path? Are you truly so full of self-righteous anger that you do not see that the London Metropolitan Police Force, with whom I am proud to serve, upholds what is right while bringing justice for the wronged? How is that not a noble profession?"

"I don't have time to waste explaining something you will clearly never understand. I came to inform you of your mother's death and to remind you of your obligations in the matter. I have done so. I will let you know when the interment is to take place and expect that you will attend, as is your duty."

"I will." Ramsey forced himself to extend his hand. "Thank you for taking care of the arrangements. If you will let me know the cost, I shall reimburse you for whatever amount you deem appropriate."

Morris nodded, face tight with suppressed emotion, then turned on his heel and left. Ramsey sank down into his chair and dropped his head into his hands. *It never fails,* he thought with frustration. *Uncle Morris has a greater ability to bring out the worst in me than anyone else I know — and that includes Superintendent Norris! Will the taint of my mother's actions never leave me?* He sighed, rubbing a hand across his face. *And do I really want to face that kind of stigma all over again if I tie myself to the sister of an imprisoned debtor?*

Anger boiled inside him at the unwelcome question. *Am I so weak,* he thought savagely, *that I would break faith with a woman of unusual character and compassion because of an unwanted family connection?* He rose, pacing the room. *Grace has done nothing to deserve such betrayal after I so clearly declared my intentions to her. How can I even consider breaking that trust? A coward of the worst kind, that is what I am.* His hand clenched and he fought to keep from slamming his fist into the wall. Grabbing his coat from the rack by the door, he flung it on and stormed out of his office. He ignored the raised brows of constables and the sergeant on desk duty as he stalked past them to the door. He shoved through the opening and turned on to the street, moving so quickly he was nearly running.

Time passed without notice, the sky darkening from late afternoon to evening as Ramsey walked the streets of London at a frenetic pace that only slowed as exhaustion rolled over him. His thoughts, at first so vehement and jumbled, had cleared and his spirit, though not quite at peace, was no longer in turmoil by the time he turned onto the street on which his boarding house was located.

Grace was more than worth bearing the shame, be it public or private, of her sister's situation. *I must speak with Grace before anything else,* he thought, mingled determination and uncertainty filling him. *Though I hate to reveal this side of myself, she must know my heart if she is to intertwine hers with it. And I must know if she is able to live with the ugliness of my past and its effects on our future.* Bracing himself, he walked into the boarding house and made his way up the stairs to the floor on which Grace, Annie and James resided in adjoining rooms. Not giving himself time to reconsider, he knocked briskly on Grace's door. It opened after only a moment to reveal the woman in question, anxiety crossing her face at the sight of him.

"Is it Annie?" She asked, her relief obvious when he shook his head.

"She is well, Grace. At least, as far as possible given her current whereabouts. I must speak with you regarding another matter, one that I find most distasteful."

"Of course." She studied his face and he wondered what she saw in it. "I cannot invite you in. That would be quite scandalous." Her lips quirked with what appeared to be private amusement over the thought. "Shall we go to the withdrawing room and discuss the matter there? The other boarders seldom use it."

"Yes, that should suffice for what I have in mind." He paused, hating the stilted formality of his tone and yet helpless to change it. "It shouldn't take long."

"I'm not concerned, Jack. You may have as much of my time as you need."

Grace closed the door to her room, locked it, and led the way through the hall, down the stairs and into the small withdrawing room. The lamps on the wall were turned low, casting shadows over both a low sofa sitting parallel to the wall and the two chairs facing the unlit fireplace. Grace settled herself in one of the chairs, arranging the skirts of her rust-colored gown with unusual care. Ramsey looked at the other chair and decided he was too full of nervous energy to sit.

"What I have to tell you is unpleasant, Grace," he began, forcing himself to meet the steady gaze of her warm brown eyes, "and you may, once I am done, find yourself unwilling to continue our association. I would not blame you if that were so."

"Perhaps you should simply tell me what it is that is so very dreadful, and allow me to decide for myself."

The blunt words were spoken with surprising gentleness and Ramsey felt some of the tension leave his shoulders.

"Of course. I'm not quite certain how to begin. I have been struggling," he stopped, wanting to find precisely the right words. "I have been struggling with the reality that your sister's temperament and thus, her predicament, are strikingly similar to that of the woman who gave birth to me. I do not think of her as my mother," he paused again, fighting the familiar rise of resentment, "because I never knew her. She abandoned me on her brother's doorstep when I was but a day old, declaring me an unwanted encumbrance, a weight that neither she nor my father, her married lover, wanted to carry."

"I see," Grace said. "Do, go on, Jack. I'm listening."

Ramsay was quiet for several seconds before he continued, telling Grace about his uncle's equation of piety with brutality. When he eventually broke off in mid-sentence, Grace put her hand on his arm.

"Jack," she said quietly, laying a hand on his arm, "I know your reasons for joining the police force and they are noble ones. While my heart grieves for the little boy you were, and the scars the man you are bears, why are you so unsettled? Did you think that the revelation of your uncle's failing and the lack of charity you experienced outside his home would make me turn away from you? Rest assured, the only fault I see is in those who should have loved you well and failed to do so."

Shame filled Ramsey as he recalled his deep conflict over whether or not to break with the woman now offering him such understanding. He felt his eyes grow moist and he cleared his throat, unwilling to release the tight grip he had on his emotions.

"Your ability to love without judgment is beyond me, Grace, but I thank you for your kindness. I fear, however," he cleared his throat again, "that even you will not have the reserves to forgive what I must tell you lingers in my soul. My uncle came to see me today, to inform me that my mother is dead." Grace opened her mouth, but he shook his head, silencing her. "Let me finish, please. It was not a pleasant visit. His words struck where my heart is still raw and, as a result, after he left, I spent hours walking the streets of London, seriously considering betraying your faith and your heart because I feared once more being associated with a shameful family connection. Ultimately, I could not bring myself to lose you, Grace, but I felt you must know the depth of my weakness. I cannot ask you to bind your heart to mine if I do not reveal to you all that it holds, abhorrent as this is."

"I need a moment to think, Jack."

Grace's face was impassive and Ramsey feared the worst. He nodded, letting silence fill the room. Minutes ticked by, and he paced, unwilling to watch what he was sure would be a dawning determination to sever their connection appear in Grace's eyes. He glanced over, studying the back of her head as she sat quietly in the chair facing the fireplace. Were her shoulders tensed and her spine stiffer than usual? *I should never have said a word,* he thought in self-recrimination. *She would have been none the wiser, and yet — could we truly be husband and wife, with nothing to draw us apart, if she did not know about my past? We could not, and my attempts to hide my weakness would only create resentment and bitterness in my heart, while its exposure by another source would do the same in hers.* He looked away to study the pictures hanging on the wall and tried to quiet his frantic thoughts.

"Jack." Grace's voice was soft. He turned to find her standing next to her chair, her smile as warm as he'd ever seen it. A flare of hope rose inside him.

"You've made your decision?"

She walked over to him and took his hand in hers, lifting her eyes to his. There was nothing but compassion in their deep brown depths, and he felt the weight in his chest ease.

"I didn't need time to decide whether or not to break our connection, Jack. I wanted time to examine my own heart. If you are willing to expose the darkest, most painful parts of your experience to me so that they might lose their power to rule you, and harm us together, then I should gladly do the same."

"Grace," he began, moved beyond his ability to express with mere words, but the look on her face silenced him.

"After a good deal of thought, I've realized that you already know what lies in my heart. You've seen the wounds I carry from family, the struggle it is to love my work in a world that does not value it simply because of my sex, and the way both of those realities affect my view of God and people. And yet," her smile softened and her eyes shone with unshed tears, "you chose to care for me anyway. How could I help doing the same?"

Ramsey touched her cheek, dropping his forehead to rest against hers. "I don't care for you, Grace," he said quietly. "I love you, with all my heart."

"And I, you, Jack."

He lowered his lips to hers, just touching them before drawing back. Their warmth lingered even as he stepped away, putting distance between them.

"I have no idea what the future holds, but I'm asking you to face it — whether it be full of joy or pain — with me. Grace Flynn, will you be my wife?"

"Yes."

The single word, low and clear, was all he needed to hear. The lamplight flickered, matching the beat of his heart as he took Grace's hand and walked with her to the door, suddenly ready to face all that lay ahead.

23

In the week that followed, James refused to speak to Grace beyond the necessary pleasantries. As if that wasn't strain enough, her first visit to her sister in Newgate Prison was particularly trying. Annie had insisted that Grace bring her items she deemed necessary for survival, sulkily remarking that Grace owed her that even if she couldn't be bothered to find a way to free the younger woman. When Grace opted to bring fresh bread, soap and a clean chemise instead of the silk hair ribbons, scented lotion and chocolate caramel sweetmeats Annie requested, Annie flew into a rage. Leaving her gifts lying on the hard, narrow bed, Grace had walked out, giving herself three days to regain her calm before returning for a second visit. Minutes into her current visit, Annie was already in fine form despite Grace's provision of another half-loaf of bread, small basket of apples, and, as a peace offering, a thin, jade satin ribbon.

"I never dreamt there was such selfishness in you, Grace," Annie's green eyes narrowed as she spat the words out. "The least you could do is *try* to alleviate my suffering, even if you refuse to lobby for my release. But no. You are too busy trying to keep Inspector Ramsey's interest to help your poor sister, and what a hopeless endeavor that is. He will lose interest in a week or two, and meanwhile, I am still rotting in this prison cell."

Grace flinched inwardly, fighting for outward calm. "I am doing all I can, Annie."

"I cannot accept that. You must find a way to get me out of here."

"There is no way." Grace's frustration boiled over. "I told you before that there is nothing I can do. You chose to keep company with Mr. Gosford. You chose to go with him to the hells and you *chose* to gamble money you didn't have. By God's grace, you are here instead of paying off your debts on your back. None of the people who helped you owed you anything, Annie. You have done this to yourself. It would behoove you to remember that, and perhaps extend some gratitude to those of us who have done all we can to save you from your own foolishness."

Annie gaped at her, sputtering incoherently. She tried to formulate a response but could not seem to form a coherent thought. Grace slipped an arm around her sister's shoulders, refusing to pull away when Annie stiffened.

"I love you, Annie, but I am done bending to your will. I should never have done so in the first place. Please," she took her sister's hand, "allow me the privilege of offering my assistance, rather than demanding it."

Annie's eyes were wet with tears. Behind the sheen of moisture, Grace thought she saw true sorrow begin to emerge. A sob caught in Annie's throat, then another, until she was crying so hard that she gasped for air. Grace wrapped both arms around her, smoothing the girl's hair, murmuring soft words of comfort. *Oh, Lord, I want to give Annie hope but I don't know what to say.*

Tears streaked the faces of both women when Annie finally raised her head from Grace's shoulder and met her gaze, drawing in a shuddering breath. There was a vulnerability in her eyes that Grace hadn't seen since they were children. She slid the curls that had escaped Annie's plain chignon behind her sister's ear and let her hand rest against her cheek.

"Gracie?" Annie could hardly meet her gaze. "I…I am sorry. Truly. I never meant for things to turn out this way. I always knew you were brilliant and I could never measure up, but I was pretty, with a little charm that people seemed to enjoy. That was enough, most of the time. I don't understand how this happened. My life was never supposed to turn out this way."

"I know. We've both allowed our insecurities too much power." Grace rubbed a thumb across her sister's cheek, drying her tears. "Let's set the past aside. You have my forgiveness, Annie, and I promise to walk alongside you in whatever the future holds. I pray that it holds good for us both. I believe it does, for God has promised good those who love him."

"I don't think I do love him," Annie whispered, her face downcast. "I've tried, but I don't even understand the words Father O'Malley uses half the time. It frightens me to think of God frowning down on me, waiting for me to do something wrong. I suppose I've certainly managed that now, if I hadn't before. He'll never forgive me, Gracie. I know it."

"Oh, Annie, he's not frowning down on you. If we confess our sins, if we say we're sorry, he's just waiting to forgive us."

"How can you know that?" Annie's face looked sullen and closed again.

"Because that's what God promises us."

"Oh, how I wish I could believe that."

"You can, Annie," Grace's heart beat faster at the look of longing on her sister's face. "All you have to do is ask for forgiveness and tell him you're sorry."

"I'm just not sure, Gracie." Annie's voice trailed off. "I need some time to think."

Trying not to look as crestfallen as she felt, Grace hugged her sister tightly and released her. "I need to get back to the shop. I'll be praying for you, Annie. I love you more than words can say, and so does God."

"I hope I will believe that someday." Annie's face was softer than Grace had ever seen it. "And Gracie? Would you bring something particular the next time you come to see me?"

Grace halted in her progress toward the door, bracing herself.

"What is it you want, Annie?"

"If you can find it, I would like you to bring me my Bible. Perhaps I shall try reading it for myself."

A small flutter of hope awoke in Grace's heart. "Gladly. And would you allow me to bring someone from my church who can pray with you and explain things better?"

"If you wish, but I'm not making any promises."

"I'm not asking for any."

"James, please, will you not come with me tomorrow? Annie feels your absence keenly."

James frowned at his sister, water dripping from his face into the basin as he tidied himself before they went down to dinner.

"Grace, I've told you that I want nothing to do with her. She has disgraced our family and even if my own feelings on that subject were different, I'm too exhausted to think of anything but my dinner and bed. Overseeing the changes at the asylum in Surrey along with my regular hours at the hospital is more than I can handle. Thank goodness the alterations are nearing completion and I no longer need to travel there on my days off. I wish you hadn't obligated me to be involved. When I think that your original plan was for me to give up London and take on that role permanently…what were you thinking, Gracie?"

Grace felt a sick weight in her stomach at the scowl he wore as he finished drying his face.

"I'm sorry, James. I thought that you might appreciate the opportunity to govern your own sanitarium. You've so often complained that working in London at the hospital is difficult. I know you desire a better position."

"Well, I certainly didn't mean I wanted to sequester myself in a tiny village to work with the mentally deranged. I know you meant well, Gracie," he softened the blow by laying a hand on her arm, "and I should have said no outright if anyone else had asked. I confess, I thought it a chance to prove I was a selfless soul, but I fear it proved instead that I am no such man."

"You are too hard on yourself. I know how deeply you care. You work yourself to exhaustion for your patients. I shouldn't have offered your expertise to Ramsey without asking you first. I will not put you in such a predicament again, I promise."

"Forget I said anything about it, Grace. And really," James smiled, "parts of the endeavor were quite satisfying. Between the two of us, Ramsey and I managed to convince the villagers that Dr. Mosley could be trusted. Did I tell you that he has committed to treat the villagers and take only what payment they can afford out of gratitude for the position?"

"That's wonderful news, James." Grace hesitated, not wanting to break the fragile peace. Compassion overruled self-preservation as the memory of Annie's shadowed eyes and pinched face filled her mind. "I will not dispute your right to feel wronged by our sister, or angry at the scandal she's caused, but it is time to put your pride in its proper place and try to forgive her. She admits her error. Is that not enough to at least begin mending the breach between you?"

James rolled down his sleeves and fastened his cuff links. Picking up his suit coat, he shrugged into it, tugging it into place before turning to face her.

"I don't see why you are so adamant about all of this, Gracie," he sighed. "How can you find it so easy to dismiss her actions? She has shamed us, you most of all. Do you not see that?"

"Of course I see it," Grace sighed, "but do you not see that it could have been so much worse? We could have lost her entirely, Jamie. She is ruined forever, but she is alive. I would rather have her disgraced and changed in heart than faultless in the world's eyes but hardened inside. Please, Jamie. Will you not try?"

"Fine." James said wearily, rubbing his temple. "I will go with you tomorrow, but I make no promises that I will speak to her."

"Oh, thank you, Jamie. You will see the change in her, I am certain, and perhaps that will help you to forgive her. I know," she held up a hand as he opened his mouth, "you make no promises, and I expect none. It is enough that you will come. Let us go down to dinner so that you can come back to your room and find the sleep you so desperately need."

"An excellent notion."

Placing her hand in the crook of his elbow, Grace allowed her brother to lead her out into the hallway and down toward the dining room.

24

It never failed to amuse Nicholas Gosford that the head of London's criminal underworld lived in one of the city's finest neighborhoods. The first time he had been invited to dine with the Rivers he had expected the carriage to stop outside an ostentatious home in a new section of the city. Instead, he had found himself alighting in front of an aged, elegant mansion. It whispered its occupants' wealth rather than shouting it—a shrewd choice for the husband and wife whose business rested largely on perception.

Gosford knew for a fact that, due to their thriving business, the Rivers were obscenely wealthy but money was not enough. They desired prestige and the praise of a society rooted in class distinction. Such an aim was nearly impossible for two individuals whose middle class upbringings were sure to show in speech and manner, no matter how hard they tried to mimic the upper classes. Louisa's cousinship with Lady Charlotte Brooke gave the pair a small entrance into society, but Gosford knew that relationship was precarious. Louisa's cousin was quite aware of the couple's moral turpitude, but, to Gosford's continual surprise, Charlotte and Thomas Brooke treated Louisa and her husband cordially enough on the rare occasion they crossed paths in the polite world. That entrance was widened by

Elliott Rivers' threat to expose the upper crust's engagement in the illicit activities he fostered unless they welcomed him and his wife in their social circles.

Gosford opened the carriage door and stepped out onto the cobblestone. Instructing the coachman to wait for him, he strode to the door and rang the bell. After less than a minute, the heavy oak swung open to reveal the expressionless face and stiff form of the butler.

"Good day, Mr. Gosford," he gestured the man inside. "Mr. Rivers is expecting you. You may leave your coat and hat with William. I will show you to the library."

"Thank you, Jennings."

Handing over his outer garments, he followed the man into the library and waited as he was announced.

"Mr. Gosford is here to see you, sir."

"Thank you, Jennings, that will be all for now. Please shut the door behind you as you leave."

Elliott Rivers rose from behind a massive desk of polished mahogany. A fire crackled in the hearth and exquisitely cut crystal decanters of brandy and whiskey glinted on a table nearby. Two chairs of dark crimson brocade were positioned on either side of the mantle, adding to the room's overall effect of discreet but unmistakable wealth.

"Please sit down, Gosford, and let me pour you a drink. You prefer brandy, do you not?"

"I do, yes. Thank you."

Swirling the liquid gently in his glass, Gosford admired the deep, rich color before raising it to his lips. His first sip confirmed that his employer had only the best of everything. He sipped again and then set his glass down on the table next to his chair, leaning forward with his hands clasped.

"While I appreciate your hospitality, Rivers, we both know this is not a social call. There is a significant problem we must address."

"Agreed," Elliott's face hardened, "a problem that has grown larger in direct proportion to your ill-advised attempt to exact revenge on Grace Flynn for refusing to sell us the supplies we required."

"Sir," Gosford kept his temper in check with difficulty, "might I remind you that you were fully aware of my plans? In fact, you and you wife were quite entertained with Annie Flynn's naïve belief that she had a gift for the cards. I understood that I had your approval to bring her and her sister to their knees in shame. Was I mistaken?"

"No," Elliott spoke slowly, his eyes coolly assessing, "but that was when I believed you capable of carrying out the task. A failure of this measure rather undermines my faith in you, Gosford."

"It was not an entire failure, sir. Annie Flynn is in Newgate Prison and ruined in the eyes of society, that much we have achieved. Furthermore, I have an idea that I believe you will find highly…diverting."

"Well, then," Elliott sat back, crossing one leg over the other and folding his arms. "Let's hear what you have to say. If you can gain your revenge, and amuse myself and my wife in the act, you will find that we are quite generous in both our praise and our reward."

"I am aware of that." Gosford leaned further forward, steepling his fingers and resting his elbows on his knees. "Here's what I have in mind."

Outside the door, unseen, Louisa Rivers lingered with ears perked attentively to the conversation. Jennings had standing orders to inform her when one of Elliott's men came to call, though, to his credit, her husband almost always remembered to let her know in advance so that she could listen under the special grate they had installed near the ceiling. When open, as it was at the moment, conversation from inside the library was clearly audible. Louisa listened with interest as Gosford laid out his plan. He was correct on both counts. What he proposed would cause Grace Flynn no end of pain and Louisa and Elliott would indeed find it excessively diverting. Murder always was.

25

Grace glanced over her shoulder as she disembarked from the carriage in front of Newgate Prison. "Swear that you will be kind to her, Jamie, and do try to keep from saying anything that will deepen the rift between you, even if you cannot forgive her."

"Grace, you are my sister, and I love you," James grasped her elbow gently, steering her toward the door, "but if you tell me one more time what I should or should not do, I will use the silk thread in my satchel to stitch your lips shut."

"You wouldn't dare." Grace poked her finger into his side, inordinately pleased to see the glimmer of fun in his eyes. His fury toward their younger sister had yet to abate, but Grace believed his teasing was a sign of his heart softening. "You'd be arrested and charged with assault. I happen to know a detective who would be quite eager to come to my aid."

"At least I wouldn't have far to go to my new home. Perhaps they would give Annie and me adjoining cells."

"Not funny, James," Grace narrowed her gaze at him, noting the mingled scorn and amusement on his face as they entered the gates.

"It was a little funny," he murmured, "and rather fitting, I thought."

They halted as the prison keeper held up a hand.

"Hand over your satchel, sir, and state your business."

"Good day, Mr. Cobb. Have you any idea how my sister is today? This is my brother, James. He's a doctor," she gestured to the medical bag James was reluctantly handing over for inspection. "After we visit Annie, we would like to visit those in ill health. Detective Inspector Ramsey was to have made arrangements granting us permission."

"That he did, miss," the man said as he rummaged through James' black medical satchel. Grace caught the look of horror on her brother's face at the man's handling of its contents and shot him a quelling glance. She'd warned him that anything they brought into the prison would be searched. He would simply have to reorganize his precious satchel afterwards.

Newgate prisoners were able to acquire whatever they wished from the outside world. The number of heavily inebriated men and women was evidence that plenty of money from the outside made it through the gates to the prisoners and then on to the tap room. There were only four keepers to oversee everything and, though she thought Mr. Cobb a decent man, keepers were often guilty of the same petty crimes as those they guarded.

"You tell Miss Annie that she should be grateful we're allowing you to visit her when her barrister just went in five minutes ago," the keeper finally closed James' satchel and handed it to him.

"Annie doesn't have a barrister." Unease churned in the pit of Grace's stomach. "We couldn't afford one and her judgment has already been decreed. She has no need for a barrister. Did you recognize the man?"

"No, Miss Flynn," the man looked confused, "but he knew all about Miss Annie's case and he had papers with her name written on the bottom. Why would a man lie about such a thing?"

"I don't know," said Grace, picking up her skirts and hurrying into the prison, "but I think we had better find out."

Annie rose slowly from her cot, her eyes never leaving the man standing just inside the door to her cell. When she'd heard the lock grinding open, she had been lying on the hard, narrow cot, reading the small Bible that Grace had brought her the last time she visited. The book had raised a number of questions and she could hardly wait to ask them. She'd scrambled to her feet, happily anticipating seeing her sister. The sight of Nicholas Gosford walking through the open door and the ominous thud of its heavy wooden weight shutting behind him caused her legs to falter and she dropped down onto the cot once more, wanting to run as far away from the man as possible but there was nowhere to go. Swallowing hard, she tightened her grip on the book and waited for him to speak.

"Good day, Annie." Gosford assessed her critically. "I see prison does not agree with you. Your pallor makes your hair frightfully bright. That might not be so offensive if it were clean, but it is most certainly not. That dowdy grey thing you're wearing does no favors. It hangs on you like a sack. If you had accepted my offer, you'd be wearing emerald green satin instead. That is," he said and smirked, "when you wore anything anything at all, and I'm afraid that would be less often than not."

Annie's cheeks burned at his words and at the recollection of how proud she'd been to win his attention.

"I've no doubt your assessment is correct, sir," she said through clenched teeth, "but I fail to see how insulting me is the behavior of a gentleman. It's your fault that I occupy this cell. Fool that I was, I thought you a man of honor."

"My dear girl, no one forced your hand. You chose to wager with money you did not have and now, you are reaping the consequences of that decision."

"Perhaps that is so. What are you doing here, Mr. Gosford? I can't imagine that you have anything to say that I wish to hear. I may have thought you a gentleman once but I won't make the same mistake again. You are as far from that as the sky is from the sea. I do not know the circumstances of your birth, but I've never met anyone more deserving of the word 'bastard' in my life."

Gosford's unnaturally light eyes flared with anger. Before she could think to yell he clamped one hand firmly over her mouth, his gaze burning into hers, trapping her arms between their bodies. The pressure of his other arm against her back forced her forward, held tight against him, to the middle of the cell.

"Your sharp tongue and heedless nature are what put you here, Annie," he hissed, his breath warm on her ear even as fear sent chills down her spine. "The world will not miss either once you are dead." Her eyes widened in alarm and he smiled, tightening his hold so that she had to struggle for breath. "You honestly believed that prison was the worst that could happen, didn't you? You should have known better."

Releasing her suddenly, he shoved her to the ground, grabbed her shoulder and rolled her to her stomach, placing a well-shod foot on her back to keep her from rising. Annie twisted wildly, dread filling her.

"Please," her voice broke as she pleaded. "I am paying for my indiscretion already. Why add to my judgment?"

"Because I must, Annie," Gosford grabbed a hank of hair, causing her to shriek in pain as he pulled her head upward, exposing her neck while keeping his boot firmly planted on her back. "My employer is most unhappy with your sister at the moment. He does not take kindly to opposition. Your losses at the gaming tables and subsequent ruin were to be a lesson to her, but he has decided that the lesson was not severe enough. Your death will accomplish what your shame has not."

Annie caught a gleam from the corner of her eye as tears of pain streamed down her cheeks. Light from the barred window near the top of her cell glanced off the thin, twisted copper wire that Gosford had pulled from his coat pocket, its brightness seeming incongruous to its dark purpose. She pushed against the dirt-packed floor, trying desperately to free herself from his hold but the grip on her hair and pressure on her back simply grew stronger. His amused chuckle brought angry tears to her eyes.

"As entertaining as this has been, I fear our time together must draw to a close. It would certainly not be wise to be found in your cell with your lifeless body."

He let go of her hair and lifted his foot simultaneously, lashing out with a hard kick. His boot connected with the side of Annie's skull and she crumpled face down on the ground. Wrapping the twisted copper wire around each of his hands, he slid the resulting length in front of Annie's already swollen face as she reached up dazed, with her book still gripped awkwardly in her right hand, to protect herself. Gosford's movements were too swift, honed from years of experience, for her attempts to avail anything more than his continued amusement as her right hand was caught awkwardly just above the wrist. He squeezed, pulling the wire taught. It cut into the cover of the book along with the flesh of Annie's neck and hand. Rivulets of blood dripped down her arm and onto her collarbones as she gagged, fighting for air.

"Your sister should have just done what Elliott Rivers wanted. It never pays to refuse him. Your death will be a warning for her and others, and I will be handsomely paid for bringing it to pass."

He tightened the wire further, smiling as white bone appeared under the torn flesh in Annie's hand. Shifting both ends of the wire to his right hand, he gripped the top of the book still trapped next to Annie's neck and tore it away, casting it to the floor. Annie gasped at the brief loosening of the wire, dropping forward so suddenly that Gosford temporarily lost his grip. She fell to the floor, blood flowing steadily from hand and neck as she crawled toward the door, sobbing hoarsely. He easily caught up with her, stepping on her skirt to hold her fast while once more pulling her head up by her hair to expose her wounded neck. Leaning down, he let his lips brush her ear.

"You are a waste of flesh, Annie." He whispered. "This gives me such pleasure that I would have killed you for nothing. Go ahead and breathe your last. Not a soul will miss you once you're gone. You may die assured of that."

26

"Open the door!"

"I'm trying, miss, but the key is stuck!"

Grace paced the narrow passage as the prison keeper and James fought to unlock Annie's cell door. Wave after wave of terror coursed through her at the sounds coming from inside. If they could not open the door soon, she was going to find her sister dead inside, she knew it. *Oh, Lord, I beg you, have mercy!* She glanced at the keeper who oversaw the debtor's quadrangle. He was sitting against the wall, hands bound behind his back. When she, James and the entrance keeper had arrived, they'd found him in the tap room indulging in ale paid for by a bribe from the so-called barrister. The pressure of James' scalpel at his neck had him revealing that he'd been instructed by the man to make himself scarce and ignore anything he might hear. Having received a half-crown with the instructions, he was promised another coin to match it if he obeyed. Grace wanted to hurt him, matching wound for wound whatever Annie was suffering as they stood helplessly outside her cell.

"I've got it."

A loud clang sounded and the bolt was drawn back with a squeal. The door swung open to reveal Mr. Gosford standing over Annie, one hand wrapped in her hair to yank her head up while the other held two ends of a gleaming wire stretched taut round her throat. Blood soaked the bodice of Annie's grey gown and her features were slack. She was either dead or unconscious, Grace couldn't tell which. A loud keening echoed in the dimness and she was astonished to realize it was coming from her own throat.

"No! Annie!" James rushed past her and threw himself at the man holding her sister as the prison keeper attacked from the other side. Shock had covered Gosford's face at their appearance, but it quickly faded into something inscrutable. He released his grip on Annie, tossing her to the floor without a second look. He held out his wrists.

"I suppose I can't convince you that this was for her own good, can I?" he asked calmly. "After all, what kind of life would a young woman have in prison, even if you have greased palms to place her on the Master's Side rather than the Common Side where she belongs? You should be thanking me for my philanthropic gesture."

"How dare you." James let go of the arm he had seized, reared back and planted his fist solidly in the man's eye. "How could you do such a thing to a defenseless woman?"

"James, stop!" Grace stretched out a hand as though she could somehow prevent the two men from exchanging blows. The sound of flesh on flesh sickened her as James sent his knuckles crashing into Gosford's sneering mouth. "Please, won't you see to Annie? She needs our attention in death," her voice broke, "just as she did in life."

James stopped, the set of his shoulders and tension in his jaw clearly showing how much it cost him to restrain himself. Gosford glared at him through rapidly swelling eyes as the prison keeper pulled his arms behind his back and secured them with a length of rope. Turning abruptly, James knelt next to his sister's body and gently brushed her hair from her face. Her skin, always fair, was ethereally pale except where it was marked with purple bruises and smudges of dried blood. Cupping her cheek, he lowered his head and, beginning to weep, laid his face next to hers. Grace placed her hand on his shoulder, fighting her own rising tide of emotion, when his head jerked up, and he turned to stare at her, wild-eyed.

"Get my bag, Grace. Hurry."

Whirling, she ran back into the passage and grabbed the bag, returning to the cell and holding it out to him. He took it and began to rummage through its contents while issuing instructions in the same clipped manner she'd seen whenever she'd visited him at the hospital.

"Help me lay her flat on her back, Grace. I need more light. Cobb, get some of your men and bring me candles and fresh water. If I act quickly, we may be able to save her."

"I thought she was dead." Grace struggled to obey her brother's orders. She felt as though she was moving through a fog. He shrugged out of his coat and removed his shirt, tearing the cloth into strips. The hope burgeoning in her was too frail to be trusted. "How can she have survived such an attack? Her neck, and her hand? There's so much blood, James."

"Trust me, Grace." James met her gaze with eyes that were red-rimmed from tears, but clear and unwavering. "She has a chance, but we must move quickly. Something must have blocked the garrotte, or she would be dead for certain."

A muttered expletive issued from Gosford's split lip. Grace saw him cast a baleful look at a book that was lying on the floor, nearly shorn in two.

"Would a small book have done so, Jamie?"

"It's possible, I suppose. Here, I need you to keep firm pressure on this cloth while I do what I can for Annie's neck. I can't have you put pressure there for fear you'll block her airway. If ever you prayed,

Grace, do it now. Her hand is so badly damaged I'm afraid I have to make an impossible decision."

"What decision is that?" Dread filled Grace at the anguish on her brother's face.

"Whether to save her hand," James said, mingled determination and grief in his eyes, "or her life."

The operating theatre at London's University College Hospital was familiar to Grace only because of James' stories, and she was grateful she'd been somewhat prepared for the sight of bloodstained tables, soiled linens, and sharp scalpels. She stood outside the doors, waiting and praying while Annie was being prepared for surgery. Ramsey and James stood with her, coats off and sleeves rolled up, both ready to enter the operating theatre as soon as the surgeon arrived. Cobb had dispatched a message to Ramsey at Scotland Yard while James stabilized Annie's condition as much as possible. They had commandeered a wagon from the prison yard, loaded the unconscious woman carefully into the wagon bed and driven as rapidly as they could to the hospital. Ramsey had arrived just as they did, hailing a ward assistant to help James bring Annie inside.

"You are certain that amputation is the only option, James?" Grace searched her brother's face.

"It's possible that she could survive without it," he said slowly, features drawn with fatigue, "but the odds are so great that she will develop infection and then gangrene that I feel we must take the hand now. There is no hope of repairing it, of that I am certain."

"I have heard that Dr. Robert Liston is noted for his speed in removing limbs." Ramsey grasped Grace's hand, his firm touch giving her comfort even as his words made her shudder. "It is best that Annie have someone quick and experienced if she must go through such an ordeal."

"I know it, Jack, but I fear she will hate us when she realizes we made the choice for her to lose a limb."

"At least she will be alive." James' voice was flat. "Dr. Liston is not called the fastest surgeon in the West End for nothing. The removal of Annie's damaged hand should not take more than a minute, quite possibly less. If she regains consciousness during the procedure, even a second will seem interminable to her."

"Jamie," Grace laid a hand on his tensed forearm. "You are doing all you can. I pray Annie will eventually come to see that as well."

"Pray all you want, Gracie," James laughed humorlessly. "Yes, she's made it this far, but Annie may not survive the procedure. Prior to our current nightmare, she was in prison. Tell me, what good has prayer done in any of this?"

"Oh, Jamie, I wish I could give you an answer that would make sense of it all. I can only say that I have seen God's hand at work within this mess, truly, even if not in the ways I had hoped."

"Pray what you wish, then," he said wearily, "for I do not have any illusions about her odds. If our sister survives, Grace, it will be an act of God. If she forgives me for my part in the amputation, it will be an outright miracle."

Grace could think of nothing adequate to say. She laid a hand on her brother's arm as a shout sounded from the end of the hallway.

"Dr. Flynn? Is everything ready for me?"

The man striding toward them was quite elderly and mostly bald, with tufts of greying hair peeking out from behind his ears and round the back of his head. His bottle-green coat flapped behind him and Grace cringed at the sight of crusted blood and other fluids staining it. James stepped forward, shaking the man's hand.

"The patient is inside the operating theatre, Dr. Liston, and is unconscious for the moment. I believe the hand must be removed and I thank you for your willingness to perform the surgery. I have a vested interest, sir, as the patient is my younger sister, but you may be certain that will not hinder my ability to assist you."

"I should hope not, young man, or you would be a shame to the profession. Let's be on with it, then. If it is only the hand, this should not take more than a minute or two."

Without even sparing a glance for Grace or Ramsey, Dr. Liston pushed through the door to the operating theatre, while James followed swiftly behind him. Ramsey stepped forward to follow them, then turned to Grace and touched her cheek gently.

"I will come out as soon as they are finished and report. Then you and I must go through your account of events. My superiors will want to know how such a thing could have happened inside the walls of Newgate Prison. I've sent word to Scotland Yard for another officer to be present, given my personal involvement with you. He should be arriving anytime."

"Hurry, then, or they'll be done before you even walk through the doors." Grace tried to smile. "Thank you for doing this, Jack. I don't think I could stand seeing the actual procedure."

"There is no shame in that, Grace. I'll be out as soon as there is news."

Without giving her a chance to respond, Ramsey pushed through the door and disappeared into the operating theatre. Grace closed her eyes, hand pressed to her heart. *Oh, Lord, please spare her.* A scream rent the air, the sound originating from within the operating room. Tears streamed down Grace's cheeks as she listened to her sister's cries turn hoarse. *Christ, have mercy.* Leaning against the wall, she wept for her sister, her brother, and the difficult path that lay ahead of them all.

27

"You promised me that he would be gone forever!"

Lady Helena Pratt turned from the window she'd been staring out of, her eyes full of accusation. Louisa Rivers, shrugging nonchalantly, idly examined her nails before answering.

"I did no such thing, Helena. I offered you a chance to remove your husband from your life without killing him and you took it. It's not my fault that those bumblers at Scotland Yard actually managed to deduce what was going on." Her eyes narrowed speculatively. "I have no doubt that meddler Inspector Ramsey was involved. Elliott will have to deal with him or he'll have the whole of the police force following his example instead of keeping their noses out of our business in exchange for a bit of brass."

"I don't care who was involved. What am I supposed to do now that Wallace is back and worse than ever? He suspects that I had something to do with his confinement, Louisa, and how could he not? It won't be long before he takes the children from me and sends them away to school. He may turn me out of his house. I won't survive if he does that. My children are all I have." She walked to the fireplace mantel and gripped the back of a brocaded chair, grasping it so tightly that her knuckles turned white. "He's already back at his old habits. I received a visit from Lady Bunting just yesterday and she was thrilled to inform me that my *husband* was seen in the company of Blanche Darling at the theatre two nights ago. When I questioned him, Wallace told me I should be thankful that another woman is willing to make up for my shortcomings."

Her voice broke and she fisted a hand against her chest, pressing it over her heart as though that would stop the pain.

"I don't know what you expect me to do for you, Helena." Louisa looked up with a bored expression from a chair matching the one Helena still clutched. "I offered you a way to be free of him entirely over a year ago and you refused. Now that Dr. Wick's is not an option, I'm afraid I can't help you find a temporary solution. As deep as our friendship runs, I cannot work miracles for you. Perhaps you will manage…or perhaps not. I wish you the best, either way. Good day."

She rose, taking a step toward the door when Helena's hand shot out, clamping down on her arm. Stopping, she quelled her satisfied smirk before turning back.

"Yes?"

"Wait, Louisa, just wait." Helena clutched her arm so tightly Louisa was certain she'd have bruises. She didn't mind. In fact, she relished the evidence of desperation. She could certainly use that to her advantage. "I don't have the money to pay for your assistance and I won't unless I can figure out how to alter Wallace's will. As it stands, if he dies before our son is grown, the money is put in to a trust and governed by his solicitors and his brother. I have not even the hope of managing a dower portion for my daughter. Wallace told my father, just after our son was born, that any woman was too much a fool to manage even a third of his wealth and he intended to leave it all to the boy. I was trying to plot a way to gain further access while he was at Dr. Wick's, but to no avail. If he is dead, my chance at his money is gone. How am I supposed to support myself and my children without it, let alone pay you to help me?"

"I am tempted to tell you that it's not my problem, Helena," Louisa said coolly as she casually pried the woman's fingers from her arm, "but I'm feeling nostalgic and our friendship is an old one. Here's what I will do: I will speak to Elliott and have him send for one of our associates who is skilled in forgery. If you can provide a sample of your husband's writing, we can provide you with a will that names you as sole beneficiary and will be impossible to disprove in court. You will still have to deal with a solicitor, but you will have enough power to pay me what you owe and support your children."

"You swear that nobody will be able to tell that the will was not signed by Wallace?"

"Do not insult me," Louisa sniffed. "I would hardly work with someone who was not the best in the field. I will, however, require that you prove to me that you are serious in your commitment this time."

"Whatever you require is yours, as long as I have enough to keep my children and myself in the manner to which we are accustomed. They shall have their place in society, and I will finally have my freedom. Whatever you require is yours, Louisa. I swear it."

"Then here is my request. Once I deliver the new will, you must take your husband's life with your own hands. I will supply you with the necessary tools, but you will be the one to end him."

Louisa's eyes glittered as the blood drained from Helena's face. The room was silent but for the distant sound of carriage wheels on cobblestone outside the London townhouse. Swallowing audibly, Helena straightened her shoulders and lifted her chin to meet Louisa's gaze unwaveringly. A cloud passed over the sun and the room darkened, the growing shadows leaching the warmth of the fire.

"You have my word. Tell me what I must do."

"How could you do this to me?" Annie's face was white with pain, her tear-filled eyes fiercely green. "I would have been better off dead than a cripple."

"Don't say that." Grace reached out to lay a hand on Annie's damaged arm, but the girl jerked it away, moaning at the pain the movement caused. Grace dropped her hand to her side, fisting it in her full skirt. "Our hearts would have been broken if you had not survived, Annie."

"But I didn't survive, did I? At least, not all of me." Annie refused to look down where her right arm ended, just above the wrist, in a swath of bandages. "How could you think that I would want to live like this? You should have just let Nicholas Gosford kill me, Grace. Death I could have welcomed. This," her voice faltered, "is beyond my ability to bear."

"I'll help you bear it, Annie, and so will James and the rest of the family. We sent for them immediately after your surgery and Father wrote that he and Mother will come as soon as you are able to receive visitors. Now that you're recuperating here at the boarding house instead of the hospital, James says that they can come. They'll arrive tomorrow and are very anxious to see you. The doctor says that your arm will be fully healed within a month or two."

"Don't you understand, Grace?" Annie lifted her head off the pillow, the tendons in her neck cording with strain and anger. "My arm will *never* be fully healed unless a hand miraculously sprouts out of the misshapen end of it! I don't want to see them! I don't want to see anyone."

Grace stood silent, searching for something to say that would ease her sister's pain and cool her anger. There was nothing.

"Get out of my room, Grace. I want to be alone." Annie glared at her. "I said get out."

"As you wish."

Grace forced herself to walk calmly to the door. She pushed it closed behind her and slumped against the solid wood frame, dropping her head in her hands. *Lord, what good can possibly come of this? Please, won't you show me something that will help me believe you're still listening?*

"I take it Annie is still unable to accept the loss of her hand?" Grace looked up, meeting Ramsey's compassionate gaze. "It's not your fault, Grace. None of this was your fault. You do see that, don't you?"

"I know," she sighed tiredly. "There's nothing anyone could have done to prevent this, and the fact that she's even alive is a miracle. I can't convince her of that, however," she rubbed her temple, trying to assuage the dull, throbbing headache that had lingered for days. "I'm quite certain if I were in her position, I wouldn't want to hear anything of that sort either. Sometimes when I hear the things I'm saying to try to cheer her, I want to hit myself; I can hardly blame her for feeling the same way."

"Perhaps not," Ramsey said with a quiet laugh, "but I would prefer it if you didn't give in to the temptation. I feel bound to try to keep you from harm. Not," he assured her, "that I mind it. I consider it an honor. Still, I would prefer not to have to protect you from yourself as well as outside forces."

"I'll do my best, but I make no promises," Grace gave him a small smile, appreciating the attempt at levity even if she couldn't bring herself to laugh. She pushed away from the doorframe. "I don't know how I'm going to broach the fact that her injury does not nullify her sentence. When she finds out that she must return to Newgate and is only allowed to recover here because your friend, Lord Brooke, used his influence to intervene, she will be devastated. I can't think about that now," she held up a hand to forestall any further attempt to comfort. "I need to get to the shop. It was kind of my friend Alice to step into Annie's place, but I'm the only one who can prepare the lotions and oils. If those are not made, I have nothing to sell."

"May I walk with you?"

"Of course. I enjoy your company. I need only a minute to collect my cloak and bonnet."

Ramsey waited in the hall while Grace hurriedly donned her outerwear and picked up her satchel. She rejoined him in the hall, closing the door to the room that had been James' but was now hers while Annie recovered. Her brother insisted on sharing the larger room so that he could oversee Annie's care. Grace was surprised and grateful at his concern for both of them. That was one reason to hope, she realized.

Ramsey tucked her hand in the crook of his arm, escorting her down the stairs and out into the still cool morning air. "Nicholas Gosford's trial is set to proceed this week, isn't it, Jack?" she asked as soon as they reached the fresh air.

"Yes," he said slowly. She glanced up and saw a hint of wariness in his eyes.

"What is it? Tell me the man is going to be tried for his crime, Jack." Anger lit inside her. "He must be held accountable for what he's done to my sister."

"It's not only up to me, Grace, you know that. Now," he met her gaze squarely despite the regret covering his features, "there's been a murder that we believe is connected with the Surrey County Asylum and, therefore, with Dr. Wick and the Rivers. There wasn't enough evidence to proceed without Gosford's testimony. He only consented to help us in exchange for leniency."

"You can't mean to tell me," her voice was flat, "that the man who nearly killed my sister, and did kill who knows how many others, is going to go free? What kind of justice is that?"

"No," Ramsey stopped, turning to face her. "He's not going to go free, Grace, I promise. He will, however, be granted his life. He will be sent to Australia, where he will work harder in one day than he has in all his years here in England. He will live, but it will be the harsh, pleasureless existence of a disgraced exile."

Tears burned in Grace's eyes. "It's not enough, Jack. I know that I must forgive the man somehow, if only for my own sake, but it's not enough for him to merely live out his life in exile. I," she shuddered in a breath, horrified at the strength of the bitterness in her heart, "I needed him to die for his crime. He was supposed to hang for this. He," her voice dropped to a broken whisper, "was supposed to hang for what he did to Annie and then rot in the ground until he was nothing but dust."

28

Ramsey raised a hand to touch her cheek but dropped it when he remembered that they were on a public street. He settled for taking her hand, stroking the back of it with his thumb.

"I wish I could say that Gosford's sentence was fair, Grace, but you're quite right. It's not fair at all. My superiors deem the murder of one peer far more valuable than the loss of many lives of ordinary men and women. I've argued the case with them, but to no avail. We simply do not have enough evidence to convict the man for anything but the attempted murder of your sister. I must abide by their decision to commute his death sentence to life in a penal colony, and do my best, instead, to bring Lord Pratt's killer to justice. I know it does nothing to soothe the anger you feel, but you must trust that Gosford will still answer to God for all he's done."

"I know that, Jack," Grace's tone was sharp, "but it does little to quell my disgust at the blatant hypocrisy of men sworn to uphold justice and defend the innocent choosing to defend lawbreakers simply because of the chances of their birth."

Ramsey said nothing. Only time would untangle the complex emotions he could see in her eyes. He pulled Grace's hand to the crook of his arm once more, and led her down the street in silence. *Lord, please comfort Grace and grant me wisdom, I pray.*

Grace's head snapped up suddenly, her gaze narrowing. "Did you say Lord Pratt's killer? The man who was being held at Dr. Wick's when we were there? He's dead?"

"He is, indeed, and probably welcomed it after what he suffered. It was not a peaceful end, I'm afraid."

"What happened to him? Was his death the result of the treatment he received at Dr. Wick's? Is that the evidence you needed from Gosford?"

Ramsey slowed his steps as they approached Grace's shop.

"Why don't you let us inside, Grace, and then I'll tell you what I can. I'm afraid," he placed a hand on the small of her back as she unlocked the door and moved through the opening ahead of him, "that I do not have many answers."

"Not many answers as yet, Jack," she replied, turning to close the door behind him, "but I have no doubt that you will uncover the truth. I have no illusions that you can perform miracles," she laid a hand on his arm, "but the fact that you are still searching gives me hope."

He placed his hand over hers and studied the face that had become more dear to him than he'd ever imagined possible.

"Grace," he entwined his fingers with hers, "every moment I spend with you only increases your beauty in my eyes. You make me want to be the kind of man who deserves a woman of such passion, piety and strength."

Her eyes shone with a deep, quiet joy as she smiled at him. "Jack, how can you be so blind to my deep and varied flaws? I suppose that blindness helps explain why I love you. And I do love you, Jack. So very, very much."

"I love you deeply as well. Now," he dropped his hand with regret,

"I had best be off to the Yard before I give in to the temptation to kiss you. As much as I want to," his eyes darkened, his gaze lowering to her lips before lifting to meet hers again, "this is neither the time nor place."

"What a shame," Grace said mournfully, "that I had to fall in love with a man of such admirable restraint and unimpeachable morality."

"Right now I don't find restraint so admirable," he confessed, "and my morality is proving a bit uncertain, which is why I must go before I forget myself completely. I will return to see you home at the end of the day, if you are willing to wait for me? I'll tell you all about Lord Pratt's death then."

"Of course, Jack. I can wait. I have much to ponder." She touched his face gently in return before dropping her hand. "I will not let his sad end occupy my mind but will endeavor to lay the bitterness that has taken hold in my heart to rest. In the face of such happiness, how can I not?"

"And that," Ramsey said, squeezing her hand before moving toward the door with his eyes still on her, "is one more reason for me to adore you. I'll see you this evening."

"Until this evening, Jack. Be careful, won't you?"

"As careful as I can, my love."

He pushed through the door, stepping out into the hustle and bustle of the crowd of shoppers. Moving down the street toward Scotland Yard, Ramsey fought to keep from running like a madman to let loose the exhilaration he felt. His heart full nearly to bursting, he walked swiftly on into the day that lay ahead.

Lady Helena Pratt stared unseeingly at the writing on the document in front of her. Mr. Warrington's deep voice had receded to a low rumble in her ears, the words he uttered unintelligible as her mind whirled. *Wallace made a new will the day before he died. Actually, the day before,* she forced herself to complete the thought, *I killed him. How can this be? Louisa assured me that I and the children would inherit everything immediately. What will I do now?* She could feel herself paling. *I owe Louisa and her husband for their assistance in ending Wallace's life, but according to this blasted will, I have no access to his money. I have no access to any money at all.*

"Lady Pratt? Did you hear me?" Lord Pratt's solicitor studied her with concern over the top of his spectacles. "Do you want me to have my secretary bring you some water?"

"No, thank you, Mr. Warrington," Helena stiffened her spine and sat forward. "I'm quite well, thank you. I'm afraid I was not prepared for the manner in which my husband dispersed his wealth. He led me to believe that I would be given authority to oversee our son's finances until Winston reached the age of majority. Still, my children and I should be able to live comfortably until Winston inherits, should we not? I presume that whomever my husband appointed as trustee of the estate will not begrudge us some reasonable provision."

The solicitor cleared his throat nervously.

"I'm sorry to tell you, Lady Pratt, that while Lord Pratt did leave your son enough to make a good start in life, he made a significant withdrawal from the estate funds on the same day he had us draw up this will."

"But why would he do such a thing?" cried Helena, fear breaking the tenuous hold she had on her emotions. "It makes no sense. Winston is his blood, his heir. He would not have wanted to risk our son's future. If anything, Wallace was too careful with his investments. He often complained of missing out and only hearing of successful schemes after the fact."

"That may be so, but he was aware of one when he came to see me last and could not be dissuaded from his intentions. I did try," Mr. Warrington met her gaze squarely, sympathy visible in his watery grey eyes, "but to no avail. He told me that he had been given inside knowledge of a fail-proof investment that would triple his capital. I warned him that it sounded too good to be true, but he would not heed a word I said."

"What are you saying, Mr. Warrington?" Helena felt her stomach clench as the man's already somber expression grew graver still. "Surely we must only wait until the investment comes to fruition?"

"No, Lady Pratt." He paused. "It will never come to fruition. I have made enquiries into the scheme and have discovered that it was all a sham. There is no money. Everything that Lord Pratt invested is gone."

"What?" She barely whispered the word. "Gone? All of it?"

"I'm afraid so."

"What are we left with? We have Winston's inheritance. We can live on that, can we not?"

"There is not," he looked at her with a face so full of regret that she wanted to weep, "enough to support all of you. The trustee that your husband chose has decided that the best course of action is to withhold the money for now and give it to your son as a lump sum when he is old enough to make his way in the world."

"But how will he live to such an age when we have no money? It's not possible!"

"I wish I knew what to tell you, milady. I can," he colored in embarrassment at her situation, "offer you enough to pay what bills you have and keep you for the next week or so, but I have my own family to care for. I'm sorry."

Shame made it difficult for Helena to swallow but she forced herself to meet his gaze.

"Thank you, Mr. Warrington. That is most generous, particularly since we both know I have no way to repay you for your generosity." She stood, folding the piece of paper containing her husband's last wishes and tucking it into her reticule. "Would you be so kind as to direct me to the trustee that will be overseeing my son's inheritance? Perhaps I can convince him to change his mind."

"Of course," Mr. Warrington looked troubled, "but I fear you will not change his mind. He is not an easy man."

"That does not matter. I must do all I can for myself and my children. Please. Give me his name."

"As you wish, milady. I have it here." He rummaged through the papers on his desk, discarding one after another until he came across the one for which he was searching. "His name and address, Lady Pratt. I wish you the best of luck." He held the paper out to her, along with a folded bank note.

"Thank you, Mr. Warrington. I will see myself out."

She walked stiffly from the office, past the secretary sitting at a desk in the waiting area and headed down the hall. Glancing down, she unfolded the paper containing the name of the trustee. Her breath caught and she halted, all remaining color draining from her face as she sought the support of the wall to stay upright. *Elliott Rivers,* she read as her limbs trembled. Fear and rage flooded through her as she realized she had been betrayed, and there was nothing she could do about it.

29

Ramsey slid his gaze downward, surreptitiously checking the pocket watch he held concealed under his desk. Sighing inwardly, he slipped it back into his pocket and returned his focus to Superintendent Norris. The lecture he was delivering was not a new one. Conversation, since it implied the involvement of two parties, would have been too generous a term for what was taking place. Ramsey wondered, not for the first time, how Superintendent Norris had gone from the dedicated detective whose case-solving exploits were legendary to a man whose concern with administration and appearances tied the hands of his own detectives.

"Ramsey? Do I have your word?"

"I'm sorry, sir. I'm afraid my mind had wandered. What did you say?"

"I ought to make you patrol the streets for your blatant disrespect." Norris' voice was tight with anger. "Do you think that you are irreplaceable? I can assure you that there are any number of young constables who would jump at the chance to fill this office and they'd be a damn sight more grateful than you've ever been!"

Ramsey remained seated, eyes on the superintendent's face. Silence, experience had taught him, was the only wise response. A knock sounded as Norris' expression darkened and Constable Blackstone poked his head into the office.

"Did I not tell you that I didn't wish to be disturbed?" Superintendent Norris asked in a harsh voice. "I am not through communicating my displeasure to Inspector Ramsey and I have no problem reserving some for you as well, Constable."

"My apologies, sir," Constable Blackstone shrank back but did not depart, "but there's a lady here to see Inspector Ramsey. She won't tell me why she's here but insists she must see him and him alone. I told her that he was busy with you, sir, but she planted herself in a chair and said she's not moving until she's said what she came to say. That was nearly a half hour ago, sir, and I wouldn't have bothered you but she looks to be a lady of some stature. I know you would hate it," he said, respectfully inclining his head to the scowling man, "if we failed to show proper deference to a noblewoman."

Ramsey bit his cheek, stifling a smirk at Blackstone's careful flattery. The young constable had a gift for tactful turns of phrase that forced Norris to acquiesce on more occasions than not. It was a skill Ramsey greatly admired but one he most certainly did not possess, at least not in the constable's ready abundance.

"Of course, Constable," Norris drew in a breath. "You may send her in. She can speak to Inspector Ramsey's superior along with him; that will no doubt please her."

"I'll fetch her immediately, sir."

Blackstone disappeared from view, hurrying back to the lady in question. Ramsey wished that he could tell Norris to leave, but he knew that would almost certainly have him walking the dangerous streets of Seven Dials. Blackstone reappeared, pushing the door fully open to admit his companion.

"Lady Helena Pratt," he announced, "widow of Lord Wallace Pratt."

The woman stepped tentatively into his office, looking around with tired, fearful eyes. She would have been quite pretty, Ramsey thought, without the fretful lines etched into her brow and the pallor of too many sleepless nights leaching her skin of color. Her black gown of fine quality had little embellishment. At first glance, he'd have thought her to be in her late thirties but after he looked more closely he saw that her face still held some of the softness of youth. She was more likely, he decided, in her mid to late twenties. Her wide blue-green eyes had purple shadows under them and the mild dishevelment of her hair bore testimony to her anxiety.

"Lady Pratt, it is an honor to meet you, though I regret the circumstances," Superintendent Norris bowed low over her gloved hand. "My deepest condolences on the death of your husband. I'm certain he was a fine man. You must miss him terribly."

Ramsey's gaze sharpened as what little color was left in her face fled at his superior's words and she dropped her gaze to the floor. *Interesting, that. Her husband's death does indeed distress the lady but with guilt, not grief.*

"Thank you," she paused, not having been given his name.

"Superintendent Norris, milady," Ramsey said swiftly, wanting to ease her discomfiture, "and I am Inspector Ramsey. Please, tell us why you're here. "Do you have questions about your husband's death?"

"No," she spoke hurriedly, "no, indeed, not regarding his death. I'm certain that was all quite natural. He was," she hesitated briefly, "a man of generous tastes, if you take my meaning. His health failed rather suddenly and before we knew it, he was gone. I do not think there was anything unnatural about his death."

Ramsey studied her taut features. The set of her shoulders and the tightness of her jaw confirmed his suspicion that there was more suppressed emotion than simple grief. His instinct told him that she was lying about something; he just didn't know what. *Not yet,* he thought determinedly, *but I will.*

"Of course there was nothing unnatural about your husband's death," Superintendent Norris' placating voice broke into Ramsey's musings. "Who would suggest such a thing? No, I'm certain your husband's death, tragic loss that it is, was the result of a full life. After all, he was a gentleman."

"Quite so," she murmured, her gaze fixed on the scene outside Ramsey's window. "However, his death is not what I wish to discuss. Superintendent Norris," she turned finally and rested surprisingly shrewd eyes on the man's face, "my dilemma is much too insignificant for your valuable time. If you will allow me to engage Inspector Ramsey , I would be most grateful."

There was no way for Norris to insist on remaining part of the case without appearing ignorant of her delicately worded dismissal. After sending Ramsey a glare meant to cow him into obedience to all of the superintendent's dictates, he bowed low over Lady Pratt's gloved hand once more and departed. Ramsey watched him walk out into the hallway, closing the door behind him, and then turned to meet Lady Pratt's gaze. Silence filled the room as they studied each other.

"I wonder," he spoke, finally breaking the silence, "if you would care to tell me why you're really here, Lady Pratt?"

She blinked at his frankness. She bit her lip in uncertainty and then nodded jerkily.

"May I sit down, Inspector Ramsey? This may take some time."

"Of course. Please, make yourself comfortable and then tell me what is on your mind."

She sat down on one of the hard, wooden chairs located in front of his desk, carefully arranging her skirts. Her spine was so rigid it didn't even touch back of the chair. She drew in a deep breath and met his gaze squarely.

"Do you promise that you will listen to the whole story before you make any decisions, Inspector Ramsey? I must have your word."

"You have it, my lady. I will hear you out before drawing my conclusions." His grey eyes were direct. "But I must tell you that I will have to act if there has been a crime."

"That is why I have come to you, sir," she said flatly. "Your reputation is that of a man who searches for justice, no matter the cost. And I fear that, for me, the cost may prove very high indeed."

He waited, pulling pen and paper toward him, while she gathered her thoughts.

"Perhaps I had better begin with the truth. My husband did not die a natural death at all, Inspector," her chin quivered but her voice was firm. "I killed him."

Grace studied the note in her hand. Her curiosity, already piqued by Lord Pratt's untimely demise, deepened substantially. She read the words over again, eyes lingering on the precise writing so indicative of its author's nature:

Grace, something has come to light regarding Lord Pratt's death that requires my full attention. I fear that I will not be able to escort you home from the shop today; however, I feel it would be inadvisable for you to walk anywhere unescorted while the investigation into the Rivers' activities is still unresolved. I'm sending Constable Blackstone with this note and he will bring you with him to the offices of Hayes & Associates, providing you are amenable. Please, Grace, do not refuse my request. I will meet you in Jonathan's office at six-thirty and I promise to explain everything then. I hope to see you very soon, my love. Jack

She turned to the young constable examining the array of drying herbs hanging near the window in her workroom.

"Constable Blackstone?"

"Yes, miss?" He turned to face her, his back straight and shoulders strong under his plainly cut jacket. His clothing, though a bit worn at the knees and elbows, was well-made and neatly kept, and his broad, kind face, reddened by exposure to the chilling wind that had descended on London early that morning, emphasized the bright blue of his surprisingly serious eyes. Though younger than her by at least a handful of years, a knowledge, likely gained from encountering the darker side of life, shadowed his eyes and made him seem much older.

"I assume," she held the note up, "that Inspector Ramsey informed you he wished you to escort me to the offices of Hayes & Associates?"

"He did, miss."

"Well, then," she placed her hands on her hips as she surveyed the workroom. It was tidier than usual due to her recent absence. There was nothing that she could not leave for the following morning. "As soon as I exchange this apron for my cloak and bonnet, we can be off."

"Is there anything I can carry for you, miss?"

The constable walked over to the table upon which she had set her satchel. It was filled to the brim with samples of her wares and quite a bit heavier than usual. Grace shifted one item, and then another, finally giving in and removing a small lavender-filled pillow so that there was space enough to close the bag.

"If you wouldn't mind carrying my satchel, Constable," she smiled at him, "I would be most appreciative."

"Of course, miss," he said, picking up the satchel easily despite the surprise that flickered across his face at its weight. "Are you ready to depart? Inspector Ramsey did say to bring you as quickly as possible."

"I believe so."

Grace hurriedly removed her apron and smoothed the bodice of her cream and blue plaid gown, grateful to discover that nothing had seeped through the apron to stain it. Retrieving her bonnet, she set it firmly on her neatly arranged hair and tied the ribbon loosely under her chin. She locked the door behind them with the heavy brass key she had removed from her reticule and placed her hand on the constable's arm. They proceeded down the street at a steady pace, the icy wind inspiring her to move as quickly as possible despite heavy skirts and a long, tiring day.

"How far is it to Mr. Hayes' offices, Constable?" She inquired after they had made their way past one block of shop fronts.

"Just two more streets down, miss," he answered, slightly breathless from the weight of her satchel and their brisk strides. "It shouldn't take us long before we're out of this blasted wind." His face, already red from the wind, deepened in color. "My apologies, miss. I forgot myself."

"Not at all, Constable," she smiled at his obvious discomfiture at having spoken so in the presence of a woman. "I have a brother. I assure you, I have walked with him in quite a variety of 'blasted' weathers."

A surprisingly boyish grin flitted across his face at her response.

"Thank you, Miss Flynn. That is very kind of you."

"I'm glad to hear that you do actually know my name, Constable Blackstone," she teased as they approached a tall building on the corner of a street just beyond a busy thoroughfare leading to a number of dressmakers and millinery shops. "I was beginning to fear that I would have to answer to 'miss' forever."

He blushed deeper still as another smile touched his serious face. *What a good friend he would be for Annie,* she thought as they entered the building and proceeded up a flight of stairs. *I wonder if there is a way to introduce them. She would benefit greatly from his kindness and I suspect that Constable Blackstone needs reminding that life holds as much joy as it does severity. Although,* her heart sank, *I doubt that Annie will see the joy in life any time soon.*

They approached a door just a few steps down the hall from the top of the staircase. Constable Blackstone knocked firmly and then pushed it open to reveal a fair-sized room with a desk in the middle and a row of chairs with their backs to the wall. A middle-aged man with thinning hair sat at the desk, writing busily. He glanced up at their entrance, made a final notation on the paper in front of him, and then rose to greet them.

"Good evening, Constable Blackstone, Miss Flynn," he nodded at them. "I will inform Mr. Hayes that you are here. Inspector Ramsey and his guest are already in the office."

He turned on his heel and rapped smartly on one of the doors behind the desk. A low reply issued from inside it and he gestured them forward. Grace breathed out a sigh, not realizing that she'd been holding her breath. She was certain that Ramsey's unseen guest held the key to the events of the past months and she prayed they would finally find the answers they needed.

30

Elliott Rivers watched as his wife hummed happily to herself while putting the final touches on her ensemble for the evening. He smiled sardonically when he caught a glimpse of himself in the mirror — a tall, lean, strong-featured man resplendent in a white linen shirt and blue silk cravat, paired with an evening coat and trousers of the finest quality black wool. His dark features were the perfect complement, he thought, for his wife's deceptively sunny coloring. Her blonde hair was artfully arranged into ringlets and liberally studded with diamonds that he knew, having paid the exorbitant bill, were real. Her pale blue satin gown was cut daringly low, as most of her gowns were. Elliott's eyes rested appreciatively on her smooth shoulders and décolletage as he anticipated the pleasure of escorting her to the theatre. Seeing other men desire his wife and then quail when they recognized her husband, his dangerous nature not cloaked by his fine clothing, never failed to amuse him.

"Are you ready, my darling?" he asked, raising Louisa's hand to his lips. "You are stunning. I will be the envy of every man there, as always."

"Oh, Elliott," she looked up at him through thick lashes, "you spoil me. I knew the minute I set eyes on you that you were the only man for me, and how right I was! I only wish others would stay out of our way. It is a never-ending trial," her full lips curved into a pout, "that my snivelling cousin Charlotte has both the wealth and influence to spoil so many of our aims. I am sick to death of her parsimonious interference in our lives!"

"I've long desired to be rid of that connection, my love," he stroked a thumb over her lower lip, "but I'm afraid we cannot sever it just yet. We need Lord and Lady Brooke," he sneered their names, "to lend us an air of respectability in the polite world. You know that continued access to the higher echelons of society is a necessity for us, both in business and personal endeavors. Take heart, Louisa; there will come a day when we will finally be able to move freely through society without them. The more noblemen and women who find themselves indebted to us, the more opportunities we will have to solidify our position."

"I do hope you're right, Elliott," Louisa sighed heavily, "because it pains me to see my cousin occupying the place in society that I was meant to hold. It makes so angry that I could kill."

"My dear Louisa," his lips quirked in amusement, "you already have. And," he added, "if I have my way, I've no doubt that you will again. I would hate for you to be deprived the opportunity to do something that brings you such pleasure."

"As I said, my darling," she laid a hand on his arm, straightening her skirts as she rose, "you spoil me. What fun it has been to lead Helena Pratt down a merry path of lies. I can hardly wait to see her face when she realizes her only option is to spend the rest of her life working off her debt to us on her back. Aren't you proud of me, Elliott?" Her large blue eyes shone as they exited the room and walked down the hall to the staircase. "It was on my instructions that one of your men convinced Lord Pratt to invest nearly everything he had in the shipping investment scheme you so brilliantly orchestrated. All his money went into our pockets and Helena is destitute. She'll be forced to work at The Dove's Cry just to survive. We gain a noblewoman as a courtesan, along with her entire fortune."

"How could I not be proud of you, my darling? There is nothing I find more attractive," he murmured into her ear as they approached the front door and the waiting butler, "than your heady combination of beauty, intelligence and ruthlessness."

"Remember that," she smiled coyly at him as they left the warmth of the manor house and entered the chilly evening air, "at the theatre tonight. Since the play will be horribly dull, you can use the time to decide whether my reward should be set with sapphires, diamonds, or both."

Climbing into the carriage that stood waiting, the pair settled comfortably under warm lap robes for the ride, every indulgence paid for by the blood money they considered their due.

"Are you certain that this is the only way?" Grace murmured close to Ramsey's ear as he stood next to her watching the tableau in front of them. "So many things could go awry and then what?"

"I admit, it's a bit more complicated than I'd anticipated but I have faith that it will work. We must at least try. Besides," his gaze landed on Lady Pratt as she stood, pale but composed, talking to a small, slim, brown-haired woman with large green eyes and a kind face, "Thomas and Charlotte have long felt the burden of their connection to the Rivers. They were thrilled that they may finally be held accountable for their crimes and offered any assistance I required."

Ramsey had introduced Grace to Lord and Lady Brook when they arrived at the Brook mansion shortly after their meeting with

Jonathan. Scotland Yard was too full of listening ears, Ramsey said, for them to make their plans there, so he had sent a note to the Brooks requesting the use of their home. Their carriage had deposited them at the door of a quietly elegant house in a genteel neighborhood. The ride was uncomfortably silent, Lady Pratt staring unseeingly out the window while Grace and Ramsey sat across from her, each lost in their own thoughts. It was with a sigh of relief that Grace alighted from the carriage to meet two more of her fiancé's friends.

The couple was surprisingly unassuming given their position in society. Charlotte's deep mauve gown was finely sewn but altogether too plain for most women of her rank. Her fingers were smudged with dried ink, a fact she dismissed with a laugh as a hazard of her novelist profession. Grace was fascinated by the woman who was by turns both eccentric and gracious. She was hardly surprised that Verity Hayes considered her a close friend, but it was the admiration and love that shone clearly from Lord Brook's eyes whenever his wife was near that she found most intriguing. Ramsey's acceptance of Grace's own work was most unorthodox. Yet here were two women who were equally, if not more unusual, and their husbands appeared delighted by it.

"I can understand," she said, recalling her mind to the present, "why Thomas and Charlotte would be eager to see the Rivers imprisoned, but I can't fathom their generosity toward my family. To pay Annie's debt so that she can go free is far more than most would do even for those they love, and we are strangers to them."

"It doesn't matter to them," Ramsey took her hand and squeezed it. "They trust that Jonathan and I have given them an accurate summation of your sister's circumstances and they desire to repair what they can of the destruction caused by Charlotte's cousin. There is also," his face softened as he smiled, "the matter of your being my intended. Though my work makes it difficult for me to see them as often as I'd like, I consider the Brooks and Hayes dear friends. They, no doubt, have countless questions and," he winced, "anecdotes that I would rather leave untold. I'm certain they will them share with you when we finally meet in a social setting."

"I look forward to it," her eyes glinted with mischief, "since your fastidious appearance and obvious intelligence lead one to believe that you have no flaws."

Ramsey was about to respond when the clang of metal on metal sounded. He looked up with surprise at Thomas, who grinned before setting down the small gold hammer in his hand and stilling the reverberating gong.

"Your attention, ladies and gentlemen," he said. "It's time that we set off. Lady Pratt," his gaze was compassionate as he turned to the woman standing next to his wife, "your courage is admirable. We are all prepared to assist you in whatever way we can. Are you certain that this is the course you wish to pursue? Not one of us would blame you if you found yourself unable to follow through on the plan we've discussed."

"I'm certain." Her voice was quiet, and shook slightly. "My only other option is going to prison silently while my children are cast out on the street. I couldn't bear that. Inspector Ramsey assures me that he will do his best to convince his superiors that I was under great duress when I," she swallowed convulsively before continuing, "gave my husband the poisoned brandy that killed him. I only pray a jury will show mercy and take into account my attempt to keep the Rivers from luring some other poor fool into their web. I know that this will ruin me completely, but it is the only way to stop them and keep my children from starving."

"We will do all we can to help you, Helena," Charlotte laid a gentle hand on her arm, "and everything in our power to protect you."

"I trust you," Helena drew in a deep breath, straightening her shoulders. "Let us be off, then. I want this over as soon as possible and the theatre will be crowded tonight. Louisa mentioned that they have reserved seating when she was gloating earlier," her face hardened, "but it may still take some time to locate them."

"Jonathan," Ramsey left Grace to join the other men, "if you will join me in escorting Lady Pratt to the theatre, Constable Blackstone and Thomas can bring the ladies in the Brooks' carriage. We will wait until everyone arrives before Lady Pratt does what we discussed."

"Of course," Jonathan replied. "Verity, you have your blades to protect yourself and the others should the situation require it?"

"I do," she replied, smoothing a hand over her left sleeve, "and I pray that I don't have to use them to give the Rivers what they deserve. If this works, what they will suffer is far more intense, and a good deal longer-lasting, than a simple knife wound."

Grace joined the ladies as they moved from the drawing room into the hallway, wrapping their cloaks around their shoulders quickly as the men shrugged into their overcoats.

31

"Well, my love, what did you think of the performance?" Elliott turned to his wife, savoring the way the candlelight played across her bare shoulders in their private box at the Lyceum Theatre. Louisa set down the opera glasses she'd been using and smiled up at him.

"Which performance, Elliott? The one advertised out front or the one taking place in the private box across from us? Flora Shackleton's attempt to catch Lord Carmichael's eye was pitiful, to say the least. I declare, I don't know which poorly cast drama was more painful to watch."

"I thought Lord Carmichael looked rather put upon when I came across him at intermission. Is Flora the pug-nosed, speckle-faced young woman with a rat's nest of black hair? Her mother is one of our clients, is she not?"

"Indeed, you are correct on both points. Flora is precisely as you described her, and Lady Shackleton has been paying us a handsome monthly stipend for nearly a year to insure some risqué letters I happened upon at their country home last fall never see the light of day."

"You happened upon them, did you?" He raised a brow. "Would that have been the house party when you sent me off riding with the entire company and stayed back pleading a headache? I seem to recall you requesting I make certain that none of my companions found their way back before mid-afternoon?"

"What an excellent memory you have. Yes, that occasion. I took advantage of the party's absence to explore and found a set of rather descriptive love letters bundled away in Lady Shackleton's sitting room. She has a small writing desk with the cleverest little false bottom in one of the drawers. She would have been better off burning the things, but people seldom do, you know."

"People are surprisingly sentimental, my dear," he said mildly. "Were these the letters that made it evident that her children were not fathered by Lord Shackleton, but by his much younger valet?"

"Indeed they were."

"Shocking."

The two shared a smile of perfect understanding, lingering a moment before Elliott rose and handed Louisa her shawl. They moved from their private box into the main lobby amid throngs of people exiting the theatre onto Wellington Street. The press of the crowd was stifling but it was an unavoidable part of the theatre experience. Though uncomfortable, it was still an incomparable chance to see and be seen. Louisa glanced around, noting a number of lords and ladies waiting impatiently for their carriages. She preened, aware of the admiring looks cast her way by gentlemen both young and old, and the envious ones of their female companions.

"Louisa!" The high, strained voice of a woman cut through the din of the crowd. "Louisa Rivers. You and your swine of a husband stop right there."

Louisa's face flushed with rage as she turned to locate the source of the insult. Elliott's gaze followed hers, his expression freezing in sharp lines of distaste. Hurrying toward them, jostling others out of the way without apology, was Lady Helena Pratt. She was clothed in the same black mourning gown she'd been wearing the last time Louisa saw her — a day dress completely unsuitable for the venue. She neared the Rivers, ignoring the frowns and speculative tittering of the crowd.

"Helena, dear," Louisa took her arm and tried to draw her away from the crowd, only to have the woman wrench her arm free, "you are overwrought by your recent loss. You should not be out in society while in mourning. It's most unseemly. Allow us to escort you home. We can discuss whatever is weighing on you in the privacy of our carriage. I know you would hate it," she raised a brow with a significant glance at their audience, "if your personal matters were made public."

"I will do no such thing!" Helena spat the words. "You two have done irreparable damage to my family. I will not grant you the honor of silence now. You requested that I give you my answer to your proposition by tomorrow and so I am here to deliver it."

She paused for breath and Elliott broke in, taking her arm in a firm grip.

"Lady Pratt, you do not know what you are saying," his expression was pitying. "Obviously, you have taken some refreshment to calm your nerves but it has had the opposite effect. We will see you safely home where you may rest until you are once again in full command of your faculties."

"How dare you insinuate that I am a drunkard." She raised her hand, slapping him hard across the face before he could ascertain her intent. "You act as though I am the one with something to be ashamed of when you and your wife are nothing but the lowest possible class of people. Do you honestly think that any in this crowd," she waved an arm at the gentlemen and ladies standing nearby with expressions of mixed horror and fascination, "will ever see you as equals? That they will welcome you into their circles? You are nothing but fools."

"You would be wise to hold your tongue," Elliott's tone became menacing, "before you say something that will bring repercussions you cannot bear. Consider my words carefully, Lady Pratt, before you dare to insult myself and my wife again."

"I have nothing to lose," Helena choked out a laugh. "You have taken everything from me. I own that I was a fool," anger and embarrassment stained her cheeks red, "to trust Louisa. I should have known, having watched her merciless abuse of others when we were at school together, that she did not have the capacity for altruism, but I was desperate. I am paying for my folly a hundredfold, I assure you."

"Not yet, you're not." hissed Louisa. "You have made a grave error coming here and accosting us like this, Helena. Don't you think that the police will be most interested to hear that you are responsible for your husband's death? What do you think will happen to you when we tell them? You have no proof that we had anything to do with that. All you have succeeded in doing tonight is embarrassing yourself."

Helena wilted visibly, face twisting as she fought to keep her emotions in check.

"I've humiliated myself, yes, but I've also caused enough of a scene that there will be talk about you and Elliott for years to come. Your hope of a place in society is gone. That is worth publicizing my own shame. How could you think that I would agree to work off what I owe you as a prostitute? And in one of your own establishments no less? If I was a fool for trusting you, your greed made you one as well," she lowered her voice, leaning closer, "particularly if you believe I do not have proof that you and Elliott assisted the hastening of my husband's demise. Enjoy your evening, Louisa. It is likely the last free one you will have for some time. I am going to the police first thing in the morning to tell them everything and by the time I'm done, they will have all the evidence they need to hang you both."

Turning on her heel, she pushed her way through the watching crowd and disappeared into the night. Louisa watched her departure through narrowed eyes. She felt Elliott's hand on her arm and she turned, uncomfortably aware that harsh disapproval had replaced admiration and envy on the faces of the gentlemen and ladies standing nearby.

"That woman was trouble from the beginning; I told you she would be," Elliott's voice was an angry whisper. "What evidence is she speaking of? Whatever it is, we must get rid of it before she confesses. If Inspector Ramsey gets a hint that there is some proof to tie us to murder, that will be the end of everything. He would build the gallows to hang us himself if he could."

"There is nothing. I haven't the faintest idea what she was talking about."

Louisa turned tear-filled eyes to her husband. He pulled her swiftly to their carriage, eager to be out of sight and out of earshot. Once the vehicle was in motion, he settled back in the seat, thinking. The streets passed by, dark and silent but for the occasional sound of another carriage or an indistinct raised voice in the distance. Finally, he spoke.

"There is no help for it, Louisa. We must go to her home tonight and compel her to tell us where and what this evidence is. Then we can kill her and remove the threat for good. You may," he touched her cheek gently, "need to bring her children into the conversation. Are you amenable to such a prospect?"

Louisa smiled grimly, reaching up to hold his hand in place as she turned her cheek into its warmth.

"Of course, my darling. Once I'm through with them, I've no doubt that her little brats will have the slightest trouble convincing Helena that she'd best tell us what we need to know. It may be," she mused, eyes brightening as a new thought dawned, "that Helena will see that the wisest thing for her to do is take her own life before things get any worse for her or her children. I believe I will do my best to convince her of that. As much as I enjoy ending a life with my own hands, it would be safer for us if she did it herself."

"An excellent notion," Elliott smiled coldly. "We should arrive home momentarily. We'll change into something more appropriate for the occasion and be off to the Pratt residence directly. No sense in wasting time."

"I do adore your decisiveness, my darling," said Louisa, "and I know that should Helena refuse to end her life and save us the grief her continued existence will bring, you will end it for her. Or, better yet, allow me to do so."

"Naturally."

Elliott tucked the lap robe more closely around his wife and sat back. It had been too long, he thought, anticipation gleaming in his dark eyes, since they had carried out such a scheme in person. It was time to remedy that.

32

The street outside the Pratt residence in Chester Square was dark, save for small circles of muted light cast by flickering street lamps. *I wonder if any of these people realize how easy it is to gain entrance to their homes? Then again,* Louisa snorted derisively, *the privileged class think no one would dare to burgle them. It's entirely too common to consider.*

"Perhaps," she whispered to Elliott as they moved swiftly and silently along the street, always careful to stay in the shadows, "we should take advantage of the laxness of these homeowners. I'm certain that a few well-placed bribes and the addition of some skilled thieves to our employ would net us quite the bounty. There are enough starving children on the streets that it would be easy to find one or two not already employed in the field who are scrawny enough to slip through windows."

"Your ingenuity never fails to amaze me, my love," murmured Elliott, squeezing her hand. "That sounds like a very profitable avenue to explore once our current endeavor is complete. Ah, here we are." He laid a hand on her arm, halting their progress as he scanned the street for movement. There was no sign of the constable they had watched until he turned the far corner of the square. Elliott estimated they had about twenty minutes until the policeman's patrol brought him past the Pratt manor again. He turned to his wife. "Are you ready?"

"I am. You will deal with the servants, as we discussed, and I'll begin my work with Helena while waiting for you to join us."

"I did not wish to give up the pleasure of watching you in your element, so to speak, and so I sent Jamison ahead of us. He will have taken care of incapacitating any troublesome servants and left the service entrance unlocked for us. He was quite certain the staff would cause no trouble. I know you convinced Helena to replace most of the staff when Lord Pratt was removed to the asylum. Since they are new, it's unlikely that any would be so loyal to the family that they would risk their lives to protect them."

"I'm touched that you still find watching me do what I love pleasing, Elliott. I shall do my best to make this worth your while."

They moved through the narrow space between homes, entering the small courtyard behind the house. A gentle push at the door caused it to swing inward easily, testifying to Jamison's competence. A lantern stood on the massive wooden kitchen table, its flame low but bright enough to light their way. Louisa blinked as her eyes adjusted and she turned her head as she caught a flicker of movement from the far side of the kitchen, near the pantry. Jamison stepped into view, shutting the pantry door firmly behind him.

"Everything is taken care of, Mr. Rivers," he said. "The servants are bound and gagged in the pantry and the lady's maid informed me, after a little friendly persuasion," his lips curved without warmth, "that Lady Pratt occupies the second bedroom on the right at the top of the stairs. The children are in the nursery in the west wing. Is there anything else you require?"

"No, thank you, Jamison," said Elliott. "You are most efficient.

Wait here for our return, standing guard in case of anything unexpected."

"Yes, sir." Jamison moved to the far side of the kitchen, near the entrance and leaned back against the wall. His casual pose belied the alertness in his eyes. Reaching into his pocket, he removed a small pistol and held it loosely in his right hand.

"Come, Louisa," Elliott picked up the lantern, gesturing to the door that led up the servants' stairs into the main part of the house. "Lady Pratt must not be kept waiting."

"Oh, Elliott, this is so exciting. We really have gone soft of late," Louisa exclaimed in a whisper. "No wonder I've been fighting such boredom."

"The thought had crossed my mind." Elliott's voice was nearly inaudible, he spoke so quietly. "Taking on some of the practical work ourselves serves the dual purpose of reminding people not to cross us and brightening your day. Your enthusiasm suits you very well. I can't recall when you've looked lovelier."

"As your determination suits you. This is the room," she murmured, placing a hand on his arm. "Would you care to do the honors or shall I?"

"Allow me," he pulled a small, folded pouch from his coat pocket and removed a small pick. "Do you have your pistol ready?"

She raised her hand, the lantern light glinting off the metal barrel of a small pepperbox pistol. The weapon had been an anniversary present three months ago, but Louisa hadn't had the opportunity to use it as yet. Elliott tried the knob and it turned easily in his hand. He placed the unused pick back in its pouch and tucked it away, letting the door swing slowly open as he removed a thin, wicked-looking knife from his other pocket. The room was dark. Only the barest hint of moonlight slipped through a gap in the heavy curtains covering the large window opposite the bed and the fire flickering in the hearth was not bright enough to do anything more than cast shadows on the wall. The outline of a woman lying beneath the blankets, her face turned toward the far wall, was just visible. Louisa cocked the pistol, the sound unnaturally loud in the silence of the room.

"Helena. Wake up." She watched with satisfaction as the form in the bed jerked awake with a gasp. Helena sat up, pulling the covers to her chin as she stared wide-eyed at the intruders. "Get out of bed. We have business to discuss." Louisa gestured with her pistol, watching with glee as fear pulled the other woman's features taut. Helena slowly lowered the covers, carefully smoothing her hands over her nightgown to be sure she was not exposing any more skin than could be helped, and climbed out of the enormous bed. She stood uncertainly next to it, clasping her trembling hands in front of her.

"For heaven's sake, Helena," Louisa mocked, "what did you think we would do when you threatened us? Throw our hands up in the air and panic? Simply allow you to go to the police? You poor, idiotic woman."

"I...I," Helena stopped, looking down. "I don't know what I was thinking. Please, don't hurt me or my children. We will leave London, tonight if you say so, and never say a word about you to anyone. I was so afraid that the police would figure out what really happened to Wallace and take me away from my children. I couldn't bear to have my babies out on the street. You must see that." She turned her pleading gaze on Elliott's face, shrinking back as if slapped at the cold cruelty she met there. "I'll leave and never speak of this again. I swear it. Please, just let me go."

"It's a bit too late for assurances now," Elliott said coldly. "You should have taken our offer and worked off your debt in one of our many pleasure houses. Your children would have been fed and clothed, and you would have been alive. As it stands, your death is the only thing that solves our dilemma. You will tell us where you have hidden the evidence you spoke of, and if you do not resist," he smiled grimly, pleased to see the color drain out of her face, "your death will be swift. If not…" he left the thought hanging ominously in the air.

"Is there nothing I can do to stay your hand?" Helena's voice shook. "Surely you are not so heartless that you would leave my children without their mother *or* their father?"

"I don't believe we are the ones who took their father from them, are we?" Louisa raised a brow at Elliott. "That was your doing, Helena. All we did was provide you with the means. When Dr. Wick's methods failed, through no fault of our own," her face hardened at the memory, "we provided you with enough monkshood to fell an army. I even told you how to mask the taste when you gave it to your husband. If you had possessed even one iota of intelligence, you would have told the attending doctor that Lord Pratt had often complained of stomach pains, and he would have ascribed the death to some undiagnosed illness. You are a victim of your own incompetence, Helena, and you must bear the consequences."

"And so must you," Helena lifted her head, eyes alight with triumph. "You were the fools, coming here tonight. You think that I would go to bed and sleep easily with the weight of my guilt and your threats hanging over my head? Obviously, it did not occur to you that I might have taken measures of my own. I hope you are prepared to explain your presence here," she raised her arm and pointed, "to the kind gentlemen standing behind you."

Ramsey emerged from the shadow of a large armoire at the same time that Jonathan stepped out from behind the curtain covering the window. Both men held pistols at the ready, Jonathan's aimed at Louisa while Ramsey kept his trained on Elliott. Fury covered

Louisa's face but she kept her pistol pointed at Helena, her hand steady despite her rising emotion.

"Put down your weapons, Mr. and Mrs. Rivers," Ramsey instructed, "or we will shoot."

"I will shoot her first," declared Louisa, tossing her head in defiance, "and though my pistol may be unreliable in its aim, Elliott's accuracy with a blade is unparalleled. Helena will not leave this room alive and neither will you!"

"I doubt that," replied Jonathan. "If you consider the odds, you will concede that if anyone fails to leave the house alive, it will be the pair of you."

Jonathan stepped to the center of the room as he spoke, his movements swift, eyes never leaving Elliott's face.

"The odds are very much in our favor," Elliott laid a hand on his wife's shoulder to silence her. "You did not think we would come here alone, when I own the best of London's mercenaries, did you? One of them is standing guard downstairs as we speak. Even if your aim was equal to ours, which I sincerely doubt, Jamison would end your lives before you knew what had happened. It is in everyone's best interest, *Inspector,*" his eyes flashed with hatred, "for you to follow your superior's example and turn a blind eye to my business. I can assure you that bringing me in will win you no favors. In fact, I would wager it will be the end of your pathetic career."

"I'm well aware of my superior's attitude, Rivers," Ramsey cocked his pistol. "You may have some sway with Superintendent Norris, but his days in the Yard are numbered. Sir Robert Peel himself is aware of the corruption in the force, and the commissioner has begun to weed out those you've bribed into silence. I've been given full authority to bring you and your wife in." His eyes gleamed with satisfaction. "It's the end for you both."

"It's the end of something," Elliott agreed, exchanging a glance with his wife, "but not us."

The pair moved in unison, Louisa whipping her arm to the left and firing at Jonathan while Elliott flung his blade straight at Ramsey's heart. The reverberating sound of the pistol shot rang in Ramsey's ears as he threw himself to the right. He felt a burning throb in his left bicep and looked down to see the small blade sunk hilt-deep in his upper arm. Forcing himself to think through the pain, he focused on Elliott's progress toward the door, praying that Louisa's shot had missed. He couldn't see Jonathan, but the sound of flesh thudding against flesh mingled with a woman's screams.

"Stop!" he shouted, stumbling after Elliott. "Halt, or I'll shoot."

"You don't have the nerve." Elliott took hold of the knob and turned it, flinging the door open. "Louisa, hurry."

Ramsey's finger tensed on the trigger. *Father, forgive me for what I must do. Let him live to receive justice on this earth.* As blackness threatened the edges of his vision and he felt his legs begin to buckle, he fired. The last thing he heard was a resounding crash and the thud of something heavy hitting the floor.

"Jack! Can you hear me?"

Ramsey heard a voice calling to him through the darkness. He tried to open his eyes but his eyelids refused to cooperate. *Grace? What on earth is she doing in the room? I must get her out of here.* With herculean effort, he forced himself to awareness, wincing as his eyelids scraped painfully over gritty eyes. He blinked, trying to bring the fuzzy image in front of him into focus.

"Oh, Jack, thank the Lord, you're awake." He looked up into Grace's face, her concern increasingly evident as his vision started to clear. "I was so afraid that there was some wound I could not find that was still bleeding. How do you feel? Can you tell me what hurts?"

"Where..." his voice sounded rusty and he swallowed to ease the dryness in his throat, "where are Elliott and Louisa? Did they escape? Is Helena safe? You shouldn't be here, Grace." He tried to take her hands in his, gasping as the movement shot bolts of pain up and down his left arm. He closed his eyes, steadying his breathing before opening them again. "You need to go now. It's not safe!"

She laid a cool hand on his brow and he sighed at her touch, despite his anxiety.

"It's alright, Jack," she said softly, brushing his dishevelled hair off his sweaty forehead. "You may rest easy. You've gotten your man, and woman for that matter," she smiled but sadness shadowed her eyes. "And your only job now is to recover from your wounds."

The image of Louisa firing her pistol at Jonathan while Elliott threw his knife at Ramsey flashed through his mind. He remembered looking down and seeing the blade sticking out of his arm, pointing his own weapon at Elliott and pulling the trigger, but that was all. The possibilities made his stomach clench with fear.

"Where is Jonathan?" He ignored Grace's hand on his right shoulder trying to keep him lying down and, gritting his teeth, attempted to sit up. The throbbing that had dulled while he lay still reawakened with a vengeance. Flashes of searing pain assailed him as he turned his head to look at his arm. The blade was still lodged there, the cloth of his coat soaked with blood. "Oh, good Lord," he murmured in surprise. "That explains a fair bit. Grace, I fear..." his voice faded as darkness settled over him once more. He thought he heard a man's voice and prayed it was his friend, alive and well, before he slipped back into the blessed relief of unconsciousness.

33

"Is he going to survive? How serious is his wound?"

Grace turned her gaze from Ramsey's unconscious face at Jonathan's anxious question. Verity placed a comforting hand on his arm, the gesture causing only the barest easing of tension in his features. A small bandage peeked out from under the private investigator's sleeve, already reddened and wet with blood. Louisa's shot had gone wide but she had still managed to graze his forearm, just above his wrist. He hadn't returned fire because of her proximity to Helena, but then he hadn't needed to. Louisa's pistol was only good for one shot without reloading and while she was struggling to do so, he had simply walked over and wrenched it from her grasp.

The ensuing struggle had been ugly. She'd scratched his face and bit his hand, only stopping when Verity, having entered the room through the sitting room door, calmly placed the tip of her blade against the tender skin of Louisa's neck. The woman's mutinous glare had transformed into raw grief when she'd caught sight of Elliott lying dead on the floor. Ramsey's aim had been true and his bullet had passed through Elliott's heart. Grace looked over to the far side of the room where Louisa sat, hands bound and hair straggling down her back, her face ashen and streaked with tears. Unexpected pity filled her despite everything the woman had done.

"He should recover," she said finally, "barring serious infection. The wound is deep and I don't feel confident about removing the blade myself, but I've bound it in place with pressure to try to stop the bleeding. You sent for James?" She raised a brow. "I'd rather have him assess Jack's condition here before we try to move him."

"I did, yes," Jonathan's expression still held concern for his friend but his shoulders relaxed marginally. "He should be here soon. In the meantime, Verity and I will tell the police what we know. Constable Blackstone and the two men he had with him are already back at Scotland Yard with Jamison, reporting to their superiors. The staff were so grateful to be rescued that they've offered whatever assistance they can reasonably give."

"There is nothing to do but wait," said Grace. "What about Lady Pratt? What will happen to her now? Ramsey said he was going to try to help her but I don't see what he can do when she's confessed her part in Lord Pratt's death."

"She will almost certainly end up in prison, I'm afraid," Verity answered, "but it's possible that, given the circumstances, she may not be hanged."

"But what about her children?" Grace's heart ached at the thought of the two little ones. "She was so desperate to keep them safe and now they are adrift in the world anyway."

"Oh, I think that things will turn out just fine for those two," Jonathan smiled enigmatically. "You don't need to worry on their account, Grace. Devote your attention to your fiancé. He will be a terrible patient. It's not too late to call off the engagement, you know, and save yourself the trouble of nursing a mulish man back to full strength."

Grace was shocked at the harsh words until she saw the teasing glint in his eyes as he looked, not at her, but at Ramsey. Glancing down, she saw that Ramsey's eyes were open again, his expression one of mingled pain and amusement.

"I am wounded in the line of duty," he muttered, shooting his friend a dark look, "and you're suggesting to the woman I love that she might be better off leaving me. Some friend you are, Jonathan. Did I ever cause such trouble between you and Verity?"

"Never," said Jonathan smoothly, "because she would have boxed your ears if you had suggested such a thing to her, and you know it."

"Apparently," Verity arched a brow at her husband, "you do not value your wellbeing as much as he does his. Is there any reason either I or Grace should not do precisely the same thing to you?"

"No," Jonathan smiled innocently, "but I wonder if I have neglected to tell you lately how delightful I find you? If so, I have been sadly remiss. It's not every man whose wife is equal parts determination and grace."

"You are incorrigible," she murmured, fighting a smile. "Come. James will not want us crowding his patient. Ramsey's superiors, excluding Superintendent Norris," she clarified, "will be waiting for our description of tonight's events. Grace," she laid a hand on the woman's shoulder briefly, "if I may, I would like to call on you tomorrow and see how you are faring. Will you send me a note telling me when is most convenient for you?"

"I will, Verity," Grace was pleased at the overture of friendship. "Thank you both for everything. I can hardly believe all that has occurred. It doesn't seem real."

"It is," replied Jonathan as footsteps sounded in the hall and James hurried through the door, "and I'm afraid it's only the beginning of the very harsh reality of prison for Lady Pratt. Louisa Rivers will probably hang by her neck in the next few months." He grimaced at the thought and then looked at his watch. "We will be off, then.

Ramsey. Do try not to be irritable while Grace is in the room. What she sees in you is already a mystery."

"Would you leave already?" Ramsey grimaced as he lifted his head. "You must tell me what you encounter at the police station. If the commissioner has followed through with his promise, things will be quite different from now on, particularly for those of us under Superintendent Norris' supervision. And," he glanced toward the wall where Louisa sat mute and motionless, "do tell Constable Blackstone to hurry up and send an officer to collect Mrs. Rivers. She may need medical attention before we can question her."

"Consider it done. Mr. Flynn," Jonathan nodded at Grace's brother, before exiting the room with his wife.

"Gracie." James knelt next to his sister. "What's going on here? Ramsey," he studied the blade sticking up from the detective's arm and shook his head, "what on earth have you done to yourself?"

"James," Ramsey gritted his teeth in anticipation of the inevitable removal of the blade, "I would hardly do this to myself."

"My apologies. Judging by what I can see," James shot him a sympathetic look, "this may take some time and cause considerable pain."

"That's what I was afraid of."

Ramsey propped his elbows on his desk without thinking, wincing and straightening as his left arm throbbed a reminder of the gash he'd received three weeks earlier. It was nearly healed, but the resulting scar still pulled painfully on occasion. *At least all I received was a physical wound,* he thought, *and one that is healing nicely, thanks to James.* He looked down at the folder lying open on his heavy wooden desk and sighed. He'd thought that finally putting the Rivers out of business would be more satisfying. He'd poured countless amounts of time and effort over the past two years into bringing them to justice. While he felt a small sense of triumph that they were no longer a threat, a deeper weight of despondency had taken hold.

Since Elliott's death and Louisa's conviction, the menace of London's underworld had changed very little. If anything, there were more reports of violence coming in as fights for supreme authority continued. He was quite certain they would not cease until there was a new man sitting in Elliott Rivers recently vacated position. Even then, there would continue to be skirmishes between rivals that damaged innocent bystanders. Sighing again, he smoothed the papers on his desk. His frown deepened as his gaze rested on the paper lying first in the file: a summation of Helena Pratt's trial and sentencing. While not an innocent, she was certainly another who would suffer as a result of the Rivers' proclivities. A knock sounded on the door and he glanced up to see Grace standing in the opening, a gentle smile on her lips.

"It doesn't get any easier, does it?" she asked quietly. "I wish I knew what to say, Jack, but there is no way to heal what is constantly being torn open. I suspect that is what it feels like to you every time you hear of another crime related to the fight to scceed Elliott Rivers."

"I'm afraid you're quite right," he rose and came around the desk to take her hand, revelling in the warmth that her touch sent through him. She could not bear his burden, but even her presence alleviated some of the darkness that weighed on him. "It's difficult to face the fact that my work is futile, but it seems I must. Every case I close is merely a drop against the wave of pain and injustice."

"Not at all," she said sharply, surprising him with her indignation. "Your work is hardly futile! It *does* make a difference, Jack; truly it does. Why, look at Helena. Can you honestly tell me that you do not see justice, and even redemption, in her case?"

"It's complicated," he scowled, turning away but not before seeing the hurt on her face. Regretting that he'd caused her pain, he turned back and gripped her hand more firmly while he searched for the right words. "I acknowledge that justice has been served, Grace. She killed her husband and she will spend years in prison paying for her crime. Still, I find myself wishing that I could unlock her cell door and tell her that she may go free, providing she promises never to do such a thing again. How," bemusement crossed his face, "can I think such a thing when she *murdered* her husband, even with the extenuating circumstances?"

"Because," Grace reached up and placed a gloved hand on his cheek, "you are a kind man who loves mercy as well as justice. You know that her heart is changed and you have met her children, who no doubt remind you of your own childhood abandonment. It's not the same situation, Jack. You were raised by decent people who simply didn't know how to love you when they knew what you came from. Helena's children are being adopted, with her consent, by Thomas and Charlotte. You know that they will love those two little ones as if they were their own and will encourage an ongoing relationship with their mother."

"But still," he insisted, "look at what remains. Annie has lost her hand and is mired in bitterness, two children have lost their parents in the cruelest, most shameful way, and Louisa Rivers grieves the death of her husband without a thought for her own sins while she awaits the hangman's noose. What kind of world is this that we live in?"

"Have I told you lately," he murmured, taking the hand she had laid on his cheek and bringing it to his lips, "that when you agreed to marry me, you made me not only the happiest man in the world, but also the most fortunate? I'm sorry I forgot that for a moment. Forgive me?"

Her warm brown eyes met his steady grey ones, heart glimpsing heart in their depths.

"Always, Jack. Always."

He smiled, lowering her hand and placing it in the crook of his elbow. The familiar touch was a balm. As he led her through the door and out into the hallway, flashes of the life that lay ahead filled his mind: Grace facing him at the front of the church in an elegant gown on their wedding day; Grace with eyes glowing as she greeted him after a long day's work with the announcement of the impending arrival of their first child; a grey-haired, stouter, slower Grace walking with him along the riverbank, her hand still tucked in the crook of his arm. A thousand other hopes and dreams mingled in between. He fully intended to savor them all.

Acknowledgements

As always, there are too many people to thank in such a small space. My family and friends, I am grateful for your love and support in every area of my life. This book would not be possible without you. Special thanks to McKenzie Spies for editing my first and last drafts, and for telling me—though I'm still not entirely convinced—that she loves to do it. And deep gratitude to my brother, Graeme J. Friesen, for his exceptional artistic ability in designing my last three book covers and his patience along the way.

CPSIA information can be obtained at www.ICGtesting.com
Printed in the USA
LVOW10s0246260516

489805LV00015B/110/P

9 781928 112396